The Potbellied Virgin

The Potbellied Virgin

Alicia Yánez Cossío

Translated by Amalia Gladhart

University of Texas Press, Austin

TEXAS PAN AMERICAN LITERATURE IN TRANSLATION SERIES

Danny J. Anderson, EDITOR

Copyright © 2006 by the UNIVERSITY OF TEXAS PRESS
All rights reserved
Printed in the United States of America
First edition, 2006

Requests for permission to reproduce material from this work should be sent to:
Permissions
University of Texas Press
P.O. Box 7819
Austin, TX 78713-7819
www.utexas.edu/utpress/about/bpermission.html

♾ The paper used in this book meets the minimum requirements
of ANSI/NISO Z39.48-1992 (R1997) (Permanence of Paper).

Library of Congress Cataloging-in-Publication Data

Yánez Cossío, Alicia, 1929–
   [Cofradia del vestido de la virgen pipona. English]
   The potbellied virgin / Alicia Yánez Cossío ; translated by Amalia Gladhart.
      p.   cm. — (Texas Pan American literature in translation series)
   Includes bibliographical references.
   ISBN 0-292-71304-5 (cloth : alk. paper) — ISBN 0-292-71410-6 (pbk. : alk. paper)
   I. Gladhart, Amalia. II. Title. III. Series.
   PQ8220.35.A5C613 2006
   863'.64 — dc22   2005031099

For my children, Katherine and Patrick

— A . G .

Contents

Acknowledgments

A translation is inevitably a collaborative work, between author and translator, but also between a translator and a variety of readers, informants, and mentors. Thanks are due to my mother, Emily Gladhart, who first bought me a copy of the novel, almost by chance, and to my husband, Sean Hayes, for his early suggestion that I undertake a translation. I am grateful to Priscilla Meléndez, for her ongoing friendship and example, and for reading my first attempts to understand *La Virgen Pipona*. Members of the Asociación de Ecuatorianistas responded to an early version of the translation with helpful comments and suggestions. My colleague at the University of Oregon, translator and poet Amanda Powell, offered encouragement and inspiration. Series editor Danny Anderson was also most supportive. My thanks also to Theresa May of the University of Texas Press. Particular thanks are due, finally, to Alicia Yánez Cossío, for her assistance, friendship, and generosity of spirit.

Introduction

The Potbellied Virgin, first published in 1985, treats the excesses of a religious sisterhood in an unnamed town in Ecuador's central Andes. The Virgin of the title is a small wooden icon, a kindly little mother in elaborate robes. The town is inhabited by rival clans, the Benavides family, which dominates the Sisterhood, and the disenfranchised Pandos. The powerful members of the Sisterhood shape the life of the town and dictate the appropriate worship of the Virgin. Seated on a park bench across from the cathedral, four old men, known as the "four old Pandos" represent the town's collective memory and establish a counterpoint to the Sisterhood's authority. The four provide a recitation of Ecuadorian history, linked always to events in the town and to the details of the Potbellied Virgin's miracles and worship. As they trace the evolution of the observances associated with the local patron saint, the Pandos refer repeatedly to Eloy Alfaro ("our father Alfaro"), and use a variety of national and international events as markers. A similar catalog of events serves to situate the town's long search for a resident priest. The history evoked covers the late nineteenth century through the 1960s, ending prior to the petroleum boom of the 1970s.

The town that houses the Potbellied Virgin is both central and marginal, a meeting point of disparate social classes and ethnic groups defined by language, custom, and tradition. Ecuador comprises three regions, the Pacific coast, the Andean highlands, and the lowland Amazon rain forest, known as the Oriente. The novel is situated in the highlands, and its characters participate, to varying degrees, in the regional rivalries that have characterized Ecuadorian history. Ecuador's population includes mestizos (mixed indigenous and white ancestry), Indians, Afro Ecuadorians, and whites. The indigenous and white-mestizo populations are the groups represented in Yánez Cossío's novel. Calculations of Ecuador's indigenous population vary widely, from 12 percent (based on self-reporting of native language) to as much as 40 percent of the national population (Pallares 6). Ecuador's indigenous groups are predominantly Quichua speakers, though many, especially among the younger generations, speak Spanish as well. Quichua refers to the northern (Ecuadorian) dialects of Quechua, the common language of the Inca empire. Numerous Quichua words have been adopted by Ecuadorian Spanish-speakers, whether or not they identify as indigenous, and many of these expressions are present in Yánez Cossío's novel.

While the Pando family is never clearly characterized as "Indian," their position in the town as the dispossessed — the family that owned everything before the Benavides clan manipulated the documents — as well as their darker hair and skin and use of various Quichua words, clearly suggests the social division between Indians and whites. As the description of racial mixing (mestizaje) in the novel suggests, racial categories blend with ethnic or class distinctions, and language or costume can be as great a marker as "race." The Pandos are identified as mestizo, differentiated from both Indians (who appear in the town at fiesta time but are not otherwise major characters) and members of the privileged Benavides family, who have assiduously protected their blond hair (and prestige) through intermarriage with white Europeans and North Americans. Still, the Pandos' sense of having been defrauded of their lands places them closer to the Indians, and their struggle for vindication becomes part of a long history of resistance to colonialism and racial domination. For example, the

Pandos allude to the Hacienda Leito massacre of 1923, in which hundreds of peasants were killed by army troops after they went on strike for better pay and improved working conditions (Gerlach 29). However, the united and increasingly powerful indigenous movements of the late twentieth and early twenty-first centuries belong to a period after the action of the novel.

After achieving independence from Spain in 1822, Ecuador was initially part of Gran Colombia (present-day Colombia, Venezuela, and Ecuador) and became an independent nation in 1830. During the nineteenth century, political power was concentrated in the highlands, where the landowning elite was closely allied with the Catholic Church. Political power shifted toward the coast following the liberal revolution of 1895, but interregional rivalry has continued to characterize Ecuadorian politics and economic development.

A central figure in the politics of the nineteenth century was Gabriel García Moreno, twice president of Ecuador (1861–1865 and 1869–1875). Fiercely Catholic and conservative, García Moreno championed religious education, organized the central government, and undertook numerous public works projects, among them initial work on a railroad to connect Quito and the port city of Guayaquil. In his second term, García Moreno went so far as to dedicate the country to the Sacred Heart of Jesus (Handelsman 28). The wide-reaching concordat signed between Ecuador and the Vatican also significantly extended the role of the church in national affairs (Spindler 65). George Blanksten describes García Moreno as "a *caudillo* who employed the Church rather than the army as his primary instrument of power" (13). García Moreno was assassinated on the steps of the presidential palace in 1875. He remains a controversial figure. The life and death of García Moreno are the subject of Yánez Cossío's novel *Sé que vienen a matarme* (I Know They Are Coming to Kill Me), published in 2001.

García Moreno's great rival (though not his assassin) was General Eloy Alfaro (1842–1912). In September of 1895, Alfaro marched triumphantly into Quito after a thirty-five-year struggle to oust the ruling Conservative Party. During much of that time, Alfaro had been in exile in Panama. Known as the "Old Warrior," Alfaro first participated in an uprising against García Moreno in 1864. Alfaro's government separated church and state, provided certain civil freedoms, secularized government education, confiscated church estates, and completed the railroad between Quito and Guayaquil. In addition, a new elite made up of coastal agricultural exporters partially displaced the aristocratic landholding class as a center of political power. Yet the liberal movement quickly fragmented. Alfaro fought his way back to power in 1906, but bitter fighting erupted again following the untimely death of Alfaro's successor, Emilio Estrada, in 1911, and Alfaro was eventually imprisoned by government forces (Schodt 46). Alfaro was killed by a mob in 1912 and his remains burnt in El Ejido park in Quito.

From 1916 to 1925, the government was largely controlled by the Guayaquil-based Banco Comercial y Agrícola. The bank's dominance grew out of the liberal government's reliance on private bank loans, a reliance necessitated, in part, by Ecuador's poor credit rating abroad. Dissatisfaction with the bank's influence on national policy contributed to popular support for the insurrection of army leaders who seized power in July of 1925. Reforms enacted under Isidro Ayora, installed as president in 1926, included the founding of the Central Bank and a devaluation of the currency, from three to five sucres to the dollar. The newly minted sucres were known popularly as *ayoras*, mocked for being cruder and less valuable than the old sucres, while the delicate fifty-cent pieces were labeled *lauritas*, after the first lady, Laura Carbo de Ayora (Salvador Lara 453). In the novel, the memory of these coins serves as another signpost in the Pandos' recollection of unexplained changes in the Potbellied Virgin's appearance.

The Four Days' War, a brief civil war lasting from August 27 to August 30, 1932, is also singled out for mention in the Pandos' reminiscence. The conflict began after congress had refused to accept the Conservative president-elect, Neptalí Bonifaz, in part because he had at various times accepted Peruvian citizenship, and installed a Liberal, Alfredo Baquerizo Moreno, in his place. Bonifaz, who had received a numerical majority of the votes, declared in turn that if he were disqualified, blood would run ankle-deep in Quito (Oña Villarreal 279). The short-lived conflict between the troops loyal to

Bonifaz — joined by armed conservative civilians — and the troops defending Baquerizo Moreno saw the first use of war planes in Ecuador, and more than five hundred people were said to be lying dead in the streets of the capital following the final battle; the *New York Times* reported that some 40 percent of the male population of Quito "had been armed and organized into rebel sharpshooter bands" (August 31, 1932). The conservatives ultimately surrendered, and Miguel Albornoz took office as provisional president.

The populist José María Velasco Ibarra (1893–1979), born and educated in Quito, is another central figure in the history presented in the novel. Elected to five presidential terms, Velasco was able to complete only one. As president, he more than once granted himself dictatorial powers. His ideology was somewhat undefined, advocating patriotic nationalism, moral regeneration, and a variety of reforms. In *The Potbellied Virgin,* he is recalled as the only president ever to have slept in the town; the fact that he addressed the population from the hotel balcony alludes to Velasco's often-repeated boast, "Give me a balcony and the people are mine" (Martz 1). He was elected to his first presidential term in 1934. Overthrown by the military in 1935, he lost the election of 1939 and took power again following the Revolution of 1944.

In 1940 Dr. Carlos Alberto Arroyo del Río, a wealthy *costeño,* was elected president. Many felt that Velasco Ibarra, exiled to Colombia following the campaign, had lost only because of electoral fraud. Peru's occupation of much of Ecuador's Amazon territory in 1941 further complicated the situation. The Protocol of Peace and Friendship, signed in January 1942 by the Conference of Western Hemisphere Foreign Ministers in Rio de Janeiro, ceded to Peru more than 240,000 square kilometers of Ecuadorian territory. Following this defeat, many felt that dignity demanded that Arroyo del Río step down. Instead, he availed himself of extraconstitutional powers granted for the conduct of the war to suppress his opposition. Following a poorly handled presidential campaign in which Arroyo del Río selected the aging and unpopular senate president as official candidate while simultaneously outlawing the candidacy of Velasco Ibarra, the military garrison in Guayaquil finally rebelled on May 28,

1944. Joined by many civilians, soldiers burned the only barracks loyal
to the government and issued a proclamation stating their aim to be
an "end to the hateful tyranny of traitors which we can no longer tolerate" and labeling the Arroyo del Río government an "interminable
orgy of crimes, thievery, and infamous mistakes which have brought
the country to its ruin" (Blanksten 45). Supporters of the uprising,
in which civilians fought alongside conscripts and junior officers,
included Conservatives, Catholics, Socialists, and Communists (de
la Torre 28–29). The uprising was a response to many years of liberal
domination as well as a rejection of the surrender of national territory. Resentment of Peru continued to fester, and a definitive peace
between the two countries was achieved only in 1998.

Following the revolution of May 1944, Velasco Ibarra replaced
Arroyo del Río and a new constitution was drafted. Velasco was
deposed by the army in 1947 but reelected in 1952, when he managed
to serve his entire term. Although he was replaced in 1956 by a conservative president who sought to redress the mismanagement and
corruption that had undermined gains brought about by booming
banana exports, Velasco was elected to a fourth term in 1960. While
initially committed to a program of major socioeconomic change,
Velasco proved "characteristically unable to convert electoral support into meaningful policy" (Martz 73). His vice president, Carlos
Julio Arosemena Monroy, turned against him and began to build a
personal following. When Velasco declared extensive taxes on con-
sumer goods in October 1961 in an effort to shore up the economy,
demonstrations in Guayaquil and Cuenca brought on a wave of
strikes, work stoppages, and military retaliation that culminated in
the toppling of the government on November 8, 1961. Velasco was
replaced by Arosemena Monroy, who was supported both by left-
ist organizations, such as the federation of university students, and
the economic elite. Though Arosemena Monroy moved toward the
center to assure his political survival once his support for the Cuban
revolution aroused suspicions, his reiteration of planned structural
reforms alarmed the elite, and allegations that his cabinet had been
infiltrated by communists as well as charges of public drunkenness
led to his overthrow by the military in 1963. (In *The Potbellied Virgin*,

the breaking of diplomatic relations with Cuba is mentioned as a chronological clue to situate the narrative of the town's search for a priest.) However, the military proved both unwilling and unable to govern in the face of student protests, labor strikes, and the opposition of the political parties, and the junta resigned on March 28, 1966. A group of national figures selected an interim president, and a new constitution was drafted. After the 1967 constitution was adopted and new election laws passed, national elections were held in June 1968, and Velasco was elected to his fifth term (Martz 75). Velasco assumed dictatorial powers on June 22, 1970, declaring that he would retain such powers until his legal term ended in 1972. As the elections of 1972 neared, army leaders feared that Guayaquil populist Assad Bucaram would run. The army pressured Velasco to postpone elections and remain in office. When Velasco refused, he was ousted in a bloodless coup on February 15, 1972, and General Guillermo Rodríguez Lara, the army chief of staff, took over.

The historical changes evoked in the novel illustrate the shifting role of the military in national politics as well as the ongoing power of the church. The two institutions appear as distinct sites of power, sometimes opposed to one another, sometimes acting in concert. Both come in for parody and criticism, although the power of the church is the more constant, oppressive force. As an icon of popular faith, the Potbellied Virgin herself is at times dismayed by the official or institutional actions undertaken in her name. Throughout the novel, the power of the church is evident at both national and local levels, exaggerated for satirical effect but repeatedly linked to historical reality. The Pandos quote approvingly a sermon by Federico González Suárez (1844–1917)—historian, literary critic, bishop of Ibarra, and archbishop of Quito—who "dominated Ecuador's social, political, and cultural life of the late nineteenth and early twentieth centuries" (Handelsman 28). Tellingly, the sermon cited deals with national honor and sovereignty, not with matters of religious faith. The link between political and religious authority is present from the very founding of the Sisterhood, for the Sisterhood is established in part to counterbalance the prestige of the Virgin of the Sorrows (La Dolorosa), whose portrait in the Jesuit school in Quito is said to have cried real tears in 1906, during the presidency of the anticlerical Alfaro. The 1906 miracle connects events in the novel to the history of Ecuador at the same time that it highlights the excesses of the Sisterhood and the rivalry between virgins (or apparitions of the Virgin Mary) that motivates the Sisterhood's decisions.

Such exaggerated yet motivated linkages are typical of Yánez Cossío's narrative, in which popular wisdom both shapes the interpretations of events and is modified in the face of social change. The four old Pandos' ritualistic retelling of national and local history is punctuated by proverbs and traditional sayings. Such refrains are used throughout the novel to convey conventional wisdom and popular knowledge, as well as to provide an often ironic perspective on the events described.

In his discussion of oral cultures, Walter Ong stresses the importance of proverbs and formulas to speech and memory (34–35). While the Pandos do not represent a wholly oral culture — one of the Pandos publishes a newspaper — the four old men in the park do pass the time with a highly ritualized speech filled with the proverbs, repetitions, and formulas central to oral cultural transmission. Proverbs also characterize the speech of the Sisterhood, so that the weight of tradition and repetition can be seen in their thought as well.

Short, formulaic, often though not always employing devices such as rhyme or alliteration, the proverbs of a community might be seen as a set of shared assumptions or beliefs, the embodiment of popular knowledge. Still, a speaker can employ a proverb with varying degrees of irony or belief. Dick Gerdes argues that "the proverb challenges its audience to better it with something more appropriate, more opportune, or even with something contradictory" (54). At the same time, "proverbs constitute typical mechanisms of repetition through which the dominant authority in a community attempts to preserve the hegemony of a moral system that is grounded in the past" (Gerdes 56). The proliferation of proverbs in *The Potbellied Virgin* also contributes to the comic exaggeration of the novel, allowing characters to express their blinkered or limited worldview at the same time that such a view is undermined or questioned.

Born in Quito in 1928, Alicia Yánez Cossío is widely acknowledged as one of Ecuador's foremost contemporary novelists. She is the author of nine novels, including *Bruna, soroche y los tíos* (1972, published in English in 1999 as *Bruna and Her Sisters in the Sleeping City*), *Yo vendo unos ojos negros* (I Have a Pair of Black Eyes for Sale, 1979), *La casa del sano placer* (The House of Healthy Pleasure, 1989), *Aprendiendo a morir* (Learning How to Die, 1997) and *Sé que vienen a matarme* (I Know They Are Coming to Kill Me, 2001). She has also published poetry, two collections of short stories, several children's books, and a memoir. Her short stories have been widely anthologized. In addition to her first novel, several of Yánez Cossío's short stories have been published in English translation.

Yánez Cossío's work displays the variety and experimentation that have characterized contemporary Latin American narrative. Her novels reveal multiple narrators, a flexible sense of time, and an agile satirical sensibility. Her principal themes have been the roles of women, the power of the church, the nature of representation, and the interpretation of the past. Her most recent novels treat controversial or little-understood figures in Ecuadorian history, such as Santa Mariana de Jesús and Gabriel García Moreno. Yánez Cossío's work cautions against either a stubborn adherence to oppressive tradition or a wholesale surrender to modern commercialism. Her work addresses the complexities of Ecuadorian and Latin American society, engaging racial, gender, class, and ethnic tensions. Yánez Cossío invites us to read — and reread — both the present and the past, alert to the dangers of easy answers, of hypocrisy and posturing; her novels demand of their readers a critical attitude leavened with good humor and a recognition of human fallibility.

Works Cited

Blanksten, George I. *Ecuador: Constitutions and Caudillos.* Berkeley: University of California Press, 1951.

de la Torre, Carlos. *Populist Seduction in Latin America: The Ecuadorian Experience.* Athens: Ohio University Center for International Studies, 2000.

Gerdes, Dick. "An Embattled Society: Orality Versus Writing in Alicia Yánez Cossío's *La cofradía del mullo del vestido de la Virgen Pipona.*" *Latin American Literary Review* 18, no. 36 (1990): 50–58.

Gerlach, Allen. *Indians, Oil, and Politics: A Recent History of Ecuador.* Wilmington, Del.: Scholarly Resources, 2003.

Handelsman, Michael. *Culture and Customs of Ecuador.* Westport, Conn.: Greenwood, 2000.

Martz, John. *Ecuador: Conflicting Political Culture and the Quest for Progress.* Boston: Allyn and Bacon, 1972.

Oña Villarreal, Humberto. *Fechas históricas y hombres notables del Ecuador.* Ibarra, Ecuador: n.p., 1986.

Ong, Walter J. *Orality and Literacy: The Technologizing of the Word.* New York: Methuen, 1982.

Pallares, Amalia. *From Peasant Struggles to Indian Resistance: The Ecuadorian Andes in the Late Twentieth Century.* Norman: University of Oklahoma Press, 2002.

"Quito Rebels Yield after Hard Battle." *New York Times,* August 31, 1932.

Salvador Lara, Jorge. *Breve historia contemporánea del Ecuador.* Mexico: Fondo de Cultura Económica, 1994.

Schodt, David W. *Ecuador: An Andean Enigma.* Boulder, Col.: Westview, 1987.

Spindler, Frank MacDonald. *Nineteenth Century Ecuador: A Historical Introduction.* Fairfax, Va.: George Mason University Press, 1987.

The Potbellied Virgin

Clip-clop, clip-clop, clip-clop, striking showers of sparks against the rocks carved by the water of the rivers whose terrifying currents carry whole settlements to the Oriente, over the round stones like hard rolls, like the bread eaten by the sweat of one's brow, the bread that is burnt at the oven door, stones that have been placed one by one by the calloused hands of the Indians, gallops Magdalena Benavides, and she thinks that the day will come when people from far away, who are the ones who discover foreign lands, will be amazed and come to see with their own eyes the hand-laid cobblestones of the town's streets and its long roads. And the stones that were domesticated by water and later tamed by the mother stone acting as sledgehammer to plant them in the ground are polished further by the blows of the horseshoes, and they are like the souls of the townspeople, blunted by life's blows so that they say at each encounter:

—Here we are, still alive, better that than be too proud.

The horse's hooves hit the stones with a contained fury, as if they wanted to pass over the prone bodies of the Pandos and flatten them into empty hides. The dark chestnut seems as though it were flying when it passes, its feet extended at chest level. The streets, entirely deserted at this most uncertain hour of the day, when the sun is rolling behind the mountain and the shadows stretch to meet the night, awaken with the clatter of this crazy gallop that rings against the an-cient stones, tearing them up, and one doesn't know if it is afternoon-evening or afternoon-night.

From all sides you can hear the shoemaker Romualdo. He strums his guitar, wasting away, *pasillo* after *pasillo,* songs he doesn't sing, no, he's crucifying himself on those trite litanies of disaster, lashing himself with the halter of heartache, he's slitting his own throat, adorning his entire body with masochistic hair shirts:

> "Not even your memoooory
> comes now to consooooole me
> because I think those memories have diiiiied
> with the cold of these last eeevenings ..."

Magdalena rides with one hand on the reins and the other trying to brush out of her eyes the golden weight of chamomile and broom that is her blond hair, because if she wasn't blond, she wouldn't be a Benavides nor would she have to take such care of her hair for the day when her turn comes to cut it all off in the dreaded ceremony, in order to give it to the Virgin who must change wigs every five years. This year it is her turn, and the other Benavides women will someday have to cut their hair, too, since they should have that terrible privilege at least once in their lives ...

Magdalena gallops to the very center of town, to the plaza, where she knows the last four old Pandos are watching her from the nests of wrinkles that surround their tiny, malignant eyes. They come from the old Pandos, the eternal opponents of the Benavideses. The two families are like water and fire, like vinegar and oil, like good and bad fortune, like night and day; they are like Ahab and Zedekiah who, "though both were enamored of her, they did not tell each other their trouble, for they were ashamed to reveal their lustful desire to have her."

The hardened, wizened old men—old age without peace is visibly rough—consume her with their eyes so as to say, once she has passed, that she is the craziest of the Benavides women, the only mannish one in the bunch, the scandal of the town, the least worthy of all the handmaidens that the Virgin has had since the Sisterhood was founded, and the words falter and stumble in the toothless hollows of their mouths:

—*Carishina, guarmishina,* pela papa en la cocina.

—*Carishina, guarmishina,* peel potatoes in the kitchen.

They've been waiting for her since the sunny midday when they heard her arrive, preceded by the long bark of the hungry dogs that point the arrows of their howls to heaven. They squirm in their impotence, because after populating the entire town and after having exercised for years their feudal rights over the unmarried Indian women, they have given out, and now they're all show. The best they can do is watch this crazy Magdalena in her wild gallop, and what they hate about her is what she represents: the strength and the power that they once held in their hands and that was wrenched away from them with the twisted force of the law, taking from them the land that had belonged to their grandfathers and that extended across every known climate. The lands that had always belonged to the Pandos, until the first Benavides arrived and changed both landscape and customs. The Pandos then had to Hispanicize their surname, exchange their rope-soled sandals for worn out shoes, their rough homespun for mended shirts and their racial pride for an anodyne mestizaje.

For years, the four old Pandos have been searching for the documents that prove their claims. They sense that although they spend their lives sitting on the park benches, they are in fact marching toward death unable to find the proofs of the lawsuit they began one day, for which — they recall — they sold two milk cows, and made their first and only trip to the capital, and went to the courts to consult hundreds of lawyers and *quishcas,* but the documents were mislaid in the notaries' offices and are no longer in their power, but rather in the hands of the Benavides clan.

Seated in the shade of an old walnut, which bears only a few stunted green nuts, they smoke their hand-rolled cigarettes, and the cut black tobacco dribbles through their trembling arthritic hands, spattering their worn trousers of ancient wool, and they retrieve it bit by bit, using the nail of an index finger as a spoon. They gather the minimal particles and the ribs of the best leaves of tobacco available on the coast, which their nephews bring when they travel to Esmeraldas, and they combine them parsimoniously with those stored in a rusty can, on which one can just make out the figure of an angel in voluminous robes, fat as a matron, with open wings, with the trumpet of judgment day in his right hand and, in the left, a basket from which fall, as if raining from heaven, boxes and cigarettes that are retrieved by boys in sailor suits and men with mocora palm hats and women with little boots and broad-brimmed, feathered straw bonnets, dressed like women from the turn of the century. One can barely make out the words:

EL VENCEDOR
Cigarrillos puros
Selecting tobacco from the best plantations
Esmeraldas, Daule, and Santa Rosa.
J, B, Nieto G.

Magdalena arrives galloping along one side of the plaza. She slows little by little, stopping at the steps of the magnificent cathedral, where she throws herself off the horse and runs up the stairs, but then pauses at the threshold of the doors carved with biblical scenes of the loaves and fishes and the parting of the Red Sea. The enormous doors bear the weight of ancestral devotion and the accumulated dust of the long streets. She knows that the four old Pandos are watching her; she senses it through her dorsal vertebrae. She can't go into the temple, still less approach the altar of the Virgin, because the gaze of the four old men has her tied, and she is wearing pants, and no woman can enter the church dressed as a man. Magdalena lets her eyes adjust to the dim interior barely illuminated by the thousands of candles that never go out, and when she sees the icon, she asks of her, trustingly, the greatest of miracles:

—Let me leave this godforsaken town. Have pity on me, Oh Potbellied Virgin, little Potbellied Mother ...

She draws back. She descends the stairs with the accumulated sadness of all the vestal virgins and daughters of the sun and of the moon who have occupied the temples of the enigmatic East and of the ancient West. She mounts her horse. Whips it and departs.

The four old Pandos spit out the thick, dark saliva of inveterate smokers and repeat:

—*Carishina, guarmishina,* peel your potatoes in the kitchen.

And they twist their necks after the galloping figure who circles the plaza and disappears. And when Magdalena has gone, the day really draws to a close, and the sun slips behind a mountain, and suddenly the sadness that has always inhabited the plaza of every Andean town built of stones and sorrows arrives all at once. And Romualdo Pando and his guitar are dying along with the day as the horse passes and once again the bleeding lament opens like an incurable wound:

> "It seems to me the breeeeze
> of these winter niiiights
> has entered right withiiin
> to freeze my soul and boooody ..."

Manuel Pando, the one from the *Voice of the People* press, sets to one side the linotypes with which he had been laying out his eternally subversive newspaper with its perennial attacks against the Benavides oligarchs: it's Magdalena again, with her mop of blond hair unraveled by the wind. Once again Magdalena, with her strange eyes the color of sugarcane about to be cut. Once again Magdalena, with the almost perfect oval of her face resembling that of the Potbellied Virgin to whom he long ago stopped praying, but that he always watches with curious interest when the local dignitaries take her out in procession, and he sees how she sways above their heads like a miniature Magdalena. A forbidden Magdalena, who in any case is his cousin, and who he can never approach because he broke all the ties that bound him to the masters of the village when he learned that he was the bastard son of one of them.

He comes out sadly to watch her pass and, leaning against the doorframe, he cleans his hand on a rag of indeterminate color while his neighbor (who is Manuel Pando's real mother, although she has never told him that, because she would die of shame) moves abruptly so as to peek through the half-open window, and knocks over the bottle of Thimolina with which she rubs the eternal and stubborn arthritis of her washerwoman's legs and of the fingers so absurdly twisted and swollen that they seem like frostbitten potatoes.

The acid deposits in her overworked veins ache, ache with the pain that will last until her death without respite or remedy, because she will always be standing among the large boulders of the river washing her clothes, the clothes of Magdalena Benavides who passes her time galloping from the hacienda into town, and who sends her so much clothing that isn't even dirty, for the pure pleasure of making her work and harassing her with the hard soap of bad fortune. The ill humors of the neighbor's swollen arteries are stirred up further when she interrupts the reverie in which Manuel Pando, the untouched son, has become lost, leaning against the doorframe with the stained rag in his hands, whistling through his teeth what he always whistles when he's laying out the linotype:

> "Life doesn't kill us, nooooo,
> what kills us are the sooorrows ..."

And the neighbor doesn't know whether to curse him for a fool or take pity on him as her son, since he's a Benavides and didn't choose to remain one, for as the four old Pandos tell, when the one from the press was young, he lived in the hacienda house with his aunts and uncles. But one bad day, when the Benavides family couldn't curb his rebellious impulses, they told him he was bad natured because he was a bastard, and he didn't need to hear more. He broke all ties, returned their surname and went off with the Pandos to earn his living, and ever since, he has understood the misery of the poor and the exploitation of the rich, and he swore that one day he would put things in their place.

And the neighbor follows him like a shadow, loving him from a distance, anxious to tell him when he watches Magdalena:

—Stop, stop looking at her, she's not for you, or for anyone. Even though she's a tomboy and doesn't even know how to ride sidesaddle, like a woman should, she's destined for the Potbellied Virgin, and as your people would say, *honey wasn't made for the ass's snout.*

And then she bends down, resigned, to mop up the Thimolina with a cotton ball she later wrings out in a delicate stream over the mouth of the bottle. The red liquid turns brown while she calculates that the Thimolina isn't going to last the month, and she'll have to go to the pharmacist again to ask him for credit, pretending not to see the sign that is the most visible thing in the pharmacy and which reads:

"Today I don't give credit; tomorrow, I will."

It is the only sign the pharmacist has added — on top of all the older signs you can barely read — since he inherited the shop from his grandfather:

If you want Strength and Beauty
Take
Doctor Huxley's
NER—VITA
For sale in all the pharmacies and
drugstores of the world
S/. 2 the bottle

and
ESPECIFICO CANDOC
from César A. Pajuelo
S/. 1 the bottle

and
BOTELLAS CALORIS
for family use
especially for children
during the period of nursing
Zevallos & Icaza

and
FOR MEN OF ALL AGES
Masculine Weakness (Impotence)

Completely Cured
New, inoffensive, agreeable, and infallible
TREATMENT
Buenos Aires, 14 December 1907
P. N. ARRATA

And as the horse passes, the pharmacist also spills his bicarbonate.
Annoyed, he throws aside the silver spoon with which he is measur-
ing out small mounds on rectangles of brown paper, since what he
sells most of in the pharmacy La Confianza is bicarbonate to soothe
heartburn caused when the potatoes eaten with their skins, with hot
pepper and fresh cheese, begin to ferment in the vigorous darkness; to
calm the colics with their spasmodic contractions when the inevitable
phase of the moon arrives and is hurried along with a tea of fig leaves;
to stifle the fierce gas pains that torment the men of the town and the
beasts of the field. The pharmacist never leaves his counter, but he
knows the intimate secrets of the entire town. He knows more than
Manuel Pando, who watches the people toil and sweat and who takes
the pulse of the town to confirm that it is dying of all possible miseries;
he knows more than the old priest Santiago de los Angeles, who cre-
ated the Sisterhood of the Bead on the Gown of the Potbellied Virgin
and who took with him to the other life the thousands of secrets that
shamefacedly crossed the grating of the ancient confessional, which is
now festooned with gray cobwebs; he knows a lot, because in curing
them of their physical ailments, he contrives to spy out the folds of
their souls, and between prescription and consultation he keeps track
of the menstrual cycles of all the young women, and he knows about
missteps and about misbegotten fruits; and he knows, above all, that
all of the men of the town are dying of love for Magdalena Benavides
and for all the Magdalena Benavideses who have been born and been
unable to marry as would have been proper; and finally, he knows of
all the fights and quarrels on account of those Magdalenas and of the
hatred the Pando women feel for the Benavides women, because their
husbands sin in thought whenever they are on top of them.

And he knows about the hatred and envy of the taffy maker
Rosa Inés who, as the horse passes, suspends in the air the golden,

twisted strap of brown sugar taffy that looks like the braid of any one of the Magdalenas, and she tosses the taffy furiously against the chonta wood hook above the door, beside the aloe branch that needs neither soil nor water because it feeds off matter found in the air, which no one sees but which the aloe eats and for that reason it brings good luck and prevents the owners of the house from being bewitched. It has been there for years, tied up with a ribbon that was once red but is now white. And Rosa Inés pulls and twists the taffy and throws it again as though it were a vertical, malleable river of gold, or a cabuya rope suitable for hanging a white neck like the elongated, heron-like, Modigliani throats that all the Benavides women have, and she doesn't stop working when she sees Magdalena pass like a flash of lightning while she has to stay in the same place, under the sticky chonta hook, working until the day turns to night, when she will sit down to wrap the candies that pile up on the shelves as if they were gold ingots, while she hears the persistent, cascading voice that sang to Magdalena—never to Rosa Inés—when she was a child:

> "Ricky gets spun sugar candy
> Roque gets a hokey pokey
> tricky tricky tricky tran ..."

And she throws and stretches the taffy before it gets cold and stiff, sighing:

—Who wouldn't want to ride like her over the green paddocks, devouring roads and distances the way you'd slurp up a noodle, lose herself behind the hills, ford the thousand rivers of the region, escape.... But the weeks of the poor have so few Sundays!

And she comes back from her impossible dreams when she hears the curses of her father who has spilled his jar of blue paint at the passing of Magdalena Benavides' horse, and she watches, both mocking and distressed, the trail of blue that zigzags between the stones and stretches from the overturned can in a thread that finally disappears in the kikuyu grass as if it were the entrance to the forest of an enchanted miniature world.

The man picks up the can and cleans it with the brush. At least he was putting the finishing touches on his rickety old truck, which was one of the first to arrive in the town and which has the image of the Potbellied Virgin on the windshield, decorated with silk tassels and pompoms of colored wool, and on whose rear bumper you can read, in the twisted calligraphy of a man who got stuck in the third grade of his rural school and of life:

"You mite forgit me but never never what we done ..."

He wrote it out and painted it thinking of Marianita Pando, because when she was still a girl, they became lovers one afternoon, and as time passed, he replaced her with a real woman and later replaced that one with another, and replaced that one with a truck into which he poured all his feelings, while Marianita Pando wasted away in oblivion, until he was widowed and asked for her hand in marriage while she was still singing rounds in school:

"Sweet rice with milk, I want to marry
a nice young lady from San Nicolás ..."

But Marianita told him he could go to hell because she was afraid that once they were joined for life, he would infect her with his old age. He wasn't all that old, but Marianita is conceited like all the Benavides women she so resembles, and everyone knows her and talks about her, because she is the most controversial woman in town. The four old Pandos say she's famous because when she was young and lived on the river bank, along came the raging current, bellowing like a fighting bull from Antisana, one of those who get hot pepper and gun powder in their feed to anger them so they'll show off well in the ring, and they say it was a Friday when the river, having already burst its banks, came bellowing and flattening every-thing in its path. It arrived at Marianita's house and tore it out by its roots and carried it off with trees, foundation, and roof; with beds, petticoats, and crockery; with the bit of patio with its sour orange trees and the chickens that laid their eggs beside the wash stone and where Marianita was bathing when the earth let go and crumbled into the furious current, and Marianita vanished and everyone looked for her downriver without finding her until the water ceased to bellow and they could launch a small gourd holding a lighted candle, and after pitching back and forth for hours and hours, the gourd finally found her. She was two leagues further downstream. They found her naked and terrified, with the block of black soap still in her hand, sitting on the biggest rock in the torrential river, where a crude wood cross still stands that the Sisterhood ordered placed so that people would remember that this was no miracle of the Potbellied Virgin, but a punishment from God, because Marianita had raised her hand against her mother when her mother reprimanded her for the affair with the truck driver who was old enough to be her father and was already married with children and "what would people say of such a scandal?" And then Marianita got angry, and her mother cursed her, but cursed and everything, Marianita knows she was saved by one of the Virgin's miracles because she never knew how she found herself seated on the rock, and the truck driver knows she was the greatest love of his life, and every time he sees Magdalena he remembers Marianita because people say Marianita looks more like the Benavides women than like the Pandos because of her long, blond hair.

And Marianita Pando has also left her sewing to one side to watch the owner of the blouse she is making pass by. It's a boring blouse to sew because even with such a fine and delicate fabric, with its peachy melon color, she hasn't wanted any ruffles or pleats, no bows or tucks, just plain, like a man's shirt. At the horse's gallop Marianita is filled with the tedium of the dressmaker's life, which affects her kidneys and which she alleviates with teas made of corn silk. And her gaze gets lost behind the mountains and when it returns from its imaginary journey, she stares at her hands, which have sewed so much clothing for the Benavides women, and she sees the battered silver thimble riddled with holes, which is like a little hat on her middle finger, next to the white steel band she wears on her ring finger to stop the spells which, as the four old Pandos say, might be cast by the wife of the truck driver, who died of *mal aire* — innocent of others' sins — giving

birth to the taffy maker, Rosa Inés. Marianita Pando thinks about the
Benavides clan, and she is filled with a strange bitterness. She takes
up the blouse that has fallen to the floor and begins making the but-
tonholes for the six shell buttons, which are the only decoration the
owner of the blouse wants. And with her bundle of sorrows, she sinks
into the dark world of the ballad that is the potion with which the
town poisons itself, clawing at its soul:

> "I reproach you nooothiiing,
> or at the most my saaaadness,
> this enormous saaaadness
> that is taking away my liiife ..."

And as the horse passes, the priest Miguel, who has arrived like
so many others who have come and gone in the place of the priest
Santiago de los Angeles, dead these many years, closes with a smack
the breviary he has been reading so as not to fall into temptation, for
the air of the town is corrupt and generates unhealthy thoughts with
more intensity than in other places. He crosses himself and begins to
jot down in a yellow notebook what he is going to say at Sunday's Mass.
He arrived recently, contracted by the Sisterhood, but upon seeing
Magdalena in a man's clothing his face twists with revulsion, because
he doesn't approve of one of the Potbellied Virgin's handmaidens riding the way Magdalena rides when she ought to be embroidering or
reading the *Christian Year,* and he writes with haughty letters: "Woe is
he who causes a scandal, it would be better to tie a millstone around
his neck and throw him into the sea," for this is how Sunday's sermon will begin, although it would be better to say throw him into the
river rather than the sea, which is so far away and so unknown to the
poor inhabitants of the town and the poor Indians who walk from a
hundred leagues around to hear the Potbellied Virgin's Mass. Never-
theless, about the river they know quite a lot, and they tremble with
fear when the rainy season comes.... And when he has worked out in
his head everything he's going to say and is about to write it down,
he becomes frightened of crossing Doña Carmen, and he decides
not to stay in town until Sunday. The president of the Sisterhood

of the Bead on the Gown of the Potbellied Virgin will recognize the sermon's allusion to her favorite granddaughter and the priest will have the same problems as the other priests who have come to town and then left. They have arrived by the hundreds and not one has lasted. They say that many have been punished and reviled by Doña Carmen. The four old Pandos say so many things ...

The whole town has awakened to the monotonous hammering of the hooves, the crack of sparks struck by the horseshoes hitting the stones, the harsh clatter, the echo over the river stones of the feet of Magdalena Benavides' horse. All of the men desire her with a shameful longing for the forbidden, but at the same time they respect her with the fear of the sacred, for this Magdalena and all of the Magdalenas will remain single without having touched a man, because they have been the elect ever since the town has been a town, and the immense cathedral was built to venerate the Virgin who walked on her own feet from no one knows where.

They, the Benavides women, must dress and undress the Virgin some fifty-three times a year, the same number as the fifty-three Hail Marys of the rosary. All of them must wear the chastity belt with which they were born, which weighs as much as the life of any of the Pando women who have to work from dawn to dusk, because such is life, because, as the four old Pandos say, *whom God loved, he made a man, and for the women, babies.*

It benefits the sad handmaidens nothing that they are the owners of the largest haciendas of the region, whose extent neither the eye can see nor the imagination grasp, nor to be the owners of the lands planted with sugarcane to one side, with wheat on the other, which have the undulations and undertows of an immeasurable yellow sea and which reach as far as the real sea so far away; it's no use to them being the owners of cornfields whose stalks bend double under the weight of the ears and of lands planted to fruit trees that burst with colored honeys, nor of the granaries full to the eaves, nor of the coffee and cacao dryers large as runways. It benefits them nothing that their domains extend across all of the earth's climates: the ranches with thousands of cattle, the stables, the coffers of inherited jewels, the wardrobes crammed with dresses, the trucks and pickups that come

and go between coast, mountains, and jungle. None of them are any
use so long as they must remain in the boring town with the furled
sails of their impossible dreams, condemned in life to a perpetual
mission. The Benavides women are like women out of Lorca, daughters and granddaughters of ferocious Bernardas, desperately barren,
sacrificed on the altar of unbreakable tradition. Although they own
the town, it is the town's strangely friendly and peaceful people who
are their true lords and masters. The Magdalenas fear them, although
once in a while, rather timidly, they go against their customs and
musty traditions and dare, for example, to gallop through the town
dressed as men dress.

They fear the town with an obscure ancestral fear, because they
know what the people who live there are capable of, and they always
remember what they have been told, time and again, so they won't
"step further than they should." They know by heart the sad history
of the Benavides grandmother obliged to feign an imaginary illness
impossible to treat in town. Early one morning, alone and in the dark,
with only the owls to notice her, she leaves for the capital, riding a
mule, allowing no one to accompany her because she is pregnant,
and she's going to the capital to get rid of the bundle that she carries in her entrails without anyone knowing. But when she returns,
pale and tearful, everyone already knows about her miserable fall, and
whom she fell with, and the town rises up and burns her house down,
unable to forgive the sacrilege of her dressing and undressing the Virgin without being herself a virgin, and afterwards they throw her out
of town and she ends her days in an asylum, poor and forgotten, and
when she dies they bury her like a dog in any old corner of wherever
she is, and having been a rich Benavides does her no good at all.

The four old Pandos say this event took place back in the year
'06, the same day Don Eloy Alfaro made his triumphant entry into
Quito, ousting president Lizardo García after the twenty-day battle
of Chasqui, when the Old Fighter left Guayaquil aboard the vener-
able launch La Montañera, outwitting the vigilance of the enemies of
progress.

Magdalena and her two cousins (freckled Clarisa and Martina, the
one who spits when she talks), all three unmarried, all three young,

vivacious, yearning for life and a husband, will never forget that awful May first of four years ago. They come to town because they have to dress the Virgin in her gown of sky-blue brocade, the mantle embroidered with wallflowers in gold thread, the sapphire crown and the pearl-encrusted shoes of the same fabric as the dress, and as they arrive from the capital, the three unmarried Benavides girls come wearing the three miniskirts they've just bought, and the dresses fall a handsbreadth above the knees and a handsbreadth below the chastity belts to which they were born. And as they're arriving, carefree and laughing with their faces turned up to catch the raindrops of the first of May, which have the power to whiten and clear women's skin, they can't even reach the steps that lead to the church vestibule, because hundreds of people are following them, because word has already gotten out of how the Benavides girls are dressed, and the respectable town waits for them with sticks and stones at the door of the immense cathedral to prevent them from entering looking like that; and old Simona, beside herself, wounded to the core, as if personally affronted — for she was Clarisa's wet nurse — is the first to insult them and throw shards of roof tiles, and this is the signal for rocks and rubble and anything else to hand to rain down upon them; and the priest Samuel, come to replace the priest Santiago de los Angeles, dead these many years, hurries fearfully down the steps of the parish house shouting curses and Latin phrases and covers them up with his threadbare cassock, saving their lives. And Manuel Pando, attentive as ever to the comings and goings of Magdalena, takes them, shielding them with his own body, back to the *Voice of the People* printing office, where he gives them shelter — since they are his cousins, and they're being threatened — while he shouts himself hoarse explaining to the furious mob that the Benavides girls aren't sluts, nor indecent, nor are they crazy, nor have they come in disguise, but rather that they are fashionably dressed. But the town wants to lynch them and drag them through the streets, and the mob can't hear Manuel Pando's explanations because the sacristan, who is weak in the head because they say the crown of his skull hasn't closed up yet, loses his mind in the tumult and goes crazy, and he climbs the bell tower and sounds the alarm on the fat bell that only tolls quietly

on those Sundays when a priest shows up to say Mass; or rings the peal
of glory for important festivals, barely moving the halter that is sus-
pended from above; or tolls for the funeral Mass when the bereaved
bring some priest who bandages his prayer for the dead, winding the
clapper in a jute sack so it will be damped; or the jute sack is taken
off to ring out in case of fire or earthquakes, because playing it the
way he's playing it now, the peals can be heard a thousand leagues
away, and the window panes shatter, sending shards flying. And the
priest Samuel — who is already packing his bags when he hears the
tumult, because he's written close to fifteen sermons and knows that
none of them will please the ladies of the Sisterhood — goes down
to defend the girls in the miniskirts who are about to be killed and
then climbs the steps four at a time to the highest tower of the belfry
and launches himself at the crazed sacristan who is shouting louder
than the bells, and he quiets him with a sprinkle of holy water that
he has to force down his gullet, for the sacristan neither hears nor
understands explanations because his mind has been clouded, and
this happens each time the moon waxes.

When silence finally returns with the presence of Doña Carmen,
who explains what a miniskirt is, because she has to defend her relatives, the town listens to reason and calms down. Meanwhile the pharmacist, who has come with his first aid kit, treats Magdalena Benavides
and her cousins, placing arnica compresses from head to foot, linger-
ing — as is only natural and human — more on the wounds to their legs
than on the lumps and swellings of other parts which don't matter so
much, being already so familiar. The priest Samuel comes down from
the tower with the sacristan and takes him to the pharmacy as well so
they can give him a potion of valerian root and belladonna, since it's
best that he sleep for a few days until the moon starts to wane.

Manuel Pando's neighbor, her maternal nature buoyed, takes pity
on the three little girls and takes out three merino shawls, and she
winds them up with a string of safety-pins around the waist, for the
poor Magdalenas cry like their namesake and it's time for them to
leave. They walk with their heads down, tripping over the long silk
fringes of the shawls. They arrive at the cathedral escorted by the
angry eyes of the people. They climb up to the main altar to change

the Virgin's clothes, which is not the undertaking of a moment, but a task of many hours; it is part of an elaborate craft and it should never appear to be a matter of guesswork, for they are closely observed by the townspeople and admonished by the ladies of the Sisterhood when they make a mistake in their work.

The unmarried Benavides girls must study the night before what the Ordinances of the Sisterhood of the Bead on the Gown of the Potbellied Virgin say about the dress, the mantle, the shoes or sandals, according to the circumstances; about the crown, the miter or the tiara, according to the occasion; about the earrings, the scepter, the rings, according to the requests of the *priostes* who underwrite the fiestas. But not about the underclothes, because according to the Ordinances in effect, since the year '26 it has been forbidden to undress the Virgin completely, which is better for today's handmaidens, who have less work and less risk of making errors.

The handmaidens enter the Virgin's dressing room. The room is sunk in half-light and smells of damp and mystery. They often want to speak but they work in silence, absorbed in a ritual that somehow does not manage to penetrate their consciousness. They open the large wardrobe of carved mahogany, and the hinges squeak like a duet of hoarse cicadas. There hang the fifty-three dresses approved by the Sisterhood, lined up on white satin hangers. On the opposite wall hang thousands of dresses, cloaks and robes that for one reason or another are not to be used. At the back of the first wardrobe is the safe with the jewels, a giant safe that was bought needlessly, because it would never occur to anyone to rob the Virgin, and it's open because the ladies of the Sisterhood forgot the combination and how to work it and precautions are taken only when outsiders come.

The other unused clothes are stored in a large wooden chest, not carved like the wardrobes but rather veneered and inlaid with beautiful arabesques of mother-of-pearl and bone, with embossed silver locks, between organdy sachets of fragrant herbs: twelve embroidered petticoats of snow-white cambric drenched with bobbin lace of the kind nobody makes any more; twelve pair of exquisite stockings, knit with silk thread, as fine as if their confection had been entrusted to tiny spiders able to nest on angel's wings; twelve pair of underpants adorned with garter belts in delicate colors that any queen would envy; twelve little jackets that aren't exactly bras, because they're not for a woman, but for the Virgin, who is neither a store mannequin nor a doll and has always been treated with the appropriate respect and circumspection, since dolls are dolls, and mannequins are mannequins, and icons are icons.

As the four old Pandos recall, the discussions about whether or not to put mothballs in the wardrobes and the trunk that hold the Virgin's clothing lasted five long, long years, from '31 to '35. And while the town is heatedly debating, the country is plunged into the greatest political agitation. The Chimborazo battalion revolts — the four old Pandos remember — provoking the fall of president Isidro Ayora, who is replaced by Larrea Alba, who governs only fifty-two days and then falls. Then comes Baquerizo Moreno, who calls elections that Neptalí Bonifaz wins, and when Bonifaz goes to take the office that is properly his, the bad faith deputies in the congress, for there have always been such, accuse him of being Peruvian, and in the face of such lies, he falls, and the furious, outwitted people take to the streets and the commotion begins, and Freile Larrea takes over and has to face the unforgettable Four Days' War, which ends in an armistice and a declaration that there were neither victors nor vanquished, but only two thousand dead who lie flat and rigid in the streets of Quito.

— Compadre, of course we remember, we lived through all that, step by step ...

And so new elections are called and, due to a tremendous fraud, the kind we've seen repeated since, Martínez Mera wins. As is only natural, the people won't stand for it, they can't bear even the sight of his picture, and to keep himself in power, he has to change his cabinet every Monday, and after ten months of yes and no, of it is and it isn't, he falls, without even being able to go out in the street or appear on the balconies of the presidential palace, because as soon as they see him, people shout brazenly: Gorilla!

—People called him Gorilla because he was a monkey from the coast, one of the old Pandos explains.

—And do you remember, compadre, what happened to the late Néstor Villafuerte who went to jail because every time he knocked back a few drinks, he began to yell: "Down with the Gorilla!" and "Death to the Gorilla!" so then there appears a squad of soldiers — in sandals, no less — who beat him until he lies on the ground aching and bruised. And, playing the clown, he asks them without fear why the beating and the club, and the soldiers answer angrily that it's because he's been insulting the President of the Republic, and the late Néstor Villafuerte, honoring his name, protests that no, that they have no right, that he hasn't even mentioned him, that he's only shouted "Down with the gorilla," that this foolishness is only because he's had a few drinks with his friends, and it's the same as saying down with the crocodile or the elephant or any other animal, and the soldiers answer that yes, he's going to prison, incommunicado, because the only Gorilla in the country is His Excellency the President ...

—Yes, that's just how it was, compadre, and when Martínez Mera falls in '33, Albelardo Moncayo takes over, and he's overthrown by our own Velasco Ibarra who also falls, as always, and this is around '35, and Velasco Ibarra is followed by Antonio Pons who lasts about as long as a sigh. And in the midst of so much commotion, in which nobody knows who will be governing from one day to the next, the mayor of the town, the Benavides who always wore riding boots, with silver spurs and riding crop, along with the men who made up the municipal council, say yes, go ahead and put mothballs and whatever else is necessary to keep the moths and cockroaches out of the wardrobes and trunks that house the Virgin's clothing, for there's too much money in there to let it be eaten by moths. The ladies of the Sisterhood say no: there is no need for kerosene or mothballs when we're dealing with garments that have touched the body of the Virgin. And the truth is that, while the benches and the confessionals of the cathedral, which have borne the weight of thousands of buttocks and have heard the sins of millions of penitents, look as if they'd contracted smallpox, the furniture of the dressing room is intact, as if the woodworms knew what they were attacking.

When the handmaidens gather the designated clothing and jewelry, they spread them over silver trays and move in procession to the altar. The ladies of the Sisterhood are seated in the first row and the townsfolk, who seem less numerous each day, keep to the back, at a

respectful distance. The handmaidens begin to climb the narrow steps
that shiver as if with cold. Their climb is a balancing act and they pout
as they get tangled up in the long fringes of the merino shawls and
their bruises and the insults still smart. Magdalena is dying to jump
down and run out of the temple, but she's afraid that Doña Carmen
will throw herself upon her and subject her to another embarrassment. And when they finish the job, they climb down from the altar
agitated and very sad, and they are made to climb into a car that waits
for them at the cathedral steps to prevent the townsfolk from starting
up again with them and their miniskirts, and they leave thinking they
would give anything to change places with any washerwoman or peasant, that never have they felt such sympathy with Romualdo Pando's
songs, that they would like to go into the shoemaker's shop to hear
up close the searing laments that sound stupid sung by real men with
hair on their chests, but sound better sung by wimps or crybabies,
and seem to have been made for the handmaidens:

> "Who could wash away all the sorrooows
> that make their painful way around the worrrrld ..."

The four old Pandos who have spent the whole day seated on
the park benches taking the sun, talking about politics, smoking,
and watching the comings and goings of Magdalena Benavides—the
best of the three current handmaidens—also ponder their lost documents. They remember clearly and will swear by the Potbellied Virgin (a vow to be taken seriously) that before the year '25, and they
remember this down to the last detail, it was sometime in the month
of March, when the river carried off entire hamlets and washed away
some twenty kilometers of the train tracks in the famous flood of the
Río Chanchán—years before the flood starring Marianita Pando—
when it didn't stop raining no matter how many public prayers they
made, when the corner post of the cathedral sprouted little green
branches and everyone said it was neither the damp nor the fertil-
ity of the earth but rather a miracle of the Potbellied Virgin, when
Don Gonzalo Córdova (better known as "button Córdova") was president, who was overthrown by a junta that handed over command to

Isidro Ayora, the one who had them mint the *ayoras* and *lauritas*, which were silver sucres and fifty-cent pieces that people saved and didn't allow to circulate, and it was the year in which they were left completely isolated and hungry, they remember exactly that in that year—because they saw the Virgin many times under an umbrella— the Virgin had a flat belly like any other image of the virgin. And it was that very year that the Sisterhood forbade the changing of the icon's underclothes, because the old Pandos' grandmother, who worked day and night making the bobbin lace for her petticoats, stopped making it. And they remember each and every one of the grandmother's lamentations as she complained that between the floods and the lack of work—because at that time bobbin work paid well, except that jobs were few and far between—it would be better if the Potbellied Virgin took pity on them and transformed them into frogs, since frogs live happily in the rain and don't need to earn their living working…. And they remember that they and others, among them the late Eleuterio Arroba Pando, nicknamed Censer, the town peddler, when he arrived with his mules loaded down with gauze and taffeta, with chintz and chambray, with thin muslin and canvas and piqués, with satins and cambrics, with mourning fabric in wool and cotton, with necklaces and ribbons, with mirrors and tortoiseshell combs, with delicate gold and silver chains, with crystal inkwells and mandolins, would spend every night serenading the young women and waking them up with trite heartache singing song after song, and he always repeated "With My Heart on My Lips" which could be heard all over the town. They remember how that time he had gone to the capital with the specific assignment to buy glass beads for a new gown for the Virgin, and he never came back, because the Four Days' War caught him there, and he died for his nosiness when the entire populace rose up in arms, for they didn't want Neptalí Boni- faz—who they called "Naptalina Malafaz," Mothball Uglyface—to be president, insisting that he wasn't Ecuadorian but Peruvian. That was back around '31, the whole thing was unforgettable.

And to get back to what they were remembering, that is, the year '25 and the beginning of '26, the four old Pandos can't forget that they, with the late Arroba Pando—may God keep him in heaven because he

played the guitar like nobody else and sang like the angels — presented
themselves to the Sisterhood and since the deceased was courageous
and never minced words, he's the one who speaks up to demand an
explanation of the Virgin's state, for if there's one thing the Benavides
and the Pando clans have always had in common, it's the Virgin, who
belongs as much to one group as to the other, say what they may.
They approach respectfully and, why deny it, also a little afraid, and
ask: "What happened to the Virgin's body that — if you'll pardon the
expression — she looks as if she were pregnant?" But the Sisterhood
made up of the town's elite who are, granted, Benavides ladies, not
Pandos, is outraged by the question and shuts them up. And Doña
Amparo, who was twenty times worse than Doña Carmen, says what
the devil does it concern them what happens among women, that
these indiscreet questions are not to be asked, that they should worry
about their own affairs, and that they are not the people to be entering with their subtleties and complaints into the forbidden territory
of the dogmas before which no one in the town or in the world has
the right to say anything, and she rebukes them irately, for who are
they to demand such explanations, and they, humbly, because they
are still inexperienced, in spite of being the sons of a heroic Chapulo,
and because times were different then, barely manage to say:

— Forgive us, Doña Amparo, it was just a question ...

And the priest Santiago de los Angeles, spurred on by Doña
Amparo, who was a real harpy, accuses them publicly, from the pulpit, of being heretics, protestants, and free-thinkers, just for an innocent question.

And they can't forget what happened in those days, for they suffered it all themselves when they were still young and didn't know
how to defend themselves, and they asked more out of concern than
anything else. So there the matter rested until everyone got used to
seeing the Virgin in the family way and instead of just calling her
"the Virgin," as they always had, they started to call her (with the
mystical respect of always): Little Potbellied Virgin, Little Potbellied
Mother, Potbellied Queen of Heaven, and even the priest Santiago
de los Angeles who died in the year '52 when the Holy See publicly
named the Virgin de la Elevación de la Peña patroness of Ambato,

the priest Santiago de los Angeles also starts to call her potbellied
in his sermons. And it's pique that kills the priest Santiago de los
Angeles because he says that over there in Rome they have snubbed
the Potbellied Virgin by giving so much importance to the Virgin de
la Peña who hasn't performed even half the miracles the Potbellied
Virgin has.

And they recall that a few days after the rivers flooded in '25, they
see with their own eyes, because they are standing at the corner waiting for the Moñuda girl to appear and show them nudie cards, they
see the Virgin taken from the cathedral protected by an umbrella, and
they are astonished to see her taken out at night, without the appropriate music, incense, and flower-petal confetti, and they assume she
is being taken out in a rush so that she will make it stop raining, since
it has rained without let-up for more than four days, but—imagine
their surprise!—there is no procession but instead she is carried
under cover of darkness to Doña Josefa's house, the one who succeeded Doña Amparo, and it's the same house where Doña Carmen
lives, and they take her because Doña Josefa is dying of a whitlow
that developed on one of her fingers, and the whitlow wouldn't burst
even after spending fourteen days under a sticky dressing of mal-
low, figs softened in olive oil, pigeon droppings, and turpentine, and
the infection spread to her whole body—that's what everyone said.
And that night, when the four Pandos remain, no longer waiting for
the Moñuda girl who never shows with the nudie cards, but waiting instead to see what happens with the Virgin, they see her return
under the umbrella looking a little strange, a little different, as if she'd
suddenly put on weight, but since the night is dark as a bat's cave or
a guilty conscience, which is the same thing, they don't see her well.
But one thing is certain, she's not the same as she was before, that
they can swear to.

And they find out the next day, from the grandson of José Gregorio Pando, who would have been around twelve and ran errands
for Doña Josefa and who, to be more exact, died that same year, not
long after the event, overcome by the worms that they say were even
coming out of his eyes, long and white, like angel hair pasta, they
learn that the priest Santiago de los Angeles and his sacristans took

the Virgin to Doña Josefa's very bedside and ordered everybody out, children, grandchildren, and servants, and only the three of them were left: Doña Josefa who has already received extreme unction and is ready for the journey, the priest Santiago de los Angeles who cries like a baby because his best friend and spiritual daughter is dying, and the Virgin who is amazed at being taken out in the wee hours of the night, in this cold and with no accompaniment, no music, no incense, no flowers.

And rolling their cigarettes with the tobacco they take out of the can labeled "El Vencedor, cigarillos puros ..." they take a rest so as to continue remembering all of the events they have engraved on their memories, and running their tongues along the edge of the cigarette paper, the four old Pandos say:

—Damn, the power of the Sisterhood is greater than that of the Masons!

And they remember that it was in the year '06, the first of January, at a formal dance at the presidential palace that Lizardo García is informed that *what was, is no more,* that he is no longer president because the troops have declared in favor of Don Eloy, and that they were dressed in mourning for the death of their late grandfather who was one of the Chapulos, and to escape their sorrow they go to see the fireworks display in the plaza, and it's in that year, in '06, that everyone is talking about the founding of the Sisterhood, how it is going to reconsecrate the republic to the Heart of Jesus, and that the Sisterhood is going to halt the advance of liberalism, that the Sisterhood has the blessing of Rome, that the Sisterhood has the authority to excommunicate, that those who oppose the Sisterhood are enemies of the Virgin, and such is the excitement and the gossipy embroidering of tales that girls born that year are even baptized Sisterhood, and that's how we got Sisterhood Pando, who left for the coast in '23, the same day as the Leito massacre, when hundreds of peasants died, along with their women and children, for demanding an increase in salary; and Sisterhood Duque, who was the mistress of the shoemaker Romualdo; and Sisterhood Arroba, the only person from the town ever to go up in an airplane, back in '29 when she was hired by some Germans who took her abroad on Panagra.... And the Sisterhood of the Bead on the Gown of the Potbellied Virgin is founded most importantly to counterbalance the Virgin Dolorosa of the school in Quito, which they say has cried real tears.

A lot of time passes talking about the Sisterhood and more Sisterhood, until we get to the year '12, a few days after the battle of Yaguachi in which general Pedro Montero — known as the Tiger of Bulubulu — is defeated, and quartered and burnt in Guayaquil, and that's how we get Don Eloy's painful via crucis, and that of his brother Medardo and his nephew Flavio, along with his generals and colonels who are sent by the cowards to Quito — on the very train that was the work of Don Eloy's own hands — and held in the prison built by García Moreno, to be later dragged through the cobbled streets of Quito and burnt in El Ejido park.

— That day had some of everything: draughts of human blood, stabbings, pickax blows, tongues and testicles torn out, and it was women who did it, compadre, women, that's how cursed they are.

— Don't go on, compadre, don't go on.

— It's since then that we don't go to Quito, because it's still stained with the blood of our father Alfaro.

And it is in the year '12, as the four old Pandos continue to recall, with trembling voices, still moved and upset by the memory of that bloody orgy, when they and the few liberals who remain in the town, to somehow express their sadness, put on mourning, and the Sisterhood fines them, and the first clash comes about when they are ordered:

— That they remove their mourning clothes immediately, and that the Pandos pay the fine ordered by the Sisterhood, for this is not a town of liberals nor of unbelievers but instead a conservative town.

And the Pandos, becoming bolder:

— We're not taking off mourning, and we're not paying any fine! They just killed our father Alfaro, and this town is *all* liberals!

— Compadre, don't upset yourself remembering those bad days, instead sing that bit that goes,

> Hail! Alfaro who one day managed
> by the force of your liberator's voooice

> to raise the sacred prayer of proootest
> that all the people felt ...

But they continue remembering that it was around 1918 when the Sisterhood ordered and counterordered more than ever, when the government of Baquerizo Moreno prohibited fiestas with *priostes*. That same year, as if to send all the liberals' laws and decrees straight to the devil, the Sisterhood begins to use the ridiculously long name of the Sisterhood of the Bead on the Gown of the Virgin—but not Potbellied, for that only began in '25, as we've already said—and that year, in '18, they hold the biggest fiesta any of them remember. And the *priostes* that year were the Indians from Huayrapata, and the poor things rose to the occasion, because the same day as the fiesta, during the inauguration of the Municipal Palace in Latacunga, they come running to say that there's no one there, that it's the last straw, that everyone is here at the fiestas which last some fifteen days, and this is certainly true, the four old men emphasize, spitting out stray bits of tobacco:

—Because, you will remember that until the year '31, with the uprisings of Larrea Alba, the Indians from Huayrapata were still paying off their debts from that fiesta ...

And they remark with a hint of bitterness and a touch of fury how the power of the Sisterhood of the Bead on the Gown of the Potbellied Virgin is so strong that it can place and replace mayors at will, that they name and dismiss the magistrates of all the towns devoted to the Potbellied Virgin, and it's not possible that they, being descendants of the first Pandos, true owners of all the land, liberals through and through—not like today's liberals who aren't good for anything—but rather being fighters of the Old Warrior in Huigra, in Yaguachi, and in Ambi, they have never been able to prevail, much as they have wanted to, against the caprices of those who head the Sisterhood, even though they're women, and old ones at that.

—But it won't always be that way, compadre, *for there's no trouble that lasts a hundred years, and no body that could bear it.*

And they remember that in the year '52, when Galo Plaza—who managed to serve out his term in peace, after twenty-nine years of military uprisings and dictatorships—was still president, and who was succeeded for the third or fourth time—it really doesn't matter—by Velasco Ibarra, they tell that when the priest Santiago de los Angeles is on his deathbed, because he's dying of the pique they say was occasioned by the Virgin de la Peña, he suddenly remembers something important, and he smacks himself on the forehead as if to revive himself, but he can no longer speak because death has him by the throat. He tries to make himself understood with desperate signs, there's something he must say that he doesn't want to carry to his grave, and he speaks with the hand already stiffened by the death rattle of his agony, indicating his niece.

—Me? she asks, startled.

—No. He answers by shaking his head and continues pointing at her.

—I haven't done anything wrong, she defends herself. And the priest points alternately to her and to her mother.

—My mother?

—No.

—Woman?

—No.

—Mother?

—Almost, almost, he says, moving his hand, and with his index finger, he points up.

—Roof?

—No.

— Ceiling?

—No.

—Lamp?

—No. And he points, desperately, further up.

—Heaven?

—No. Yes. No.

—Mother … heaven … The Virgin! They all shout in unison.

—Yes. And with his last breath he touches his belly.

— The Potbellied Virgin?

—Yes.

—Do you want us to bring the Virgin to you? they ask, kindly.

—No.

—The Potbellied Virgin ... ? What? The sad relatives try to guess what he means while the priest Santiago de los Angeles keeps pointing desperately at his belly.

—Does it hurt?

—No.

—Your belly ... ?

—No.

—Her belly ... ?

—No.

—Her belly, or hers, or hers ... ? They point at each of the assembled women in turn as they also agonize over the question.

—No. No. No.

—The Virgin's belly ... ?

— ...

And there falls the silence of silences, and the priest Santiago de los Angeles exhales his last sigh and passes over to the other side, and everyone is left dismayed at having been unable to guess what he was trying to say, and there's no help for it, he dies carrying his tremendous secret with him into the next life.

And then, starting in '52, the Sisterhood's real problems begin, because a month after the priest Santiago de los Angeles (who was the real agent behind the Sisterhood) is dead and buried, another priest comes, who is delayed two weeks by the uprisings occasioned by Guevara Moreno who was the mayor of Guayaquil and one fine day took over the airport along with all of its planes. The new priest lunched with the ladies of the Sisterhood who threw him a banquet, and the leftovers were eaten by the four old Pandos because old Simona who was at that time the cook in the big house and was also wet nurse to the freckled Clarisa, took them what remained, the first and only time they ate stuffed turkey. But so much preparation and attention were all for nothing because the priest left the next day saying the old ladies of the Sisterhood wanted to violate the secrecy of the confessional.

And in '53, while Velasco Ibarra is president, when the Pope makes Archbishop de la Torre a cardinal, the Sisterhood asks for a priest, and the cardinal sends a young one, freshly ordained, who only lasts three days and bursts into tears after talking with Doña Carmen. And since the ladies keep up their requests, the cardinal sends three or four more who likewise beat a hasty retreat, frightened off by the Sisterhood's proposals.

And in '54, when Monseñor Proaño is made bishop of Riobamba, they ask him for a priest, and when this one arrives, he can scarcely exchange greetings with the ladies of the Sisterhood who have gone to meet him. They tell him what he must and must not do, and the priest, frightened, without even resting after the lurching of the mule, without opening his suitcases or taking a sip of water to quench his thirst, returns on the same mule, leaving the town on tenterhooks and the ladies furious.

And in '55, on the same day they learned that the savage Aucas had killed five North American missionaries on the banks of the Curaray, and the news spread all over the world and people said this was a country of cannibals, another priest arrives who seems likely to last, because he's old and they say he has oceans of patience, but he leaves at the end of three months after having discovered a microphone installed behind the screen of the confessional. He leaves stooped, worn down, and pained and with his hair entirely white, and he shuts himself away in a nursing home insisting that he is not himself, but instead the Holy Trinity, and he dies searching his body for the other two persons.

And toward the end of '56, another one arrives, rather nasty-looking, and they say that under his cassock he carries a pistol. He stays five months trying to defeat the Sisterhood, but the ladies themselves order him to leave, and since he refuses to go, they put his luggage out in the street and padlock the doors to the parish house, and they shove him into the first car that appears, and he threatens them with the pistol, and there are shots and stonings and finally the police intervene.

And in '57, when Camilo Ponce is president, they approach him, and he sends a few more who come and go with the same outcome of fights, arguments, and escapes.

And in '58, as a result of the death of Pius XII, a very young one

arrives, barely ordained, and he says a solemn Te Deum for the soul
of the departed Pope, and he is the first one to organize mass baptisms
for the newborn *guaguas* and other already half-grown *langarotes;* he
performs marriages by the bundle for couples who've been shack-
ing up for years; he hears confessions from repentant penitents and
habitual sinners face-to-face and not behind the screen, and when it
seems that finally everything is going as it should, one Sunday, with
the cathedral packed until not one more soul will fit, the people learn
that he made his escape at two in the morning leaving a letter in his
own hand in which he threatens the ladies of the Sisterhood with
excommunication.

And in '59, the entire Sisterhood journeys to the capital and asks
the new papal nuncio, Bruneira, directly for a new priest, and he listens to the ladies very diplomatically and sends an Italian who after a
few days escapes to the Oriente to live with the naked and terrifying
Aucas, saying they are preferable to the ladies, who are more papist
that all of the popes and antipopes put together.

And in 1960, during the fourth presidency of Velasco Ibarra, the
Sisterhood turns to him and the president sends one who has had
considerable experience in public jails and in mental hospitals, but
as soon as he arrives, he has an argument with the ladies who continue to insist in the matter of the secrecy of the confessional, and he
leaves for Peru and never comes back.

And in '61, the desperate Sisterhood again asks for help from
President Velasco, and he sends one with an escort—so he won't
think of trying to flee—but he spends two months struggling like
a devil in a bottle, shut up in the parish house looking over the
mountains until the day a group of climbers gets lost on the snows
of Chimborazo, and they send rescue teams from every city in the
republic, and one sets out from the town, too, under the command of
the priest, who seizes the occasion to go deep into the frozen wilds of
Zumbahua with the fiercest, most distrustful and rebellious Indians
of the region. There he remained missionizing after his own fashion,
far from the ladies of the Sisterhood.

And in '62, in the same week that diplomatic relations with
Cuba are broken, during the presidency of Carlos Julio Arosemena
Monroy, two come, as if to keep each other company, but they also

escape: disguised as Indians so as not to be recognized, they slip away into the shadows of the night. And in that same year, during the days of the military equipment scandal, one arrives who becomes gravely ill within a few hours, and he says the climate doesn't agree with him, that he's going to die, and he leaves in an ambulance, stretched out trembling on the gurney, but no sooner has he gotten a few leagues away from the center of town than he recovers. He jumps out of the vehicle and disappears on foot into the solitary sands of Palmira and is never heard from again.

And in '63, during the time of the Military Junta, when the military names the Virgin de las Mercedes—who is made of stone and comes from Quito—Generalísima of the Army, the Sisterhood asks them for a priest, and when he arrives and makes himself comfortable and sends for his family, the Sisterhood realizes he doesn't even know Latin, nor how to say Mass, that he's not good for anything, the only thing he knows is how to play soccer, and he organizes game after game, and with his cassock hitched up he'll kick any old ball or piece of junk he finds in the street, and he goes so far as to play soccer in the very atrium of the cathedral, and he becomes the idol of the town, for there's no one who can block his shots on goal and he can score from any distance, and with the money from the collection plate he buys colored T-shirts for all the men in town and forms fourteen teams.

And in '64, when the Military Junta is up to its usual tricks, and there's a great fire on the Benavides sugarcane plantation, and the cathedral is covered with ashes, three more priests come who simply repeat the same old story.

And in '65, they appeal to Tulcán, since Pope Paul VI has, from Rome, named Luis Clemente de la Vega bishop, and he promises the Sisterhood that he will attend to their needs, but the designated priest keeps them waiting week after week. They make and remake the arches with agave stalks covered with flowers, with streamers and with brightly colored paper from the station to the cathedral, yet the long-awaited priest never arrives.

And in '66, when it seems that everything is going well with the interim president Clemente Yerovi—for good is always fleeting—when Archbishop Macarios arrives from Cyprus, the Sisterhood,

more desperate than ever, turns to him, and Macarios responds that
it is not his responsibility.

And in '67, during the time of Otto Arosemena, during the
Eucharistic Congress in Cuenca, they publicly request a priest over
the loudspeakers, and one shows up who begins by wooing the Virgin's handmaidens and the next month he hangs up his habit and
takes off with Marianita Pando's cousin who has just turned fourteen
years old.

And the four old Pandos, who are the living memory of the town,
remember how in the years that followed the never-ending story was
repeated. And it's going on thirty years that the town hasn't had its
own priest, but only those willing to come from neighboring towns,
who come and go as if they were peddlers. They administer the sacraments any old way, casting their benedictions to fall where they
will, they hear confessions as if it had nothing to do with them, they
throw the baptismal water at any part of the body, without interest,
without ever feeling themselves the leaders of the flock, they perform
the sacred mission as a formality, and without being able to get along
with the ladies of the Sisterhood of the Bead on the Gown of the
Potbellied Virgin.

The town has seen and put up with all kinds of priests: evangelical and apathetic, fat and thin, shorties and beanpoles, pre-conciliar
and post-conciliar, learned and ignorant, prudent men and scoundrels. They all resemble one another in that none of them lasts;
some because they won't submit to the Sisterhood which refuses
to recognize the secrecy of the confessional; others, for fear of getting themselves into theological problems; others out of self-respect,
because after all, they're human; others out of common sense and
because under their cassocks, they wear trousers. They all come
to see for themselves how things are and when they confirm what
they've heard they pack their bags and leave. The four old Pandos
comment spitefully that the only priest who hasn't come to town is
the scandalous Father Almeida — they don't know who he is, but he's
famous. The Sisterhood is worn out by the complaints and claims
of every sort. The parishioners have to travel to other towns lest the
guaguas die unbaptized. Proper customs are disappearing little by

little. Poor couples don't have the money to marry elsewhere and they prefer to shack up, imitating the Indians who first "get settled" before they get married, and when they're at the wedding party they sing shamelessly:

> "Santo San Juaniiito
> from San Sebastián,
> if the priest won't perform the marriage
> the sacristan can."

There is no one to hear confession or celebrate a miserable Mass. The worship of the Potbellied Virgin is waning while the pernicious new doctrines brought to town by Manuel Pando who got tired of so much fuss that he became a communist and doesn't mind saying it, they're thriving. And the worst of all is that the good people of the town, longing for what they can't have, secretly join the protestant churches that are struggling to get into the town and take everything for themselves so as to end the devotion to the Virgin, but the Sisterhood is on the alert and the *Watchtower* and *Awake* and *End of the World* magazines are confiscated and thrown in the wastebasket, and the addressees' names are taken down so as to put them on the blacklist that is growing daily by alarming proportions.

The four old Pandos tell how Doña Carmen has sequestered three of her favorite great-grandsons in order to force upon them a priestly vocation. They say they are on one of her haciendas with special tutors, they say the three boys go around dressed as altar boys and that they're treated like kings, but that the three are more incorrigible than the worst kids in town, that they play poker with the holy cards, organize card games with the majordomos that last into the wee hours, and run about the countryside lifting their tunics so as to chase the chickens and pee on them. None of this is news to their grandmother—she already knows she'll get nothing good out of the three—but the need is so great that she persists.

Doña Carmen writes to the Holy Father in Rome almost daily, asking for authorization to found a deaconry in the Potbellied Virgin's town, for there is more than enough cause and justification to do so.

She has sent, one after another, more than two thousand certified letters with return postage included in the envelope, believing that over
there in the Vatican they are poor. But the Vatican doesn't answer: it
remains deaf and dumb as a post. She thinks that this is a dirty trick
played by the Pandos, she is almost convinced, although sometimes
she begins to think that the end of ends is approaching: the end of the
world, and that the best thing to do, so as to be at peace with her conscience, would be to go to the Potbellied Virgin, undress her and ...

— No, no, get thee behind me, Satan, things aren't as they were in
the past. Not like when imported waters first arrived, Perrier, Hanos,
Rubinat, and Vichy.

She knows that the townsfolk have thrown themselves into the
arms of impiety and atheism and that they have become communists
over night, and she is the chosen one, the predestined one, the one
anointed to combat the apocalyptic beast. She brandishes the knife
of Judith in front of the monstrous body of Holofernes in Bethulia
and she feels lyrical, but later she becomes frightened and she feels
weak, unsure how to get out of the morass. She feels insecure and
threatened. There are Pandos everywhere: in the post office, violating
her personal correspondence; among the police, meting out justice
as they please; in the clinics, handing out boxes of contraceptives as
if they were candy; among the radio announcers and those who write
for the newspapers, who never make known the important news,
but instead other items that nobody cares about, and she knows that
those who write meet daily at *The Voice of the People,* property of that
cynical Manuel Pando who gave up a brilliant future on account of
four crazy ideas he got into his head, all because in one bad moment
of anger, one of the aunts told him he was conceived in sin and that
he wasn't a purebred Benavides, and they say that he has said that the
Potbellied Virgin has too many jewels and that with one little nugget
from one of her crowns he could arm the whole town and make the
revolution, and the ladies, who were his relatives once upon a time,
have disowned him and demand his head on a platter.

— Did you ever see such a brazen half-breed cholo?

But if the letters don't reach Rome, it may be because the address
isn't correct, and for that reason no traveler from any part of the

country goes to Rome without the charge to deliver a letter into the Holy Father's hands, or at least to leave it in the hands of reliable people. But it is in vain; everything is in vain, Doña Carmen doesn't understand it, she's even sent lists of candidates for deacon and subdeacon, for she'd be content with any old subdeacon. And the letters contain all the details they would want to know, along with the promises she would fulfill in exchange for the favor, and they contain the offerings—which, considered carefully, look more like bribes—because if you have to pay for this, Doña Carmen would pay double what they ask. And enclosed with the voluminous letters go the curriculum vitae of her candidates accompanied by hundreds of signatures clamoring for spiritual aid, and there are seals and prayers and panegyrics and the testimonies and complete histories of the particulars of the miracles that the Potbellied Virgin has performed for her faithful followers.

And Doña Carmen has even, driven by desperation and urgency, nominated herself. The only possible objection might be her sex, but aside from the skirts, who in the town would be more suitable? She has sent to Rome all the papers that list her honors, her qualities, and the works she has performed in the course of the apostolic years; a color photo the size of a postcard in which she looks very handsome, very dignified and circumspect, in a black dress buttoned up to her chin, with a high, stiff collar, trimmed in purple as if she were a lady bishop, for she's never seen a photo of a deaconess, and it occurs to her this must be how they dress. She is seated in front of a writing table of black mahogany on which there stands a reproduction of the Potbellied Virgin. She holds a half-open prayer book, which is meant to represent a breviary, and between the pudgy hands that hold the book spill the beads of a rosary of pearl and tortoiseshell threaded with gold. Her eyes are thoughtful, and on her opulent bosom (which she would rather not have) rests a cross of cabochon emeralds set in gold filigree hung on a heavy gold chain. Her hair is neatly combed and reveals a distinguished note of white. And along with her picture goes a curriculum vitae which spills over eight pages of beautiful English calligraphy, including everything that she would want to make known, with the exception of her date of birth, and where one

reads that she has performed extensive apostolic and cultural labors
and, in her free time, also literary works, for she has written a novel
titled *Dawn in the Countryside* in order to extol right-living and Christian piety. She has written twenty-seven Marian panegyrics published
in various religious magazines. She has given seventy-two magiste-
rial speeches about the temporal and spiritual power of the church,
about dogma, chastity, celibacy, obedience, and similar topics. She
has delivered forty-three cultural lectures ranging from the cultiva-
tion of geraniums to the lives and works of the saints that the nation
has given to Christendom and innumerable talks on various themes
which could be compiled in several volumes of Collected Works. She
also holds important offices: she is president-for-life (unremunerated)
of the Sisterhood of the Bead on the Gown of the Potbellied Virgin.
She is founding president—active for life—of the Feminine Institute
for Decency. She is a founding life member of the Diocesan Academy
of the History of the Miracles of the Potbellied Virgin. She is president of the Apostolic Society of Ladies and Young Ladies to Comfort
the Dying. She is president of the High Wardrobe of the Potbellied
Virgin. She is a founding life member of the Social Foundation of
Marian Ladies. She is honorary member of three municipal councils
and wears the insignia of the Spanish Government of the Ribbon of
the Order of Isabel the Catholic. She is a full member of the Academy of the Language corresponding to the Spanish Academy. She
founded the town's chapter of the Eternal Patriotic Front, a political
party imported from Brazil that has spread to every city in the country,
and they go on and on, pages and pages of works done for the common good and for the benefit of morality, and reviews and clippings
from newspapers and magazines, and she has even sent her physical
measurements: height, weight, bust, hips, and waist. And with such
a raft of documents weighing who knows how many kilos, still there
is no answer, neither a yes nor a no, not even an acknowledgment of
receipt, as if they had all died, which means that perhaps even Rome
has been touched by the sinister hand of the communist Pandos.

Slowly and rhythmically, for nothing can stop the calendar, the fiestas of the Jubilee of the Potbellied Virgin approach. It has been fifty

years since the last ones were celebrated and people are still talking
about them. The four old Pandos remember all the particulars of the
great festivities.

—Because at that time, the town inaugurated the electric plant
and there were bullfights and they paved the streets around the
cathedral which up until then were just tamped earth and became
an absolute quagmire when it rained, and the doors of the cathedral
would be locked and padlocked and nobody was allowed to enter, not
even to hear a Mass for the dead because they might soil the marble
floors, and at that time these very benches were placed and the New
Bridge was built which was left useless because the river changed
course and they had to build another bridge, and since they never
agreed on the name it should have, it's always been called the Newer
Bridge, and that was back around 1910. The Newer Bridge was inaugurated the same day as the attack on the Peruvians, when the most
illustrious González Suárez gets tough and says from the pulpit of the
cathedral of Quito:

—"If the hour has arrived in which Ecuador disappears, let it
disappear, not tangled in diplomatic threads, but rather on the fields
of honor, in the open air, with weapon in hand: it will not be dragged
into war by greed, but by honor."

—Yes, those and other words from history, compadre, we know
them by heart, and people nowadays don't even know who González
Suárez was.

And the four old Pandos repeat in unison the patriotic words,
slowly and deliberately, and they almost come to attention as they say
them, as if they were going to war, and afterward they remain pensive
and nostalgic, and after a silence they spit out bits of tobacco and
murmur longingly:

—Damn, the old cleric was on the same level as Eloy Alfaro!

And they remember that was the last fiesta in which all of the
Pandos took part directly and actively, and they pulled out all the
stops, for in the matter of being generous, not even the Benavideses
with everything they have can beat them, because they gave the Virgin the best of all the crowns, the diamond one, which at that time
cost a fortune, and which she wore during the most solemn fiestas

before the Pandos fought with the Sisterhood, and which is the one
she ought to wear now for the Jubilee, and if the handmaidens don't
put it on her, they should give it back, since accounts pending with
the loansharks for that enormous crown won't be paid off before
judgment day.... And they remember that it was in 1920, just as the
first airplane — named "El Telégrafo" — flew out of Guayaquil, when it
passed over the cathedral and seemed about to crash into the cupola,
that the townsfolk enter the cathedral to see if any of the stained-
glass windows have broken, and they surprise two Colombians trying
to steal the crown and the thieves are trussed up and sent elbow to
elbow to the panopticon in Quito.

Doña Carmen is sick with nerves and hysteria. She doesn't have
a moment's rest, she has even begun to bite her nails and she has
developed an intermittent and revealing nervous tic in her left eye.
For that reason, when she talks with the Pandos, she has to wear dark
glasses — God forbid they should think she was winking at them, and
given how bold they've become, it's best to take some precautions, for
an Indian in gloves, nobody loves.

Awaiting the letter from Rome that doesn't arrive, she has written
to all of the bishops asking — for the love of the Mother of God — for
three priests, only three, to celebrate the Mass of the great Jubilee.
And after a long time, the most unexpected bishop answers that he'll
send one, only one. The remaining bishops pretend not to understand. Doña Carmen suffers uncontrollable impulses and she is over-
taken by an insane desire to throw herself against the walls, all the
while muttering:

— This is the work of the Pandos.

And the ladies of the Sisterhood answer:

— Envy, it's pure envy and nothing but.

And they calm her down saying:

— Ay, Carmita, *if envy were mange, half the town would be scabby.*

Doña Carmen is losing weight and she can't touch a bite thinking
that they can't celebrate such an important Mass with only one priest.
Not even the bishoprics of Peru and Colombia have answered her,
and she'd be satisfied even with three bumpkin priests from Pasto.
And she can't overlook the date, nor even postpone it, because that

would be clear evidence that things are going wrong. And it is impossible to fix another day because all of the other festivities are ready.

The symphonic orchestra from the capital is already promised and contracted in writing, with its forty internationally renowned musicians who will play the most magnificent Te Deum ever heard in the town. Also ready are the "castles," enormous frameworks of reeds fitted out with firecrackers, squibs, pinwheels, and mortars that have been carried on men's shoulders from the outlying areas and are standing in front of the cathedral waiting only for someone to bring close the tip of a lit cigarette in order to explode on the eve of the great Mass, filling the skies with colored stars, with showers of sparks that will scatter as if they had trapped all of the fireflies on earth and which will rumble as they explode like corn toasting in lard. The multicolored balloons are ready; shaped like animals and birds they will rise into space nodding in the air, the little candles lit between the reeds burning until they are lost to sight. The sponsors for the drinks, for the bulls, and for the music are chosen and ready; all of them have their new clothes and their respective retinues, while the four old Pandos, wanting and not wanting the fiestas, comment sententiously:

> "The Indian to be a *prioste*
> and the cholo to be a lieutenant
> would both willingly hang."

The gala banquet to be attended by all of the Sisterhood's invited guests and the important people of the town has been prepared. The breakfast to be served after the Mass is ready. The bands from seven neighboring towns that will come to play in the streets and plazas are ready. The pictures, holy cards, and mementos that will be distributed to the invited guests and which will have to be given as well to the importunate whiners are ready. The sweets that will be thrown to the town's children as they leave the Mass are ready. The *agrados* of the Indians are ready which, lacking a *taita* priest to whom to offer them, and as a sign of respect and obedience, they will carry by the dozens to Doña Carmen's house, and these *agrados* are fat chickens, large guinea pigs, fresh eggs, and many other things ... and it is only five days until the Jubilee.

The four old Pandos see José Gregorio running like a crazy person. They note that he has worked in Doña Carmen's house ever since he came into the world. They remember that he was already nearly grown when he was one of the first people in town to reach Rumi Loma to see the train when it passed by for the first time back in '08, when the first locomotive reached Quito. That was the greatest: there were big celebrations all over the country marking the magnum opus of Don Eloy, and it was José Gregorio Pando who brought the news and described how big and red the locomotive was, how it whistled at every curve and threw columns of smoke, and everyone listened to him open-mouthed, and from then on people went to Rumi Loma to see the train pass until they gave up the custom, but José Gregorio was left with the taste for carrying news and messages.

—Right now he must be taking something good to the old ladies ...

José Gregorio Pando bursts in without knocking at the door that is always closed, without cleaning the mud off his shoes as he has been ordered to do, without asking *may I come in* as he usually does; like the head bull of the herd, he invades the forbidden office of the Sisterhood, which is carpeted in red and blue, where the large portraits of all the presidents of the Sisterhood are framed in gold leaf and where the anxious ladies are meeting, seated before identical cups of an infusion of lemon balm with valerian root, orange blossoms, and fifteen drops of passionflower that they have prescribed themselves because they no longer trust the pharmacist, who has become a compadre and crony of the Pandos.

José Gregorio comes running, with his tongue and his shirttail hanging out, and almost out of breath he leans on the conference table so as not to rush at the ladies, and the cups clink against their saucers and spill and helter-skelter, almost shouting, he says that two gringo missionaries are dining at the Little Sugarcane Inn at this very moment—on spicy chicken and iced fruit juice, to be exact—and they look like gringos because they have light eyes like granadilla seeds and they talk funny and they've told the people who've asked that they're going to the Oriente to do missionary work, that they're going to convert the Aucas, and they have three mules loaded with baggage, and they seem like decent folk, and any minute now they'll finish eating and leave, and they say that they say ...

Doña Carmen and the twenty ladies rise to their feet propelled by the same thought. They don't hear any more. They spill their teas on the polished table and rush out, running as fast as they can through the cobbled streets, and the townsfolk, who see them run, run after them, because they think they are going to confirm a new miracle of the Potbellied Virgin.

Half the town arrives out of breath at the ancient tavern. The missionaries freeze with their spoons in the air when faced with so many people staring at them. The ladies incoherently tell them their troubles and, almost on their knees, they implore them to stay five days longer in the town so as to celebrate the solemn Mass. The missionaries say they can't, that people are waiting for them in Archidona, and they get nervous at Doña Carmen's tic, which makes it look as if she were insinuating something else ...

Doña Carmen moves without preamble from the humble Christian entreaty to the irate, hyperbolic threat and, unable to control the nervous tic in her eye, she rebukes them like bad-mannered children. The missionaries refuse to negotiate and lowering their spoons, they return to the spicy chicken, which is getting cold.

Then Doña Carmen Benavides, with the authority of the deaconry that has not yet arrived — but is bound to arrive eventually — orders all of the parishioners and travelers to leave the inn. She orders a padlock placed on the eyebolts of the doors and without further ado informs them that they have been abducted, and her manner is imposing, as if to say *where the captain commands, sailors don't give orders.*

The missionaries are furious. They pound the table. The ice jingles in the tin cups, and they holler and protest and beg. Doña Carmen sends her servant José Gregorio Pando to bring the rifle her nephew used to hunt tapirs years ago, and when he returns with the

rusty and lethal weapon, she directs him to stand guard at the inn
and orders that no one come near the house.

They move the three dejected mules to the patio. The innkeeper and her family come in to clean and air out the "presidential"
room that no one has occupied since the memorable year '33 when
Velasco Ibarra stayed there with two politicians during the electoral
campaign, and he spoke to the town from the balcony of that very
room. And he was the only president who ever slept in the town.
The innkeeper opens the wooden shutters and sees for the first time
the famous room, which is in no way different from the others, save
that it has balconies facing the street, is larger, and has three old-
fashioned windows. She opens the shutters so that six bats and their
young can escape, and to air out the scent of age and oblivion. She
uses a long broom to clean the cobweb curtains that hang from the
crumbling, water-stained ceiling and industriously sweeps the floor,
singing:

> "Little white dove
> with your little brooown breast
> I have never seen in doves
> so much bad faaaith ..."

She cleans up the accumulated dust of memories with the broom
made of marco leaves to kill the fleas, and she mops the floor with
creosol water to scare off the bad odors and shakes out the old mattresses where history has made its nest with the rats.

Meanwhile, the ladies of the Sisterhood have scattered throughout the town and return bearing: one, two pairs of painstakingly
embroidered starched sheets, blued with balls of methyl alcohol, that
were part of the trousseau that she stitched between the ages of fifteen and twenty-five; another, pure woolen blankets with red, green,
and yellow stripes that were woven in the mills of Quero and which
she stores with mothballs for when guests arrive from the capital;
another, a wooden washstand with its rosewater soap, antique porcelain washbasin, and pitcher which she has been told are very valuable and which she displays in her living room; another, two table

skirts made in the mills of Guano that were woven from memory without a pattern; others, towels with tassels knotted by hand that are a bit scratchy but dry thoroughly; another, a bulb for the open mouth of the socket that dangles from the extremely high ceiling beside a streamer of gummed paper studded with flies; another, a candlestick with a candle, in case the electric light goes, which has happened rather frequently ever since the ladies brought a complaint against the municipal bosses; another, a mirror with a wooden frame carved in San Antonio de Ibarra, which is poorly silvered, but which is a marvel for its garland of leaves; another, a vase with Castilian roses and lilies to brighten up the room that doesn't want to give up that certain melancholy patina of old hotel; another, two antique porcelain chamber pots, because the inn doesn't have a bathroom or anything close; another, two crocheted bedspreads that drag on the ground but are blindingly white. And they come and go, exulting in the abduction, while the missionaries watch the goings-on open-mouthed, and in an aside, they say to Doña Carmen, trying to convince her by rational arguments, that this act of disrespect is going to start an international incident, because they are foreigners and they have their papers in order. Doña Carmen laughs at national problems and international difficulties don't trouble her; what matters is that the Potbellied Virgin have her Mass as she deserves and as the Sisterhood had planned, for *he who has noble blood lets no one twist his arm.*

When the day of the Jubilee arrives, the missionaries are pale and emaciated, although they have eaten well, because Doña Carmen has taken great pains to send them the best food and the innkeeper has bent over backward with her attentions, but they have not closed their eyes once because at midnight the good people of the town serenaded them, and they stayed awake thinking that it can't be possible that, in the midst of so much happy uproar, the people should begin to sing such sad songs:

> "I go to driiink the water from the fountaaaain
> and the waater of the fooountain is poiiiisoned ..."
>
> or

"Tears are the mysteeerious liquid
that calms the sooorrows of this wooorld"
                        and
"I took my corn outsiiide
thiiiinking it would not raaaain
and I caught the veeery dooownpour
with all my corn outsiiide ..."

And the noise of the crackers, torpedoes, and rockets has startled
and frightened them, for they thought them the shots of José Gregorio Pando's rifle although he, for his part, has not left his sentinel's
position for a moment.

When the day of the Jubilee arrives, all the townsfolk are in the
streets and everyone from the surrounding areas has come to town.
The missionaries are carried with due consideration, surrounded by
the principal band as if they were the sponsors of the fiesta, passing
under the arches of *chaguarquero*, decked out with bunches of flowers, streamers, and garlands of kite paper toward the cathedral which
rises above the town in its full splendor. They enter amazed, and they
see the main altar which is lit with thousands of elaborately molded
candles and stuffed with flowers, and they come up against the image
of the Potbellied Virgin who is radiant in her white gown embroidered with gold threads and baroque pearls; with her crown of one
hundred and thirty-six diamonds and eighteen emeralds as big as
cymbals and her scepter of solid gold that she can't hold up which
they have had to tie to a post; and they are speechless with wonder.
They fall in love with her round, childish face, with the blond locks
that fall to her heels, with the grace of her beringed fingers, and they
address her with their Latin phrases:

—"Tota pulchra est, o Maria et maculanon est in te quam specioa,
quam suavis in deliciis conceptio allibata."

For such beauty there was no need to twist their arms or to kidnap
them. Doña Carmen should have begun by showing them the cathedral in which it is a glory to say Mass, for there is nothing in this style
or of such richness in all of Europe, there is nothing in the world
that resembles it, and they know art, thinking that with the Chiesa

del Gesù in Rome they had already understood the Baroque.... But this miniature Virgin, so elegant, in spite of her weight, so graceful, in spite of her richness, so much the Mother of God, in spite of being so much a girl ...

They are led to the dark sacristy. They allow themselves to be dressed and indulged by the ladies, who are still afraid they might escape. They put on the albs with their exquisite lace, they knot the belts, they place the capes around their shoulders, the copes, the amice. They hang the stoles on them, and they climb up on a stool to put on the chasubles that are also as white as the Virgin's gown, with chrysanthemums embroidered in gold thread following the design of the brocade. And when they are ready and looking very handsome, along with the other priest who arrived the night before from Mocha and who has had to get dressed alone, they go in single file through the small door that leads to the main altar, and the people who know how they were acquired can't contain themselves and applaud. And the conductor of the symphony who is up in the choir, baton poised, ready to begin, upon hearing the applause wants to leave that very minute, but he sees the packed church, the people kneeling with their hands together and their eyes glued to the icon and, hitting the music stand with his baton, he rises up on his toes, gives the signal and begins ...

José Gregorio Pando, who is the other hero of the fiesta, never for a moment stops pointing the ancient rifle at the missionaries. Although just this morning he realized that it had been unloaded for years and that it could no longer be loaded because there were no longer any bullets available for such an artifact.

The three officiants, in spite of everything, are pleased, for the faith of so many people seems incredible to them. But might they agree to remain as the town's parish priests — either the one from Mocho, or the other two? Never!

The red that here is crimson, the sulfuric blue, the green of the cane leaves, and the yellow of ripe corn shine as if colors had just been invented. A thunder of musical notes like the fireworks of the night before shatters into thousands of aniline shades. The music has the colors of barium chlorate and lacquer, it explodes with strontium bicarbonate and copper sulfate, it rises to the cupolas like white glitter and sulfur, the notes emerge from the pipes of the ancient organ and they crash against the gold-plated altarpieces and the walls hung with slabs of marble from Cuenca producing an exorbitant explosion of jubilation.

—My God, what a Mass, what a town! What country is this ... ?

Faced with so much color, the kidnapped missionaries can't concentrate on the service, and they turn their heads from time to time to stare at the Virgin's altar. The cathedral is packed. People have come, and keep coming, on foot from the communities of Cataló, Huambaló, Puñapí, Huayrapata, Punllo, Tisaleo, Pataló, Casahuala, Llipiní, Leitillo. They have come and keep coming from Mochapanta, Quisapincha, Anzahuana, Guynacuri, Yanayacu. They have come and are still arriving from Sicalpa, Penipe, Licán, and Pongalá. They have come and are about to arrive from Guanjo, Pindilig, Tutupamba, Turupamba. They've come with their ponchos and shawls in all the colors of the rainbow, and when they enter the immense cathedral men and women alike take off their hats.

Everyone is here: the rural chagras in their best Sunday clothes, with their leather *pinganillos* and their jangling spurs beside the women with their braids tied with colored ribbons, *polcas* of chintz, and heavy shawls; the dolled-up cholas; the doñas with their strings of necklaces and earrings of fine stones; the Indians with their best ponchos; the Indian women with their wide *mamachumbis* wrapped around their waists, securing their skirts, with their coral *huallcas* at their throats, their glass *cunga huallcas,* their red *maqui huatamas,* and their *shigras;* the young *longos* who wriggle impatiently, anxious for the Mass to end so they can go out to the somersaults of the *vaca loca;* and the small, powerful clutch of the Benavides' relations who have come from all over the country.

It is a drunkenness of color, of music and art. The Baroque is at its zenith. The luminous flares of Mozart's Hallelujah sung and performed by the Quito Symphony explode against the coffered ceiling of the golden cupola. The director closes his eyes and dries the drops of sweat from his brow with the full conviction of having been inspired. The principal musicians clear their throats quietly,

signaling their approbation to one another with the tips of their eye-
lashes. They forgot about playing for a motley audience that never
goes to concerts and played for themselves and, who knows, perhaps
a few of them for the Virgin. They have fallen silent remembering
perhaps the uncomfortable and weary trip with their instruments
on their knees and the clouds of dust from the long road getting
into every crack. And the stops in each and every village, waiting
while sacks of wheat are loaded and unloaded, along with cages of
chickens, bundles of luggage, bunches of bananas ... stretching out
the trip as if they were making a circuit of the entire country. And
the months of demanding rehearsals for what is already over in a
moment, while below the church empties with the low murmur of
the crowd that will continue the celebrations under the hot sun of a
provincial morning.

It has been a fitting end to the great Mass of the Jubilee that com-
memorates the appearance of the Virgin, who wasn't yet potbellied at
the time, to a handful of frightened young Indians, half dead of their
age-old hunger and of sadness.

One day—the four old Pandos know the story by heart—they
find her standing, very quietly, at the entrance to a hole in the rock
and the children spend the whole day chatting with her. When they
return home, their mothers beat them because the little Indians have
neglected their work, and the children beg the Virgin to heal their
wounds. The next day they go back to talk with the Lady and on their
return, they get another beating, and the Lady heals them again, and
so the days pass until their parents go to confirm what the little Indians have been telling them, and they see the icon and go to inform
the religious authorities about the discovery, and they come running,
because icons don't appear every day, and they carry her in procession to the nearest church. The next day, when they go to the church
to offer her bunches of wildflowers, they see that the Virgin has disappeared in spite of the padlocks on the doors. They look for her
everywhere and find her once again at the entrance to the cave. They
once again carry her in solemn procession to the church, and the
stubborn doll escapes again. They bring her back once more, they
wash her mud-splattered feet and they tie her with cabuya ropes to

the altar pillars and leave her under guard, but the guards fall asleep
in spite of themselves and the little statue flees yet again, walking over
the rough ground and through the brambles. And so they pass many
days, fighting by fair means and foul, until the Indian children say
that what She wants is to be there, at the entrance to that dark hol-
low and not in the old church. And they begin to build her a modest
sanctuary and She begins to perform uncountable miracles, offering cures that confound the doctors, reviving dead people who were
already starting to rot, providing solutions to problems that seemed
by any reckoning impossible. And for every miracle she performs,
heaps of carved stones arrive, slabs of polished marble, cedar timbers
brought from Lebanon by Kalil Nader to make the altarpieces that
are later covered with gold leaf. And the sanctuary gets bigger and
bigger, as if to accommodate the entire town that is also growing in
the shadow of the immense cathedral, which has to be the largest and
most sumptuous of all the cathedrals ever seen.

The four old Pandos remember that back around the year '11 when
the construction of the cathedral was almost finished and the military coup against Eloy Alfaro erupts and there is conspiracy everywhere, Colonel Luis Quiroga shoots General Emilio María Terán in
the Hotel Royal, which was the fashionable hotel in Quito, and the
mob kills Quiroga and drags him through the streets, that's when
they begin to forge the heavy bell that has to be the largest bell ever
made, and they tell that all of the women file by and fling into the
forge — from a distance, because the forge is like a huge volcano —
their gold rings, bracelets, pendants, and necklaces; their bronze
chocolate pots, pans, and vases; their silver cutlery, serving platters,
and candelabras, saying that what will only be lost in the revolution,
ending up in the hands of who knows who, is better off with the
Virgin.

And when the heavy bell is forged with the names of those who
donated the metal inscribed on the edges, no one can move it and it
spends ten years at the foundry, and there are even three consecu-
tive attempts to steal it, but it is so big and weighs so much that the
thieves fail. They finally raise it to the bell tower, back in '21, the same
day the remains of Don Eloy arrive in Guayaquil to be deposited in

the Central Cemetery, and they have to use fifty team of oxen to raise the bell, and when it begins to peal, the inhabitants of the town are left deaf and the youngest babies cry in terror, and the walls vibrate down to their foundations, and the adobe rooms of the old houses crack, and the windowpanes shatter, and the birds fly off in flocks, never to return.

After the Jubilee Mass, the musicians of the symphony begin to wrap up their instruments. The empty cathedral is even more solemn. The little naked angels of the magnificent altarpieces pee a holy grace against the twisted barley-sugar columns that gleam like candied gold. The cherubs fan their flying heads with the tips of their wings. The biblical faces of Luke, Matthew, Mark, and John remain absorbed in the old canvasses of classical severities, and they want to speak out from the carved frames overlaid with gold leaf. The unaffected scenes of the hundreds of miracles of the Potbellied Virgin of today and of the not-yet potbellied Virgin of years ago, reproduced on large canvasses, take on the normality of those times when the laws of nature, impelled by the mental force of faith, fail; to the eyes of everyday perception, such laws cease to be, and they reach backward in time and become inexplicable for everyone, even for the minds of the Pandos themselves who want to combat obscurantism and don't know how, who call themselves liberals and feel themselves among the most pious, conservative *curuchupas,* who proclaim their atheism and yet believe in the miracles of the Virgin.

The townsfolk are squeezed into the vast atrium, where the process of Christianizing the infidels was begun. The people have attended a voluptuous fiesta and in the middle of this ever more amorphous mass, Doña Carmen Benavides, the president of the Sisterhood of the Bead on the Gown of the Potbellied Virgin, awaits her sisters and guests with the zeal of a loving hen. Clucking to and fro, she gathers them up in their turn, and when the whole group is together, they congratulate themselves yet again on the idea of kidnapping the missionaries. José Gregorio Pando has finally stopped aiming the ancient rifle at them and, satisfied, rubs at the joints of his hands and fingers which are cramped after five days of never lowering the weapon.

— The Mass was most solemn, they remark. The attendance sur-
passed the timid count of four stray nobodies that the Pandos and
their followers had predicted, although the four old Pandos observe
that nothing the old ladies of today do comes close to the old days.

Among the mantillas of black lace with a high, tortoiseshell
comb, after the style of the Andalusian beauties, among the city-
made suits of the Benavides men who have come from every corner
of the country to attend the Jubilee celebrations and the miniskirts
of the Benavides women which have now been accepted and are even
starting to be worn in the town, what stands out are the tinsel of the
epaulettes and the gold buttons of the officers who are in the government and who attend en masse so as to demonstrate with their
presence that they never miss a fiesta and that they are allied with
the Holy Mother Church, to make it known to all the Pandos of the
republic that the two powers are unassailable in a town that has a
Madam President like Doña Carmen and the world's biggest cathedral. And thus one of the officers expresses it to Doña Carmen and
she thanks him for his presence and for the compliment, but she can
say no more, because she is left thinking that no woman, not even she
herself, who has four chests crammed with jewels, bedecks herself
as these officers do themselves: what jeweled sets of little shovels
and hoes with miniature rifles on their lapels, what gleaming buttons with coats of arms on their sleeves and everywhere else, what
epaulettes lined as if with mirrors, with gold braid and buttons and
tassels of twisted gold thread, what jewels and precious touches on
the hilts of the swords with gold pompoms that look like little bells,
what rings holding stones worthy of a bishop on their hands, what
straight yellow bands on their trousers, what fancy in the decoration
of the tilted cap, what curves in the handsome visor, what refinement
in the gold braid that hangs across his chest like a set of necklaces,
what a gala display, what elegance, such trappings, such fripper-
ies, buttons, and bows, what adornments and embellishments, such
decoration, ornamentation, and embroidery! The Potbellied Virgin
would look so charming if she had such an outfit made for her, with
all of these fancy details.... And she already imagines her dressed as
a general. But no, she reflects, how could she wear pants with a body

like that? She'd lose her mystical aura and look like any old doll, but nothing like a virgin. And she rids herself of the bad thoughts, wiping them from her brow with her gloved hands, and she submerges herself in the compliments and congratulations of the crowd that surrounds her.

The members of the Sisterhood of the Bead on the Gown of the Potbellied Virgin are fatigued by the effort of having their own way in the face of the portents, bad omens, and predictions of disaster from the underhanded enemies of religion who have multiplied from one day to the next just as the children of Abraham multiplied in the desert. They feel stifled by the mass of the faithful who have arrived from the *páramos,* from the mountains, from the ravines, from the hillsides, from the canyons, walking a day, two days, four days; by all those who have come from the provinces, from the cantons, from the outskirts, from the hamlets, from the villages; leaving their houses, their farms, the *llactas,* the home-plot *huasipungos,* and who have arrived on foot, by mule, on horseback, by train, by bicycle, by bus, traveling the entire geography of the world. All have thrilled to the orchestra's tremolos and arpeggios, which have loosed them from their seats and made them travel who knows where, and which for some have even made the time seem long as they hoped the orchestra might play at least a *cachullapi* or a *sanjuanito* as the sacristan does during the Christ child's Masses. Happy and rowdy, with all the invited guests, they set out for the town's principal house, which is the home of Doña Carmen Benavides. It is an opulent home occupying an entire block very close to the cathedral as suits the taste of the Madam President who sets her schedule according to the playing of the hours and the half hours by the bells of the tower clock, at the foot of which the unmoving eye framed in its stone triangle is watching what it sees and what many would prefer it not see.

When they arrive at the old house in which the entire town could fit—though they've never tried it—and which has so many rooms closed with padlocks and eyebolts that the bunch of keys weighs fifteen pounds, a ray of sunlight divides in two the generous stone patio surrounded by flowerpots. Ten energetic and imperative *tan tan tan tan*s announce the hour of ten in the morning, and the group begins

to climb the great stone staircase to the second floor, and everyone
pauses at the landing to look at the old, old canvas of the Virgin
that was painted centuries ago, when she was not yet potbellied, and
which belonged to Doña Amparo. The crowd spreads out through
the corridors of turned railings forming a single file to enter the
immense banquet hall which overlooks the main street, beside the
parlor which is next to the small parlor and beside the grand salon
which has been opened today, after being closed for five years, ever
since the wedding of Doña Carmen's third granddaughter, the happy
girl who wasn't destined to dress the Virgin, but who had to marry a
gringo to keep up the family tradition of blond hair.

On starched, snow-white tablecloths embroidered by the nuns
of seven convents, some of which no longer exist, there is another
baroque explosion of sugar: it is the largest cake of all the Jubilees,
and it is decorated with a pastillage of sugar in homemade gothic
style. It does not represent the town's cathedral, but it rises just the
same in the center of the main table and it has entrances and exits,
transparent windows with stained-glass panes made of candy and a
pointed tower so tall that it touches the iridescent tears of the twelve-
armed crystal chandelier that arrived from Paris when they built the
house, and which was transported along with those of the salon, the
parlor, the small parlor, the chapel, the sewing room, the library, and
other rooms by an entire train of Spanish mules, and on the front of
the cake cathedral, over the portico, on top of the archivolts and the
tympanums and the rose windows, there is a frame of sugared filigree
with a miniature reproduction of the Potbellied Virgin, all in white
icing, with her splendid gown, her mantle, and her crown, with her
scepter, her long hair, and her clogs. And around the cake are piled
mountains of pale blue, yellow, and pink coconut candies; pastries
filled with almonds and walnuts; meringues, shortbreads, marzipan,
and nougats sent from the convents of Cuenca; and there are cookies, ring-cakes, cheese tarts, rolled wafers, candy kisses, and sugar
sighs, and small silver dishes overflowing with candied almonds, pine
nuts, and pistachios, sugared almonds, bonbons, and lemon cakes,
and crystal plates with heavy syrups made of every kind of fruit, and
there are dozens of glasses of rosé that play keep-away with the rays

of the sun that fight to enter from the plaza through the high windows in defiance of the lace curtains, of the drapes, of the canopies, of the awnings and fringe; and there are platters of fruits exquisitely garnished with grapes from Pomasqui and avocados from Guayllabamba and pears from Leito and guaytambos from Ambato and peaches from Gualaceo and pineapples and taxos and babacos and a whole earthly paradise of apples and watermelons and strawberries, and there is homemade egg bread, water bread, and sweet-savory *lampreados,* and there are cheeses, curds, and custards, and once in a while, it is as if the arthritic hands and gnarled fingers of the neighbor of Manuel Pando — the one from *The Voice of the People* — had appeared, inopportune and indiscreet, the neighbor who washes the tablecloths in the icy water of the river, stooping over the hard rocks. She spreads them to whiten on the kikuyu grass and rinses them walking into the river up to her thighs, and she starches them with rice starch or cornstarch according to the texture of the cloth, and she wrings them out, twisting them like gigantic skeins of thread. And damp, big-bellied, and heavy they go into the reed basket brought from Colta, they ride on her head; rocking with the rhythm of her slow and clumsy pace they go to be ironed with six old-fashioned irons which she sets to heat over the charcoal fire, for electricity is very expensive for her budget, and she has to use the six irons in turn at just the right temperature — which she's learned to calculate over the years — and on which she leans both her arms when she is worn out so that the heat will really penetrate the fabric, and so she appears, tired, sad, and angular like the oil painting *Woman Ironing* by Picasso, which looks as though he had come to the town, with his brushes and canvas on his back, and had used her for a model when she was ironing and thinking about her son and about life in general. And she can be heard singing, very softly, under her breath, as if it were the complaint of an old pain that had given her the most bitter and most beloved fruit:

"How could your looove make me unhaaaapy
in this poor wounded cooore of my beeing
say, if another looove, say, if another looove
say, if another looove like mine you've ever haaad ..."

And she remembers, racked with grief, the times she went to bathe in the river to carry out the ritual that might make the child she carried in her womb be recognized, and she sees herself as a young woman gathering elder leaves, guarango, and ripe spikes of atuxara to bathe herself in the river early when the waters — perhaps for having slept — are not cold but rather tepid, and she sees herself with her body covered in the green lather of the elder, and later untying her heavy braid she submerges herself three times in the deepest part of the stream with her hair covered in the white lather of the guarango and the purple lather of the atuxara and later she sees herself kneeling before the Potbellied Virgin, and she changes one iron, and then another ... for someday, life will surely come to an end.

Three silver services with everything necessary for drinking café con leche are in the hands of three pages, rendered impersonal and asexual by this moment, one of whom is José Gregorio Pando, standing in a corner, stiff, like a broom. He looks like the original mock-up for the first monument to café con leche, holding, immobile, a tray that weighs more than the old rifle.

José Gregorio Pando is the right hand of the Benavides house; he is the chauffeur when the lady of the house goes out, he is the confidant in times of trouble, the majordomo of the household goods, the trusted one, the master of the keys to the two hundred locks, the secretary, the messenger, the *huasicama,* and for that very reason, the sharp and idle tongues of his own relatives have spread the rumor that he is Doña Carmen's lover, but this is calumny, because ever since she has been president-for-life of the Sisterhood she has too many problems and too much hustle and bustle to waste time on sex and romance and still less with a Pando born and bred to be a servant who never left the Benavides house even to go to school or to military conscription, and he even believes that Doña Carmen and the rest of the Benavides women have no sex, and if they have it, it's their business and nothing to do with him, because not now when he's old, but rather when he was a boy, when the Benavides women went to bathe in the river making a great game of their shrieks, José Gregorio Pando went along carrying huge baskets filled with the enormous sheets they used to dry themselves off, and the washbasins they used to pour water on themselves (for they were afraid of the strong currents) and the colognes and the soaps and the combs, and when the Benavides women dressed and undressed they would order him:

—José Gregorio, close your eyes.

And he closes them tightly and doesn't open them until he's told. And only once does he dare to peek, out of pure curiosity, not naughtiness, and he is astonished at that milky whiteness, damp and shivering, and he feels more disgust than anything at that ridiculous beard around the pubis that they hide, and he feels no desire, because these bodies look like raw bread to him, before baking, like leavened dough without the flavor or the aroma or the firing of the bread that he likes to taste when he also goes to the river with the *longas* his own age who don't shiver or squeal in the water like these bland Benavides women who in no way tempt his hunger. And he shudders to think that if he had to lie down with one of them — if he were ordered to do so — he would be buried in that flesh and the bulk of white dough would flatten him with its weight and it would spread over him and he would feel the hard angularities of the skeleton beneath, for such fleshiness with all that black hair in *those* places must be as tasteless as the oca tubers that haven't felt the sun, or the guásimas that you have to eat when there is nothing else. No, José Gregorio Pando has his hidden loves that he recalls when he sings outside of work hours, when he is tired and uncertain whether he did the right thing remaining single so as to serve his mistress:

—"How anxiously I seeek your compaaany
so that you might waaarm my saaadness ..."

The group, the people, the place, the breakfast, might seem ridiculous, but they don't. They are saved by a touch of unaffected small-town aristocracy, the two former captives comment quietly; you couldn't ask for better in such a remote place. Everyone gathers around the table, and when all have in front of them a plate and a cup and a glass of rosé, they remain standing to hear the speech of the president of the Sisterhood of the Bead on the Gown of the Potbellied Virgin who looks magnificent in her new tailored dress and

the black mantilla embroidered with silver threads that falls across
her shoulders, just brushing the double ply of the carpet woven in
Guano, a carpet so large, so fine, so thickly tufted, so full of arabesques that they must have sheared who knows how many thousand
sheep in order to weave it.

Doña Carmen has had her hair done in an elaborate chignon
held in place by dozens of hairpins. She wears on her bosom the
great cross of cabochon emeralds which is not a simple cross, but
a patriarchal cross, so as to fit a larger number of precious gems.
She taps the edge of a crystal glass with a teaspoon and there is
silence. She speaks and — as was to be expected — relates the history
of the Sisterhood, since there are so many outsiders present. She
tells how on many occasions, people of discernment have suggested
they change the name of the Sisterhood, because it is very long and
because it can sound almost ridiculous when heard for the first time.
But they will never change it. First, because it is a historic name and
secondly, because it holds great significance: they are determined
to demonstrate to the whole world that, in spite of being who they
are — because they are members of the Benavides family — they are
tiny and humble as the beads on the Potbellied Virgin's gown, beads
which are no longer used because, thanks to the faith of thousands
of worshippers, the old beads have been replaced by precious stones.
She informs her listeners that if they have not yet achieved that Fran-
ciscan humility so pleasing to the Virgin's sight, they struggle daily
to achieve it. And it is possible that this might be true in spite of
the opulence of their flesh, a product of the well-laid table; and in
spite of their respective fortunes, none too honestly acquired, as the
Pandos affirm with their gossip and through the printed word of *The
Voice of the People* and in the yearnings of the four old Pandos who
know the story of how the fortunes were made, but who can't prove
it until the old legal documents reappear.

Doña Carmen keeps on describing the glories and the ups and
downs of the Sisterhood. She tells how the group survives the attacks
of the enemies of religion. She affirms that it is no sin to be rich
and tells how her ancestors worked themselves to death, and the vio-
linist from the symphony thinks there are thousands of people like

him, working themselves to death without ever getting rich. She tells
how her ancestors had the vision to value the land, and the cellist
thinks there are thousands of people who value the land as he does
and will never own it. She tells how her ancestors were sufficiently
intelligent to accumulate material goods, and the conductor thinks
there are hundreds of capable people like himself who will always be
poor. And she explains that she speaks of the disagreeable topic of
wealth because the town that used to be Christian is beginning to go
astray under the disastrous influence of atheistic, raving communism
and in order to combat it, the Sisterhood has developed its plans,
and when she is about to unfold those plans, she notices that among
those present are many unfamiliar faces who might be friends of the
Pandos, so she decides to keep quiet.

Since she is a great hostess and respects the rule about *guests first,
miserable though they may be,* and she perceives that they are dying to
start eating what is on the table and she surprises a ray of sunlight
diving into the rosé, she raises her glass and offers a toast to the
success of the Sisterhood's plans and to the greater honor and glory
of the Potbellied Virgin; and the wine cleans the pipes of the last
leftovers of the Hail Marys of the Mass and arriving smoothly at the
wrists makes hands break out in applause. The pages set aside the
trays of hot milk and freshly brewed coffee essence and pull back
the chairs so that the ladies might settle their snow-white bottoms on
them and they begin to serve, impersonal and erect:

—Sugar? Hermesetas? Saccharin?

So much syrup amidst so much diabetes. So much creaminess
where one watches one's weight. So much toffee where there are
so many old people. The varied delicacies on the table might seem
inappropriate, even in poor taste for a breakfast at ten o'clock in the
morning, but it is a traditional custom and tradition is never tacky; it
is the typical First Communion breakfast and Doña Carmen considers it most appropriate to what they are celebrating.

The guests begin to eat, commenting upon the events of the day
and Doña Carmen's speech, which they say was longer and meatier
than the homily at the Mass, because Doña Carmen just said whatever came into her head, she is in her own home and need temporize

with no one. She didn't struggle with words nor with her ideas like
the person seated on her right who gave the impression that he was
picking out his words with tweezers; it seemed as though he looked
at them against the light before casting them out over the braids finished off with cords and colored ribbons; over the tangles dressed
without benefit of mirror or comb; over the tufts and bald heads of
the variegated faithful, and the sermon came out a bit ridiculous, but
it was a sermon.

The diabetics drink their café con leche with Hermesetas, a few
little slices of cheese and homemade bread, they eat fruit and deco-
rously pass the napkin over their lips, while the others defy Gargantua,
gobbling up anything they can. The enormous gothic cake remains
intact. The guests think it will end up in the gullets of Doña Carmen's
forty grandchildren but she, maternal and honorable, has planned
to give it a more Christian fate: she will send it well-wrapped in the
box left over from the town's first refrigerator, which is installed in
Doña Carmen's pantry and which is a novelty because you can make
ice cream without the shallow bronze pans that spin on a cushion of
highland straw and rock salt. The cake will go to the little orphans of
San Vicente, and the little orphans will make a good account of it but,
accustomed as they are to a congenital malnutrition, like all abandoned children, when they have finished eating it — if they actually get
to eat it — they will suffer in the twists and turnings of their intestines
the disasters of a revolution; the butter and the chantilly cream will
commit sabotage, their guts will jump with indignation at the novelty;
the little orphans will spend an entire week sitting on the toilet.... If
Doña Carmen were a fortuneteller she would know about these and
many other things which she can't know about because she is very
much above them and it's a bother to go down to the slums and dirty
one's shoes and smell the stink of human misery.

Meanwhile, in the plaza, the *priostes* compete in splendor with
Doña Carmen: four pairs of *curiquingues* have come with tight pants,
large wings covered with colored feathers moved by their arms, and
a long neck that ends with a pointed beak. The measured beat of the
bass drum sounds, and the same Indian who is the one-man band
beats the leather drumhead painted with colored birds and striped

tigers and red and green circles and other geometric designs, and it is the same person who also plays the sad, howling reed flute. The *curiquingues* begin to dance, as the people join in on the chorus:

"Get out and dance, *curiquingue* ..."

They move in circles with many small hops, imitating the male bird pursuing the female, and the knowing chorus sings:

"Turn yourself around, *curiquingue* ..."

The people laugh with a happiness that is ancient, distant, pre-Incaic. The little *longos* play at imitating them and become tangled up in the onlookers' legs. The *priostes* share out the chicha that the gods teach them how to make:

"Pick up your feet, *curiquingue* ... "

The dance and the uproar reach their climax when one of the man-birds spreads his legs and with his arm-wings tied behind his back with a piece of rope, picks up the gourd filled with chicha using his clenched teeth and lifts it off the ground, dancing all the while, and drinks it down without spilling a drop. Everyone applauds, laughing and commenting, and the drum and the reed flute mark the monotonous, melancholy rhythm, as if even at the heart of pure happiness, of laughter and clamor, there remained a sediment of old sadness that doesn't let go even when they urge the dancers on:

"Pull out the worm, *curiquingue* ..."

Gourd after gourd of chicha is passed around, and as each earthenware jar is emptied it is immediately replaced, until the dance is finished:

"Pick up your feet, little master,
Pick up your feet, little lady ..."

The fair has the look of the biblical years of the seven fat cows, when one eats everything there is so as to endure the lean years. There are platters of guinea pig bathed in peanut sauce that look like drowned mice. There are potatoes in their jackets, beside the pots of hot pepper with cheese sauce to be eaten with the chiricaldo. There are baskets of steaming hominy — to be eaten after the probana — with ripe peas, with toasted corn, chochos and chopped onion with parsley and cilantro. There are giant clay pots where golden corn simmers with green fava beans and mellocos. There are roast pigs laid out on beds of lettuce with red peppers coming out of their eyes and snouts. There are pans of potato llapingachos frying in the lard colored by the cracklings that chirp and sizzle like cicadas in the bronze pans. There are enormous pots of mondongo broth and others with beef tripe stew. There is tripamishqui hopping on improvised brick stoves. There is murunchi, there are mashuas. There is bread of obligation in the form of rings and there are cakes and cornmeal arepas and sweets and candies from Ambato and more jars of fermented chicha, each with a gourd floating in it like a drunken boat wanting to sail more distant and more ancient seas, and the gourd is passed from mouth to mouth as though today everyone were one big family, children of the same small mother who stands on the altar because the true mother, the *Mama Pacha* of the ancestors, is dead. And they suffer every variety of orphanhood, which they want neither to address nor to recognize, nor to know what they are like, for in their dictionary the verb to steal does not exist, for if one Indian is hungry and sees a chicken, he takes it and eats it, knowing the owner of the chicken would do the same, for what to the whites is theft, to the Indians is a loan, and the jails are filled with chicken-stealing Indians ...

And among the multitude of Indians, who are beginning to fall down drunk with the drunkenness that is neither habit nor acceptance, but rather rebellion and contained fury, the last few remnants from the highest slopes arrive, the barefoot and desolate and under-fed *guasharangos* who were not invited, those who have nothing even among the wretched of the earth, who have found out through rumors that there is a fiesta and who turn up in swarms to gather the remains of the remains of the remains ...

And the people set aside their food and drink, because the dancers hired by the *priostes* have arrived, and every one of them is a
castle in motion, and they get ready for the dance to the sound of the
drum, the reed flute, and the fifty bronze jingle bells that they wear
around their knees. And they begin to dance, turning by themselves
and around each other, and they move in circles, in zigzags and arabesques, and the contraption that they wear on their heads barely
moves with the beat, so that all can see the rain-bird in the shape of a
pelican, and the phallic symbol represented in the bull, and the lightning bolts and thunderclaps, and the ritual, mythic serpents formed
with shells and snails and beads and mirrors and earrings and coins,
all of which carry a hint of feathers and of reeds that are meant to
represent corn flowers.

And they dance priest-like and solemnly an untiring dance that is
a whole ritual and its own poetry:

—*Ñuca culqui mana minishtini, ñuca shungu.*
—I have no need of money, and I say this from my heart.

And the silk ribbons in every color of the rainbow that hang
down behind them move in soft waves, and under the wire masks,
half hidden by a shower of pierced coins that hang over their foreheads, you can just barely see their fierce black eyes, with a look
that tries to catch hold of a right to be, to exist, to know themselves
respected, to possess the seized land, which they would like to carry
with them on the red back-support covered with old coins, or in the
apron decorated with golden suns and animals and birds and flowers
embroidered with silk and tiny glass beads, and in their gloved hands
they brandish a cutlass that is sign, symbol, cross, and defiance.

The rockets shred the morning air and explode among the clouds
in peals of laughter that only last an instant. And out comes the *vaca
loca* charging at those who want to grab the fruits and banknotes
pinned to the framework of reeds covered with colored cloths
donated by the sponsors.

And the tired sun begins to set, though it will reappear for the
next fiesta when other *priostes* begin to save their entire lives in order

to pay the expenses of feeling themselves kings for a day, so as not to
suffer the stain of being called *longos,* although they know for a cer-
tainty that *he who was born for a nickel will never see a dime,* although
they are painfully aware that *he who was born for sorrow is unhappy
even when drunk,* although they are perfectly convinced that *he that
was born for darkness, though he go about selling candles,* yet:

   —*Huasharangu cashpa, allucanata cargungapag saquirín, caraju.*

   —They won't let a poor man even carry a dog, damn it.

   Everyone has eaten and drunk. The whites at the home of Doña
Carmen Benavides, the cholos, the chagras, the Indians and even the
guasharangos at the *prioste*'s house, in the plaza or on the streets. But
there is one who has refused to try even a bite since the eve of the
fiesta when the fireworks with their multicolored flames are burnt in
front of the cathedral, and music is heard all night long, and there
is a lavish squandering of aguardiente. He has not even come to the
window to see the multitude of outsiders who don't stop arriving, and
the next morning, after the great Mass when everyone is celebrating
the dancers and the *curiquingues,* he remains stretched out on his
bed, with his crossed arms serving as pillow or with an open book
on his chest that he is unable to read, or smoking one cigarette after
another. His mother-neighbor, who watches his every move, enters
softly and places within reach a plate piled high with food:

   —Don Manuel, eat something ...

   Manuel Pando, who in another era was Manuel Benavides, scorn-
fully tries to explain that he will eat nothing at the expense of the
Indians who are poorer than he, and that it disgusts him to eat the
food of the rich, but that when the time comes, he will take what is
his, asking permission of no one. And the good woman insists on
making him something, but she isn't sure what because she knows
that his are upper-class tastes. And she wants to understand him
yet she can't, and she never could have imagined that between them
there would be such an enormous barrier ...

   And before the fiestas of the Jubilee come to an end—for they
will last eight full days—after the copious breakfast, as afternoon
falls, the luncheon of the Sisterhood of the Bead on the Gown of the
Potbellied Virgin is served, which only a few guests attend, for it is

a gala luncheon with five sets of monogrammed silverware and rows of cut crystal glasses for the wines and the liqueurs. The entrees, the soups, the main courses, the desserts pass in a veritable parade.

The missionaries beg to be allowed to leave. Doña Carmen consents. They saddle the three dejected mules, say their good-byes like close friends, and walk away with a bag full of banknotes given to them by the Sisterhood. The whole town follows after them for more than four leagues. They reach the outermost boundaries of the town, and they go singing hymns along with another class of song altogether, which the Pandos intone from time to time, so that it won't seem like a pilgrimage or a procession, for they say they're fed up with so much sanctimoniousness. But they will join in wherever there is excitement and food and free drinks, and they don't want the fiestas to end.

From the bell tower, where the heavy bell that is never tolled the way a bell ought to toll hangs—although the last time the scatterbrained sacristan rang it he did so out of pure panic when the town rose up because the Benavides girls made their entrance wearing miniskirts and the peals shattered windowpanes all over town—a great eye enclosed in a stone triangle watches unblinking the movements of this motley crowd and thinks of what the immense eye that sees everything in the present rather than the past must think, as if it were Borges' Aleph; it knows about the Indians that which the whites and the mestizos don't know, for he who considers himself white cannot enter that world, and the mestizo can only just sense it. And the eye knows that the Indian has played at being an Indian for four hundred years, allowing the whites to know of his world only as much as he wants them to know. The white man is set above nature and is at best a transient through the landscape, while the Indian is nature itself, he translates goodness as if nature were good: he is goodness and has only one verb: *kausana* which is the being and becoming, the getting and having of the whites, he is the sequence of life and of the living, of that which lives, because the dead does not exist.

And when the fiestas end at last, because everyone's pockets are empty, the town begins to disappear into its hard work and daily toils and obligations. Manuel Pando goes back to thinking about the revolution of the oppressed, for he was born a revolutionary, he didn't become one. And the first struggle was with himself until he became hard and strong like the wood of the chonta, incorruptible and upright like the pambil palms. Able to soar to the heights to catch the prey that can only be spied by those who have the eyes of the Andean condor, not a buzzard that contents itself with any old carrion it might find in the ravines. He is resolute like granite and he knows the paths he walks. And when no one else eats, he begins to serve himself his food, food of a good bourgeois, although the four hundred years of hunger of his people cause him pain, for no one can give what he doesn't have, for the revolution must come from above, although those from below must make it, for it will come like rain and like the morning, for the revolutionary must have some charisma, he can't be just any old makeshift fellow nor one who doesn't understand renunciation and sacrifice.

And out of the whole town, only Manuel Pando could have been a revolutionary because he threw overboard everything he had in order to struggle alongside the poor and he was able to reclothe himself in dignity and pride in order to frighten the great Benavides dynasty and instill a natural respect in the ineffectual Pandos who are up to what they're up to out of greed, not because of ideological principles nor because their hearts are bursting out of their shirts.

Manuel Pando returns to the struggle, returns to fight for his principles, putting together one by one the linotypes to upbraid all those who took part in one way or another in the Jubilee fiestas. He prints his subversive sheets and while he turns the crank, he realizes, once again, that he is alone, terribly solitary and alone just as Jesus was many afternoons, and he knows that he is alone against a citadel that ought to collapse, he is removing one by one the ancient stones of the foundation, he knows that he should clean the mortar with which they are joined and he knows he should build a new town that does not sleep in the shadow of an immense cathedral, but instead a town where people live according to the rhythms of the heart and of nature, a town with schools, hospitals, and gardens where the air would be thinner and cleaner.

Everything returns to its accustomed course. When the fiestas are over, the windows are closed. Trash from the festivities piles up in the deserted cobblestoned streets. But this time the calm doesn't last long. As soon as a few days have passed, the entire town begins to get worked up about the continual arrival of new outsiders who come without Sunday clothes and show up on foot, covered with dust and sadness. And they arrive from the North, crossing over the Newer Bridge, they come from all of the outlying villages with their homes on their backs, as if they wanted to settle down in the town that has just finished celebrating the Jubilee of the Potbellied Virgin.

Hundreds of cowed and fearful people come, fleeing the drought that has loosed itself upon them, fierce and merciless. It is a drought the likes of which has not been seen for years and years. They tell sadly that up there in the North there's not a drop of water, the most torrential rivers are dry, that the channels of the irrigation ditches are lost in the dried grass, that the fields are barren and cracked, that the leafless trees reluctantly hold up the few nests of the downcast birds who lack the strength to emigrate to the Potbellied Virgin's town, that the bridges feel worthless and idle because the rivers can all be forded at any point, that the lakes have closed their borders, that the wells hold only a sediment of wormy mud.

They say that they've been told by those who know their history that this drought is just like the drought of 1714 when it stopped raining for over seven years.

And it is true, the present drought extends to the four compass points as if it were a yellow sheet. The four old Pandos, seated on the park benches, take a dim view of the stream of people arriving with suitcases and bundles. They say there have always been droughts like this one in the north, in the south, on the coast, and in the jungle. But they're certain — no doubt about it — that in their town, which is the town of the Potbellied Virgin, never but never were there frosts, droughts, or blizzards, but that in exchange, it always suffered the plague of all plagues, the arrival of outsiders with loose morals, who come hungry to eat up the savings and the harvests, who want to live idly, with their hands folded, on the work of the poor, that lots of slutty *carishinas* come to sell their bodies or to look for a husband

among the young men of the town, that they take advantage of people's good hearts because one has to offer them food and shelter.
And as they watch them arrive, grumbling, they note that there are
many more now than came in '41 during the war with Peru whose
causes will someday be fully explained. That year so many outsiders
showed up that they even slept in the park, on account of the Peruvian bombardment of Puerto Bolívar, Santa Rosa, and Arenillas, and
they tell how they and almost all the Pandos took in whole families of
refugees.

The bishops, archbishops, and parish priests of the affected cities call for prayers at the national level, although the Indians have
already made their pleas to the mountains, have crucified the few
toads they've been able to find on the arid farms, they have made the
burros rub up against the fence posts, but all in vain: it doesn't rain.

Then the corresponding bishop orders that a virgin as miraculous as the Potbellied Virgin, the Virgin of Quinche, go out on pilgrimage. The faithful, sympathizing with their neighbors in their
misfortune, promptly change the sky-blue gown embroidered with
precious stones for the dark traveling costume. They take off her
crown of pearls and put on the tiny, broad-brimmed straw hat,
woven especially for her; they tie it with a ribbon under her jaw so
that it will stay on firmly and the wind won't carry it away. They give
her two long braids so her hair won't become tangled on the journey. They put away her golden scepter and give her a walking stick.
They take off her embroidered sandals and put on a pair woven from
cabuya.

And when She is ready to go out on the long, long pilgrimage
through all the parched and withered fields, her followers say goodbye
to her with tears and melancholy songs. The drought victims from
the neighboring villages come to carry her on their shoulders, and
with her on their backs, rocking on the special litter used for such
occasions, which is like her work cart, She goes forth followed by
many priests and acolytes, which She never lacks, who fall off one by
one along the way. And the faithful carry her through zigzagging can-
yon shortcuts and open paths, through towns and hamlets, through
valleys and hollows, and wherever She goes She runs into the ash

crosses with the toads nailed to the center that the desperate peasants have placed so that the rain will fall. And the Lady of Quinche sees a few statues of St. Bartolomé Bendito buried up to his neck so that he will feel how the earth burns and the dust irritates and will make it rain sooner. And She politely moves aside so as not to step on them and says nothing. She is accompanied by hundreds of people who throw out torrents of Hail Marys, and She sways between the women who now and then toss paper confetti on her because they don't have even a handful of flower petals to throw — just try to find rose petals, or dahlias, or even wildflowers in this drought! The women carry in their devout hands clay plates in which they fan the coals so that the southernwood, the incense, and the dried rosemary will smoke. And they sing to her and ask her to make it rain.

When night falls, the Virgin asks for shelter in convents, in hermitages, in churches, in the great houses of the haciendas, and in the homes of those who were *priostes.* They let her rest and they clean the dust off her gown and they wash her feet. And wherever this daughter who is not the daughter of any old Joaquín nor of any Ana, but rather the daughter of Diego de Robles passes, a resuscitated frog sings and the clouds begin to appear, they turn gray, they swell, and finally they burst with downpours. But when the procession moves on and the thirsty ground has absorbed the water, the drought that doesn't want to leave comes back, and the Virgin of Quinche has to return to the same spot, and the inhabitants of other villages that have already been waiting for days demand her, and the others won't let her go, and then those who have tired of waiting for her show up, and with sticks and stones they try to take from one another the small icon that allows herself to be pushed back and forth with an expression somewhere between smiling and satisfied. And the anguished peasants begin to shout and to insult each other and to moan:

— They yanked her right out of our hands with her litter and everything.

— C'mon, loan us the Virgin.

— Wait a little, it's our turn, don't be so greedy.

— We'll give her to you, don't be so anxious.

— They're hoarding the Virgin as if she were all theirs.

And the religious authorities and the magistrates and the mayors and the *priostes* all have to intervene, and they have no alternative but to toss a coin up into the air:

—And if it's tails, the Virgin of Quinche stays with us.

—And if it's heads, you take her.

—Agreed?

—All right, but no funny business.

But the Indians, who aren't treacherous or quarrelsome like the chagras, wait patiently to be given the Virgin so that she can pass through their lands, and they don't intervene in the fights, but from afar, with tears in their eyes, they beg her:

—*Bonitica,* we'll give you many offerings.

—*Amu mía,* send rain.

—*Mamitica,* by your fault we'll have no harvest celebration.

—Little one, little star, there's nothing left in the sown fields.

—*Bonitica,* where is the corn, where the potatoes?

And on the bishop's desk the letters and telegrams asking for the image pile up to the roof and spill onto the rug. And the committees come from far away line up to explain the Virgin's favors to the bishop. And the bishop, helpless before so many claims, covers his face with his hands. And then someone suggests that to be done with all this bother they should have a replica of the Virgin of Quinche made, what with so many talented woodcarvers in San Antonio de Ibarra, or they should send a similar virgin and there's an end to the matter …

And the bishop gets angry and asks how are the natives, "native" as they might be, not going to notice the deception, how will they fail to see it's not the real thing; when they see that the false one doesn't make it rain—because she can't—there will be real trouble and that he cannot allow.

And then the solution appears, when someone remembers another virgin reputed to be as miraculous as this one, and suggests that while the Lady of Quinche is working in the north, the Potbellied Virgin can put herself to work in the south. And the same bishop, knowing with whom he will have to deal, puts aside the mounds of urgent letters and telegrams which haven't even been opened, since they all say the same thing: "Send us the Virgin of Quiche so she can drive away the drought."

In his own hand he writes a very polite letter to the selfsame president of the Sisterhood of the Bead on the Gown of the Potbellied Virgin, Doña Carmen Benavides, and among other things, he affectionately suggests that she lend the Virgin, because the country is suffering an emergency, and he gives her other patriotic reasons and motives, he sends her his paternal benediction, and he passes the flap of the letterhead envelope over his tongue—which is not so parched as the earth because he has just finished a glass of lemonade—and he orders that the letter be delivered that same day.

And at dusk, while Doña Carmen is drinking hot chocolate with fried cakes and fresh cheese, she receives the missive and right away she sends José Gregorio Pando to summon the ladies of the Sisterhood, and since the call is urgent, they arrive running, just as they were at home: some wrapped in shawls because the afternoon is chilly and it looks like they'll have a downpour; others in aprons, because they had been arranging supper in the kitchen; others in curlers, because they'll have visitors in the evening and they have just washed their hair; another in slippers because her varicose veins are bothering her; another in overcoat, wool stockings, and a scarf, because she has pneumonia.

When everyone has arrived, they begin the plenary session. The bishop's letter is read, the matter is considered and submitted to a vote. The majority says yes, that when all is said and done it's an honor that the miraculous gifts of the image are recognized from so far away; that by going on a pilgrimage and making it rain with her passing, the numbers of the faithful and devout will increase; that think of those poor people with their sown fields ruined; that this is a good opportunity to obligate the bishop to send a permanent priest, for it's no longer possible to continue as they are, without a priest to help them stop communism in its tracks; that it's a good thing that the Virgin will leave the town for the first and only time in history. But, and make no mistake, she will return immediately because they can't be left abandoned and exposed, threatened by droughts and earthquakes.

But then they realize that it can't be, that she can't leave immediately as the bishop requests, that the Potbellied Virgin can't leave
tomorrow or the day after, that it will be ten days, at least, because
she can't just leave the way she is, because since she's never once had
occasion to leave the town, she doesn't have traveling clothes like
that other roving Virgin and the Potbellied Virgin can't be less than
the other, she has to go in appropriate clothing, because otherwise,
what will the people of other regions say?

And immediately, in that very instant, no matter that night is fall-
ing, they send for scissors, for thimbles, for fabric and for thread,
and as soon as the orders arrive, they set to discussing the style of the
dress, and they make drawings, design clothes, and conclude that the
fastest thing would be to knit a tiny wool sweater in miniature.

—But, wool? In this heat? And how common!

—Then a crocheted dressing gown?

—That won't look good on a body like hers.

In the end they decide on a simple dress of embroidered piqué
that can be washed after the journey and a black velvet cape. And
when the velvet is cut, they realize it's going to get dirty with so much
dust and she's going to look terrible. Then they decide on a light
brown velvet, the color of the barren, dusty fields, and they get down
to work, forgetting all about their other obligations, the visitors, the
supper, their rest.

And the next day, they order a pair of moccasins, because they aren't
going to put rope-soled sandals on her like the other one, who is a very
common virgin, and neither is she going to wear silk slippers over the
mountains. They send the pattern and the measurements to the shoemaker Romualdo Pando, lamenting that they must appeal to him rather
than making the moccasins themselves. And the shoemaker Romualdo
Pando sends back to say that there are no lasts for that size and it will
take two days to make one. The ladies send back to tell him that it is very
urgent. The shoemaker responds that it isn't because he doesn't want to,
but only for want of the last, and besides, he's out of brown leather. The
ladies send to ask what material does he have. The shoemaker responds
that he has only black leather, a little brown deerskin, and red chamois.
The ladies send back to say that he should make the moccasins out of

the brown deerskin which will go better with the brown of the velvet cape and besides deerskin is softer than leather for so much walking.

And the one who can't take any more walking is José Gregorio Pando who likes to deliver messages quickly and exactly and when he's relaying messages he is very professional, he gets right to the point and doesn't allow himself to gossip. Finally, he brings the message that the moccasins will be finished in six days, because the shoemaker wants to do a job worthy of the Virgin and he won't charge anything because it is his own gift to the Mother of Heaven. Immediately he gets to work, and although he's happy, he can do nothing without the frame provided by the wounded sadness of his agonized ballads, which slow down the work rather than hurry it:

"I reproach you nooothiiing, or at the most my saaaadness,
this enormous saaaadness that is taking away my liiife
so that I resemble a pooor man on his deeeath bed
who praaays to the Virgin, begging her to cuuure his wooound ..."

And one day, when the young Pandos pass by Romualdo's, who doesn't lift his head from his work (which is a miniature wonder with incredible details, rubber heels, silver buckles, inner soles of cork, gathered toecaps, and silk laces) they discover that the Potbellied Virgin is going on a journey—and she's going without their having been consulted—and they become furious because the Sisterhood has not counted on the fact that they are the people, the sovereign people, and they say that it cannot be that the Sisterhood disposes of the Virgin as if she were private property. They are fed up with so much petty intrigue and antiquated customs and with so much obscurantism and with so many sanctimonious old ladies who have appropriated what doesn't belong to them.

And they go in a bunch to complain to the ladies of the Sisterhood and they tell them that they can't stand for this arbitrariness, and the ladies tell them to leave at once because they are very busy and they should come back tomorrow or the next day.

And very much offended, they go to the town council to present their complaint, and that body installs itself in plenary session,

Alicia Yánez Cossío

for the matter is serious, for the Virgin can't leave the town without popular consensus, and they summon the ladies who must attend because they are going to be formally questioned by the representatives of the people, and the ladies decide to attend — to avoid problems because they already have plenty — for it's better to be patient with these uppity cholos.

Each one brings her work, because first things first: one is embroidering the flowers on the skirt, for doing the petals in raised stitches is a question of concentration and patience; another is hemming the cape, which can't be done any old way, for the thread should not pierce the fabric; another, lining the miniscule buttons of the cape, for you can't just have them done by machine; another, making the stockings for the moccasins, which she is knitting with five little needles, and since the stitches are invisible and almost impossible to find, she has to carry the count in her head and cannot be distracted even for an instant; another, threading diminutive pearls to make a simple necklace, and she's working with a hair-thin needle and the pearls jump out of the box as if they were flies when she tries to hook them; another, finishing the lining of the cape, for everything that belongs to the Virgin must be done by hand, though if she did it by machine she'd have already finished; and they are all so busy that they scarcely hear the questions put to them and, without pausing in their labors, they set forth their reasons, which are not capricious, and have nothing to do with sending the Virgin out as a tourist. This is a patriotic undertaking, one the bishop has asked as a special favor, for he finds it impossible to fight the drought with a single virgin, and the two can very well help each other out.

And the members of the council argue that the committees of the affected towns shouldn't be going to the bishopric about public matters, that they are no longer governed by the concordat of the days of García Moreno, nor the Modus Vivendi of 1937, for religion is one thing and politics another, and public calamities should be resolved at the presidential palace or in one of the innumerable ministries, and that they ought to oblige those in the government to send one of those military aircraft that only fly for sport or tourism, and that for once they should do something positive, bombarding the idle and stingy clouds with dry ice, as would be done in any civilized country, and they should leave our Virgin in peace since she has no reason to take on such projects when more modern methods are available.

They discuss the matter for three full days. The ladies have finished their handiwork and can argue and respond, for *reasons draw out reasons*, but neither side is ready to give in. They talk of miracles and tall tales; about how if they want rain, they shouldn't cut down so many trees; about what are they to do if the trees are already felled and there are no more forests; they talk of supplications and politics; they accuse one another of being pious old biddies or impious communists. The discussion spreads everywhere. The town and its families are divided between those who want the Virgin to go out on her mission and those opposed; between those who want to fight the drought with the aid of heaven and those who accuse the government of indolence. Manuel Pando is the only one who keeps a cool head and laughs at one side as well as the other.

The newspapers of the entire country take up the noisy brawl and give their opinions, and even an intellectual of note writes a long editorial in which he suggests that the best thing that could be done to fight the national scourge of the drought would be to ask the Mexican government for Chac Mool, the god of rain. The editorialist assures his readers that when the Aztec god went to Europe as part of an exhibition of Mexican art, he unleashed such storms on the high seas and such tempests in every region he passed through that the European peasants also began to fight over him, and Chac Mool had to remain in Europe longer than his allotted time.

The angry ladies of the Sisterhood protest in writing, sending paid insertions to all of the newspapers in which they demand to know how could anyone even mention foreign and pagan gods when the country already has the image of the Potbellied Virgin. They accuse the papers of being antipatriotic and of propagating superstitions with stone idols.

The four old Pandos comment that the commotion occasioned by the departure of the Potbellied Virgin can only be compared to the stir that originated in '55 when Velasco Ibarra was president for the third or fourth time — it really doesn't matter — and the first car race, called "The First Circuit of the Republic," was initiated and the cars were supposed to pass through the town, and the people got up at dawn and sat on the sidewalks saying at every noise: they're coming, they're coming ... and the cars never came.

Then the young Pandos decide to act on their own account and send those crazy old ladies to the devil, and they spread the rumor that the Virgin is leaving for good, never to return, because the Sisterhood has had the nerve to put her on the market and has sold her to the bishop for who knows how many millions of sucres. And the town, its sensibilities and pride cut to the quick, rises up in fury and begins to organize against such an outrage:

—Those Benavideses will see what we're capable of.

—*Muleteers all, we all carry cargo, and on the road we'll meet again.*

And when the day arrives on which the ladies finish everything associated with the wardrobe for the journey, and the shoemaker Romualdo has delivered a pair of precious moccasins that fit in the palm of one's hand, and the Benavides handmaidens are ready to change the Virgin's clothes, they begin by removing her golden scepter, the crown of amethysts that matches the necklace and earrings, they take off her gown of yellow moiré to put on that of embroidered piqué with her traveling cape of brown velvet, they put on her silk stockings, they slip Romualdo's moccasins onto her feet, and the townsfolk step into the streets, silent and determined, ready to oppose the icon's leaving, murmuring:

—If the Virgin leaves us, the drought will come ...

And the ladies are afraid when they see the resentful crowd, and they go to and fro showing everyone the bishop's letter in which he begs them to loan the Virgin and never a word about payment. But no one wants to be convinced, and just in case the ladies try to deceive them and remove her, the people decide to stand watch that night and guard the Virgin. Worried, the ladies of the Sisterhood retire to their homes. And the people haul their mattresses out onto the streets, for they aren't about to sleep standing up or sitting on the cold stones. They arrange themselves as best they can in the atrium, on the steps, on the adjacent streets, and they sleep mattress to mattress, body against body, and to bear the cold they take along their blankets and here and there a demijohn of aguardiente that circulates among them as they say:

—They'll have to step over our dead bodies before they carry off our Virgin.

—She's not leaving, even if the Pope demands it.

—Our Virgin isn't one to do miracles for just anybody.

And in the freezing night, the guitar and the songs of Romualdo Pando underscore the note of tragedy that goes beyond the pains of love and disillusionment and digs into the depths of one's being:

> "I will settle our account when I am able
> to give back to you the life you gave to me ..."

And there they remain three days and three nights exposed to the elements with the streets paved with mattresses that, begging your pardon, are pushed to the sides to make room for the stoves, for one has to be prepared for anything, for *hardships with bread are not so hard.* And they make improvised hearths. And other belongings begin to appear, emerging from the houses behind their owners little by little.

And there is one who takes along his best fighting cock in its cage. And the basket with the angora cat that just last night gave birth to six kittens who aren't going to be left alone in the house. And the cupboards with the new china, for the town is plagued with thieves who have come along with the refugees of the terrible drought. And the Singer sewing machine which can't be idle while this troubling situation drags on, for if one's poor, one has to work. And the RCA Victor radio with an extremely long cord which stretches from the living room for one has to remain informed and know what's up with the drought. And just as the bedroom and the kitchen came out, out comes the dining room and behind that the parlor, for the people of the town are beginning to acquire a taste for this living on the street. They make booths and stalls with poles and canvas roofs to achieve greater intimacy and order.

And every night, Romualdo Pando strums his guitar and sings sorrowfully:

> "There are afternoons on which one would liiike
> to take a boat with no fixed destinaaation

and silently, from any foreign pooort
head out to sea with the dying of the liiiight ..."

And the bishop, irritated and offended because the Potbellied
Virgin doesn't appear, begins to send telegrams and messages, and
word comes back from the town that she hasn't left because of trouble
between the Benavides and Pando families. His holy prelate's patience
runs out, and exercising his purple influences and his powerful taffetas
he gets the government to send a squad of soldiers so that, by reason or
by force, they can get the Virgin to the dry fields, and this one can do
the same as the Virgin of Quinche, who has left her comfortable sanctuary and hasn't rested even a single day since the drought began.

And the news spreads that an entire battalion is coming, and the
people get ready to fight, and the ladies of the Sisterhood are horrified and cross themselves at the mere thought that the soldiers might
place the sinful hands of filthy barracks men on the immaculate body
of the Virgin which no one has touched besides the Benavides handmaidens, unmarried, well-born and without the stain of carnal sin
that—so they say—makes of men, beasts.

And when the soldiers arrive, sooner than anyone expected,
under the command of Captain Quinteros who comes with orders to
remove the Virgin at any cost and who is dying to go into combat and
earn a well-deserved promotion, the frightened Pandos vanish and
those who spread the rumor take refuge at *The Voice of the People* so
as to see what happens from a distance.

The soldiers arrive in an armored truck and they look surly, grim,
iron-willed, implacable, transformed into walking machines. They line
up in battle formation. They begin to march with rifles at the ready
over the mattresses, with no respect for what they find in their path,
crushing the newborn kittens along with their mother, knocking over
the sewing machine, smashing the dishes, overturning the kettles of
food. They advance like a human tank firing their machine gun bursts
into the air and leaving behind them the tracks of their boots.

The tumult begins: the dogs launch their long howls; mothers
hurry to collect their children; the owner of the fine fighting cock
hides it under his shirt. The people cry out in terror and run to take

refuge in the cathedral begging the Potbellied Virgin for mercy. The whole town just fits in the cathedral, and when the last of them have entered—the four old Pandos, the lame Macías, and fat Maruja who can't run with her seven children and her abundant flesh—Manuel Pando, without losing his calm, runs in search of the sacristan, remembering what happened in the riot of the miniskirts, and he shuts him up under lock and key in one of the rooms of his house so that, if he loses his head, he won't be able to ring the large bell:

—Just relax, we don't want you losing your head again and ringing the bell, then we'd all have to buy windowpanes.

The soldiers begin to climb the stairs of the immense porch and their climb is a mechanical march. They aim for the jugular, risking life and death, feeling like the small gods of a cut-rate Olympus, abject, run-down. But the heavy doors are closed, and the soldiers are left in confusion with their smoking weapons, standing in the midst of hundreds of mattresses of every color and size, with no one to shoot at. They are amazed, they are not programmed for such situations, they don't know what to do because they were never trained for the times when the enemy vanishes or takes refuge in a sacred space. Captain Quinteros takes off his cap and scratches his head:

So, now, who the hell do we shoot?

Inside the cathedral, in a tumult of bodies, both human and animal, Doña Carmen Benavides, without having to think twice, nervously clears her throat and climbs up to the pulpit on the steep staircase that only priests have trod. The people fall silent when they see her. She raises her voice and with great indignation says to them:

—Soldiers, arms, and bullets against us, the peaceful inhabitants of this town! Who are they who want to take away our Virgin? We cannot permit, brothers, that such …

And she cannot go on. The peaceful parishioners who are inflamed because they cannot bear that their Virgin be taken away, believe that Doña Carmen—deaconess—is asking them to go into combat, and blind with indignation and heroism, they put their hands to the job. They destroy the ancient, worm-eaten benches and the confessionals that aren't good for anything, since there is no one to listen to or absolve sins, and each one, armed with whatever is to hand, goes out the door that leads to the sacristy and is connected to the parish house, which since the death of the priest Santiago de los Angeles has had no fixed resident and is almost in ruins. They nearly demolish the house in order to equip themselves with stones and bricks, and thus armed, they charge the battalion that doesn't know what to do in the face of the closed and holy doors.

—Men! Half-turn and fire!

The soldiers make a half-turn as they have been told and begin to fire. And when all is said and done, their weapons have the last word as always, since that is what they were invented for.

Amidst the mattresses, among those killed by bullets or wounded by poor aim, in a colossal disorder and motley crush, the soldiers penetrate the cathedral and, with a total lack of consideration, as if she were simple war booty, grab the Virgin—who is clean of any stain or sin—with hands still dirty with dust and powder, hands accustomed to force and to violence that ought to be crippled, unable even to caress their own children. They wrap her up in a greatcoat that stinks of barracks and foul language and they carry her off hidden in a cardboard box that until recently held the candles that the sacristan sold more cheaply for the Potbellied Virgin because they had already been resold several times.

—They're stealing the Potbellied Virgin!

It is a howl that reaches to the heavens and stirs the very entrails. They are stealing the people's daughter and their mother, taking away their reason for living in this life and the next, for the town without the Virgin is a barren field and the people without her are like the cattle of the dry pastures, more orphaned even than the Indians.

The few Pandos who are trapped, who are like the very devil in a bottle because they are not allowed to get out, are meeting with Manuel Pando, learning from his lips about how religious alienation works, and they can't figure out how he manages to know so many things, and no sooner do they hear the howl that fills the streets and penetrates the walls than they forget about the mirror game of the social imagination where reflections take on the consistency of the real and the real the consistency of reflections—which Manuel Pando is patiently explaining to them—and they leave him with the words still on his lips and rush out, unstoppable, to the scene of the action, and they tear the stakes and the sticks out of the hands of the fighting women and the children, since that's what the men are there for, and they fight like wild beasts beside fat Maruja who has left her children face-down in a confessional and has gone out to the field of battle, and unable to find either a blunt or a cutting weapon she takes up a handful of hot ashes from the brazier where she was cooking corn on the cob before the soldiers showed up, and without fear of the bullets that fall like hail and burst like toasted corn, she hurls the ashes into Captain Quinteros' face leaving him blinded and disconcerting the troops who don't know what to do when they see the captain throw his weapon to the ground and walk blindly, cursing and tripping over the mattresses until he finally falls down on them, and on top of him is fat Maruja, who smothers him with her bulk and, underneath her, the captain thinks the entire cathedral has come down upon him.

The young Pandos, at the side of the Marian townsfolk, also throw handfuls of ashes into the soldiers' faces, and when the ashes run out, they begin to throw boiling-hot corncobs at the troops, and when there are no more corncobs, they scatter, with the giant ladle, the boiling water over anyone wearing a uniform.

But what gives the greatest results in the uneven and ferocious combat are the mattresses. With bare mattress blows they charge the sacrilegious troops calling them thieves, faggots, and all the son-of-a-bitches they can muster. A cloud of dust obscures the sun and the sheep's wool of all the disemboweled mattresses covers the streets and the plaza. The soldiers, now without weapons and some without cap or uniform, covered with scratches and swellings, continue fighting for the cardboard box that holds the beat-up icon who goes from one side to the other as though she were a ball. And when the people finally retake her, she lands like rain from the sky, who knows how or why, in the arms of Doña Carmen who also takes part in the fight, beating the cops with her broomstick. She drops the broom to take up the box and runs with it to her house, escorted by the mob, and she goes in and shuts the gate, bolting it with its iron bar.

The battle won, the people chase off the nearly naked soldiers. The taffy maker Rosa Inés, who hasn't stopped working in the midst of the skirmish and the uproar so that the taffy won't set up, cursing her bad luck for being unable to help as she would like, and who hasn't taken her eyes off the battle as she throws the taffy against the chonta hook and twists it, when she sees the naked, scratched soldiers pass, blackened with ashes and some wearing only their boots and covering their privates with their hands — for a naked soldier is not the same as a soldier fully dressed — throws with all her might the golden cord at the head of one of them and traps him, and several more fall down along with him. And hundreds of small children appear like flies and climb on top of the naked, fallen bodies, burnt by the hot taffy, and tear the taffy off piece by piece to go on stretching it and eating it, while the whole town pursues the disbanded troop well beyond the spot where only a few days before they accompanied the kidnapped missionaries. There, according to plan, the armored truck awaits.

And when the people return, sweaty and triumphant, they organize an unheard-of procession for their own satisfaction and reassurance, with canticles, incense, candles, and prayers, to place the Virgin on her throne. And then they notice that the Virgin is no longer potbellied, and they don't know whether or not it is a miracle, and moreover, they observe that she has lost a joint of one finger. Confused and saddened, they call the unmarried Benavides girls so they can change the Virgin's clothing and burn the sullied gown and cap and comb her and adorn her and generally give satisfaction. The three cousins set to work and see that the Virgin is flat ... and they touch her and prod her and look to one another in confusion.

And when the people have done their duty by the Virgin, they take on the unpleasant task of assisting the wounded who are piled up in the plaza and they apply arnica compresses from head to foot and the doctors in training remove the bullets from their bodies and give them to their patients as souvenirs, and the others set themselves to burying the dead without tears or lamentations, without washing of the bodies or special prayers, for they have died for the Virgin and are already seated at the right hand of God the Father. Everyone is in a hurry, because they have to search through the sheep's wool and the rubble for the tip of that miniature finger, and they hunt for it for three entire days, for the Sisterhood has promised a gold ring from the icon herself to whoever finds it.

Doña Carmen is out of her mind. She rushes to and fro those three days and three nights without eating or drinking, without sitting down nor lying down to rest; with her hair loose and tangled, pale, aged, haggard. The people step aside when they see her appear, murmuring sadly:

—She doesn't find it, doesn't find it, not even *searching with a rosemary branch.*

—*She's like a hired burro,* the enemy Pandos comment, and the friendly Benavideses try to console her, saying, *better to lose a finger than the whole arm.*

She pays attention to no one and hears nothing, searching—she says—for the Virgin's finger. Her zeal is edifying, her constancy moving, her Marian devotion touching. But the four old Pandos, who have finally left their park bench as a result of the failed attempt to steal the Virgin, follow her like bloodhounds. They know she's not searching for a finger, but rather for the reason the Virgin used to be potbellied and no longer is. Doña Carmen is dying of anxiety and searches and searches. She goes through the torn-up sacristy, covers the cathedral inch by inch, climbs up and down the stairs, scrutinizes the porch, circles the entire plaza and even prods the chest and pockets of anyone who comes within her reach. Her eyes are bulging and teary, her lips bruised purple where she has bitten them. She moves with the terror of one possessed, hunting for what she cannot find, searching without even a clue, and she feels as though her life is draining away in the search. And with her go the shadows of the four old Pandos, glued to her heels because they guess what she is seeking.

Then the word goes out that during the battle the Virgin gave birth to a tiny God who must be hidden somewhere, and the people are moved to tears of tenderness and fill the altar with flowers and prayers. Some women make precious little baskets with diapers and tiny sweaters and place them devoutly at the foot of the illuminated altar. When the town recognizes as fact that the Virgin is no longer potbellied because she has had a child that has flown up to heaven

or has died — for the details are secondary — Doña Carmen, so as not
to arouse suspicion, stops hunting, but she begins to live on tenterhooks and she is unrecognizable: she neglects her distinguished
appearance, her clothes hang from her like rags, she no longer seeks
the object but rather the conjecture and she neither eats nor sleeps,
nor can she tell anyone what she is looking for, not even José Gregorio Pando who, after forty years in her service, considers leaving
the Benavides household, because he is tired of all this hysteria and
cannot forgive them keeping secrets from him, and to keep his spirits
up he hums through his teeth as he runs his errands:

> "Ave Maria my laaady
> this I really do not caaare for
> with her whims and her bad huuuumor
> she scares me more than the deeevil ..."

The people of the town have begun to buy mattresses, no longer
of sheep's wool which balls up with use, taking on the sleepers' bad
posture and molding itself around their fatty bodies, but of the kapok
wool that the nephews of the four old Pandos, who have acquired a
taste for business, bring up from the coast in their trucks. No sooner
do the people see Doña Carmen than they approach her to demand
that she have the Virgin's finger restored. They are convinced that it
causes her pain, and they can't bear that after the pains of childbirth
she should suffer pain in her hand, for those pains are their responsibility and they feel guilty:

— The piece of finger has to be somewhere, this isn't the end of
the world; if it doesn't appear, it doesn't appear; for *beside the seven
cardinal sins there are seven cardinal virtues.*

Doña Carmen is out of her senses, she hears them as if in a dream
and it takes her three full months to do as the people ask, and finally,
at the urging of the Sisterhood, which has also echoed the demand,
she has a notice placed in all of the country's newspapers (with the
exception, as is only natural, of *The Voice of the People*) calling for an
artist of proven honor, celibate, Catholic, and without vices, who can
restore the finger of the sacred icon.

After a period of time, Figueroa presents himself, bearing letters of recommendation that attest to his honor, one of them signed by the Nuncio; he brings along newspaper clippings that prove his reputation as an artist and master craftsman; he comes with his tartan cap and his air of seeing beyond mere material things; he speaks with the ladies of the Sisterhood, answers the questions they put to him and when he realizes that no one has ever dared subject him to such an examination of his conscience and habits and that it is an embarrassment, and very unmanly, to play along, he decides to take the job anyway because the price they will pay goes well beyond what the Nuncio paid him for the three quarters of a dog of an old San Roque that the relatives of a cloistered nun had sold him. They write up a contract in the book of the History of the Life of the Potbellied Virgin and so that there will be a record of the historic event, the ladies of the Sisterhood and Maestro Figueroa affix their signatures, and right away head for the cathedral. They go at a solemn pace, and the townsfolk, who know what they are about, step aside respectfully, because after the Battle of the Mattresses the Sisterhood once again inspires confidence and occupies the same place as before, for it has been demonstrated that it is more powerful than the army or than any old bishop; it is evident that the Pandos are a bunch of liars because it couldn't have been true that the Sisterhood was going to sell the Virgin, who didn't leave and has remained in the town, even if they made her traveling clothes.

The committee arrives at the cathedral with the whole town behind it. Figueroa stays behind, overcome with astonishment before the gigantic pile, and he measures with slow steps the size of the vestibule, enters the temple, he takes off his tartan cap, puts it under his arm, and stands in an ecstasy of wonder. He thinks he has been transported to a medieval cathedral. There is in the close of the rural afternoon a mysterious light that filters uncertainly through the high windows and leaves an absurd spot of color on the undaunted coldness of the marble and the warm splendor of the golden reredos. He feels himself submerged in the Baroque and he has to walk on tiptoe because he is afraid of his own steps, which seem to him untimely and profane. The heel taps of someone walking beside him irritate him. Annoyed, he turns to ask the person to be quiet or to walk in some other fashion and he forgets what he was going to say because he sees Magdalena Benavides who is going to hold the icon while he works. She has to go alone without the other handmaidens because her cousin Martina has eaten a full basket of cherries and is throwing up her guts and can't come out of the bathroom; she has to be treated with large quantities of infusions of *matico,* mint, plantain, and *caballo chupa;* and Clarisa, the other handmaiden, has a cold that makes her sneeze constantly, and she has to stay in bed drinking teas of horseradish, garlic, and ginger.

Figueroa goes as far as the communion rail covered with a long, starched white tablecloth and, squinting his nearsighted eyes, he is just able to make out the lovely image of the Virgin which is some three meters above them and whose finger he is to restore in the shortest time possible, according to the contract stipulated by the ladies of the Sisterhood.

Doña Carmen doesn't want the unknown outsider to be alone with the Virgin, and the unknown outsider doesn't want to work in the presence of so many people, for works of inspiration, sex, and digestion should all be done in private, without witnesses, in quiet, protected places. Doña Carmen cannot agree that the strange artist place his hands on the immaculate body of the Virgin, so for that reason she obliges her granddaughter Magdalena to remain in the church as long as the job lasts, and the poor handmaiden obeys with an ill grace because she has no other choice. If she were free like any other woman in the town she'd be galloping on her horse and running races with the wind. Doña Carmen can't tolerate that the two be left alone, so she orders the sacristan to go up to the choir and play the organ to inspire the artist and, by the way, keep an eye on the two who will otherwise be all by themselves. They begin to work as soon as the ladies of the Sisterhood and the curiosity-seekers have left the church. The sacristan, rolling up his sleeves, attacks the organ with the music he most enjoys:

"Saalve, saalve gran Señooora,
Haaail, haail oh great laaady,

Hail oh Empress of heeeaven
Daughter of the Eternal Faaaather ..."

The temple shudders with the melody. Figueroa, entirely moved, feels his insides stirred and feels an old, hot tear slip down his cheek. It is an intimate, native music; more than liturgical it resembles an indigenous lament, it is a moan of mother earth, a howl of the *Mama Pacha*, a desolate and orphaned *yaraví* with all the sadness and beauty of the Andean *páramos*, with the sorrow of the drizzle of the icy early mornings, with the poverty of the stunted corn of the *huasipungo*, with the emptiness of the dusty hamlets, with the exposed ribcage of the thin dogs, with the misery of the drunken Indians fallen in the ditches of the long roads home every Sunday afternoon. But the breath of Magdalena who is at his side and who — since she is not an artist, but rather a vital woman — doesn't share his emotion, returns him to reality; he recovers himself and is embarrassed by his tear and asks Magdalena — without looking at her — to bring down the Virgin, for he can't work up in the heights trying to balance on the skinny little stairs.

And Magdalena begins to climb up unconcerned, and he, from below, sees the high heels of her fine shoes, which number two: the right and the left; he sees the well-formed ankles, also matching; he sees the articulation of her knee and the undulating tendon at the back of the knee of the two legs at eye level, he sees the rounded flesh of the thighs that disappear in the fine linen of the slip, and he wants and yet doesn't want to see more, because what he doesn't see, he imagines. He moves without transition of time or space from the aesthetic, mystical emotion of the medieval place with its intimate music to the brutal desire of the flesh with all its weaknesses, miseries, and grandeur, and he begins to sweat profusely and he has to sit down on the first rung of the altar steps because these emotions come very strong and close together after such a long and tiring journey. When Magdalena comes down with the Virgin, he sees it all again, in reverse, from the linen that circles her thighs down to the high heels of her shoes and his eyes meet her luminous eyes, and when he tries to help her — because she has asked him to — his hands bump into hers that still support the body of the Virgin and they establish a current of neurons through the mantle embroidered with pearls and threads of gold. And in a single look they say everything that has to be said in such cases. For a long moment they are lost in the forest of their thoughts and feelings until the sacristan hits a wrong note that sounds as if it were the seldom-heard fire siren destroying the spell and asking:

—What are you doing down there?

And then Figueroa remembers what he came for and reaching into his jacket pocket takes out ten or twelve small pieces of cedar. He chooses one and begins to destroy it with a very delicate gouge until the finger is shaped, but it doesn't come out as he would wish, for he is far from being a Legarda in such circumstances, and he makes another, which doesn't please him either, and another, and another, and another…. And the job that should have taken three days at the most, from shaping the tiny finger joint, slipping in a delicate fingernail, painting it until it resembles porcelain and afterward gluing it on the hand, stretches out over an entire week during which Figueroa and Magdalena find each other, discover one another, and fall in love.

The sacristan is furious, he wants to hang from the huge bell rope and let the whole world know what is going on. It no longer matters to him what he plays on the organ, sometimes he surprises himself when he realizes he is intoning brazen *pasillos* or romantic *boleros.* The damned work of the clumsy artist is never-ending, and in addition to being sacristan, he has other things to do: he has a nicely placed business in fresh eggs, and hens lay every day, for a machete under the nest that is hidden among the leaves of rue to avoid any illness of the chickens is never lacking; he needs to collect the eggs, place them in baskets padded with straw from the *páramo;* give the hens water and corn; put ashes on the backs of the little chicks so the *chucuris* won't carry them off; place the eggs in the clutches by odd numbers, so they will all hatch, and never in pairs, which is bad luck, for then few hatch; keep count of the eggs he leaves at the shops and above all look after his candle business, about which the four old Pandos comment maliciously:

"Sacristan who sells candles
If he doesn't have a waxworks
Where on God's earth do they come from
if not from the sacristy?"

But he plays dumb in the face of the malevolent and sarcastic comments and keeps on selling and reselling candles. But now the business is abandoned, he can't do any of his daily work, which is what he lives off of, for being sacristan and playing the organ whenever he's asked is something he does out of devotion to the Potbellied Virgin and because of a promise that he has never failed to keep, and for that reason he does it for free. But this business of spending the whole day sitting in front of the organ can't be, this way there are no promises that can be kept. He tires of playing hymns when he sees that Figueroa isn't working as he ought to, but instead is talking with Magdalena; he becomes uncomfortable and bangs the key that squeals like a fire engine and seems to say:

—Hurry up with your work, you loafers, this is no place for idle chatter!

But they don't even notice his presence, they are concerned with their own business, as they say, *for the burro will get into the wheat and the hen into the corn.*

Every day, at exactly twelve noon and at precisely four p.m., for *under the master's gaze, the horse gets fat,* Doña Carmen and the full Sisterhood go to supervise the job, and they think the slowness of the artist is effort, and they think such clumsiness is care. They suspect nothing, for how could they suspect such a thing? The Potbellied Virgin also says nothing. On the contrary, she is happy to give Magdalena what she has asked for each time she has dressed her or visited her; she is happy that poor Magdalena and poor Figueroa should fall in love at her feet and at the cost of her finger, for although tiny she is a mother and she wants to make everyone happy.

But the sacristan can't go on neglecting his business, and when at last Figueroa has glued the finger on the graceful hand, he swears by the Potbellied Virgin that he will take the gossip to Doña Carmen. The glue is still fresh, the Virgin placed on her high throne, when

Figueroa grabs Magdalena and they leave the cathedral running as if pursued, across the park where the four old Pandos are smoking and talking. The old men drop their tobacco box when they see that the outsider is supporting Magdalena around the shoulders as if he were embracing her, for she can't run in her high heels, and they see them climb into a bus that will take them who knows where, for it's obvious they are fleeing, that they go as man and wife, that this is the last straw of last straws.

When Doña Carmen and her entourage arrive at the cathedral at precisely four p.m., they find it quiet and empty. The Virgin's hand is finally complete and she is in the place where she has always been. There is a suspicious and complicitous silence. They begin to call very softly.

—Maestro Figueroooa ... Magdaleeena ...

They look at the Virgin as if to question her and the Virgin doesn't utter a peep. They begin to look for them. They don't appear. The ladies look at one another, worried. Suspicion sneaks in. They all rush to climb the spiral staircase that leads to the choir and find the sacristan asleep over the keys of the harmonium, for the poor man has a weak head and has succumbed to an unbearable, pandering fatigue. They go out to the streets, shouting for them. They arrive at the park, and the four old Pandos tell them—more than a little amused, because of the expressions the women take on—that they saw them run, hand in hand, in the direction of the buses and that they even had their arms around each other. And when they go to the buses, the neighbors tell them that the two climbed onto the "Kleber Alfonsito" that left ten minutes ago for Quito.

Doña Carmen burns with indignation and fury, she can bear the embarrassment and the bad news no longer, she would like to die at that very instant, and since death isn't prompt, she thinks it prudent to faint in the middle of the street, and she does so into the arms of the solicitous Sisterhood that encircles her with concern and finally revives her with a bottle of ammonia.

Meanwhile the town, feeling itself wounded in its own flesh, begins to spread the scandal to the four winds, for it is the first time in the history of the town that a handmaiden of the Virgin dares so much:

—Those Benavides women don't even respect their mothers, *a tree born crooked can never grow straight.*

—*Seeing is believing.* It's the bad company of those trips to the capital, for *he who shacks up with wolves will soon learn to howl.*

And when Manuel Pando learns of the scandal, which to him is no scandal, but just one more of life's low blows, he shuts himself up in the last room of his house. He doesn't want to see anyone or hear anything about anything, he wants to mourn the flight of his cousin Magdalena and he wants to do it without witnesses, because he needs to cry even though he is a man, for he loves Magdalena in spite of everything.

Days pass, filled with malevolent and indignant remarks, for *a small town is a great hell.* Doña Carmen is ill, body and soul. José Gregorio Pando says his boss *resembles a Jew on Good Friday,* that broken-down laughingstock of the Holy Week procession. Doña Carmen suffers because she loves Magdalena and would have given anything to make her happy, but give her a husband, never! It hurts her that she has abandoned her position for an unknown outsider. She cries because she doesn't know what will become of her. She sighs because she understands that she has died while still alive. The comments of the townsfolk wound her. She doesn't understand that Magdalena could have fallen in love. She can't get her mind around the notion that, between Figueroa and the Virgin, she could have preferred the former—meaning, in short, sex. When they told her that off in the fabled Llanganates the suro, which blooms only every two hundred years, had bloomed at last, she was happy, thinking her sorrows were at an end, and she even took it to be decided that this would be the year in which they finally had the long-awaited priest to help them stop communism. But everything goes from bad to worse, the misfortunes come all together, in a bunch: one after another, like in the time of the Pharaohs when there came the ten plagues that laid waste the banks of the Nile; she doesn't find what she is looking for, nor does she know where it is or who has it; Magdalena, the best of her granddaughters, the most beautiful, the most worthy to be handmaiden to the Virgin, the most loved—in spite of her protests—the most intelligent, the best dressed, runs off with an unknown nobody; the town remains hungry for Masses and sacraments; she hears nothing from Rome; the Pandos are more stirred up every day and are more insolent; her liver suffers and she thinks she has gallstones; the infusions of taraxaco, boldo, rosemary, cacao leaves, and artichoke taken on an empty stomach have no effect; so many disasters heaped together on her shoulders, as if the Pandos had cast a spell on her and had been dealing with the very devil, and to top it all off: there are no longer as many handmaidens as there were before.

There remain only Clarisa, who is a crazy girl and you can see how much she wants a husband, she doesn't concentrate on her work, and Martina, who is a fool, who never gets straight what the Virgin is supposed to wear and since her head is full of little birds, they always mess up on her account, for she doesn't understand that this dress goes with that mantle and those sandals, and that this crown goes with this necklace and those rings and earrings.

Doña Carmen has to find another handmaiden, and the only one left in the whole town is Marianita Pando, of whom it is said that she is the one known misstep of the Benavides men—without taking into account the father of Manuel Pando, for that one has been erased from the list, and turning a blind eye to the unrecognized children, of whom there are probably thousands. Marianita is the only one left, for the Benavides women were always good breeders and those of today are like the dry fig tree of the Bible, Doña Carmen has to admit, even if they are her own flesh and blood. Marianita is pure Benavides, that's plain to see, the whole town knows it, and she has blond hair, and there is none other available in the whole town, and say what they may about what she has done or not done, she's in her forties and she's single, and they have to get with the times and admit one who isn't a Benavides.

—And what else are we going to do, when there's nobody else? Let's see if this way the viperish tongues of the Pandos stop talking.

—But, this is impossible.

—And what can I do, when you're the ones at fault, when for every baby "your worships" have, the Pandos have seven. And don't tell me that at night, in bed, they do what they do and you just pray the rosary, *for things are as they are, and we must bear what we are sent,* no one's going to *pull the wool over my eyes or sell me cat meat for rabbit,* nor do I *drink borage tea* and *I'm not wet behind the ears.* If I keep quiet it's out of prudence, and if I only had one son it was because I was widowed without the good-for-nothing even having died, everyone knows what my life was like … and a touch of sadness invades Doña Carmen and she remains pensive.

The other ladies of the Sisterhood also voice their objections:

—A village woman like Mariana can't be handmaiden to the Virgin, when we know she isn't a virgin and she's no longer young.

And Doña Carmen confesses to the ladies. Lowering her eyes to keep from blushing, trying to soften the circumstances, she murmurs what she has never told anyone:

—I have great esteem for poor Marianita, who isn't at fault for being a child of sin; when all is said and done she is the love child of my late brother.

And everyone knows Marianita Pando is dying for them to make her a handmaiden and is willing to cut off her long hair so that it can be made into a wig for the Virgin, and she yearns for them to hold the haircutting ceremony. For it's not just a matter of taking the scissors and cutting it off in front of the mirror, but rather it has to be done according to the Ordinances of the Sisterhood by a distinguished man who can be the mayor, or a town councilor in the worst case, or any important man. In the past it was the parish priest who did it, but since there hasn't been a parish priest for thirty years, another man has to take his place, but he has to wear gloves, and the woman who is giving up her hair has to dress all in white and arrive at the altar preceded by a boy carrying the scissors on a silver tray. She has to be covered in white tulle, and the officiant has to remove her veil, take the cruel scissors and hack any which way while the locks are gathered by the president of the Sisterhood of the Bead on the Gown of the Potbellied Virgin and deposited on another silver tray. The cathedral is full of people and the old organ overflows with music. And Marianita Pando wants to be the victim so that there will be a record of her beautiful hair and so that the Virgin will wear it as a wig, and she can show off her dress, like a bridal gown, even if she is a frustrated bride, for *if she can't have the cat, she may as well have its hair.*

And when the Sisterhood, after long discussions and much commentary, gives the appointment to Marianita, she receives it as the best gift of her life. And Clarisa and Martina are furious because they will have to treat her as an equal from then on, when she is only a Pando dressmaker. And when they see that the Pando dressmaker's hair is longer and blonder and more luxuriant than theirs, they become obsessed with their own hair, because they won't permit anyone to put the ordinary hair of a Pando on the Virgin.

And Martina, who hates Clarisa because she's a flirt and has more boyfriends and grabs every opportunity to go to parties and soirées when she is not in the town, and because she caught a cold by going around in a low-cut dress and so it's her fault cousin Magdalena fled, and she has freckles and is stuck up, goes to the pharmacist and bribes him with all her savings so that, when Clarisa goes to pick up her preparation of chamomile, rosemary, and weeping willow to dress her hair, he will put in a few drops of alum with the tears of the sambo plant to ruin it so that her hair will all fall out. The pharmacist has her come into the back room and there the two swear to keep the secret. The pharmacist pockets her savings and Martina is nervous, because if anyone finds out what she's done, she will be severely punished.

And Clarisa, who hates Martina because she is stupid and can't memorize the order in which they are supposed to use the Virgin's gowns and which mantle and jewels and sandals go with each one, and because she is always poking around what her cousin does so as to carry the gossip back to Doña Carmen, and she is cross-eyed and spits when she talks, and is capable of swallowing, like any vulgar Gargantua, an entire basket of cherries and so it's her fault cousin Magdalena fled, goes to the pharmacist and bribes him with all her savings so that when Martina goes to pick up her concoction of chamomile and other herbs, he will put in a bit of alum and tears of the sambo plant so as to ruin her hair. The pharmacist makes her swear by the Potbellied Virgin that she will keep the secret, pockets the money, and Clarisa is left trembling because she knows what she has done is an assault.

One day, the two cousins meet in the park. Each begins to make fun of the other's hair, they begin to fight for real and throw themselves at each other like sluts fighting over a husband, they destroy their dresses, they scratch each other like tigers, they pull each other's hair and come away with entire clumps in their hands; the locks of blond hair fall out like straw and from then on they are bald, bald as hen's eggs, bald like the moon, bald like the cupolas of the cathedral. And the people begin to talk, saying that it is a punishment from the Virgin for having tormented Marianita who is no longer a Pando but signs her name Benavides by order of Doña Carmen who has ordered the official registries changed, and everyone agrees that she has hair just like Magdalena did, and she no longer wears it in a bun or in braids, she lets it hang loose like a cascade of liquid gold, while the cousins Clarisa and Martina appear from time to time with scarves over their heads to protect their skulls on which they smear beef marrow and pigeon droppings every night. Every time they see them appear, the four old Pandos whisper:

—Serves them right that they ended up bald because they are pretentious and stuck up.

And:

—Serves them right that they ended up bald for going around looking down on the poor.

The respective families intervene, Benavides against Benavides, on account of the social-climbing Marianita:

—For if she's a Benavides now, it's out of pure pity and because of Christian charity.

Clarisa's relatives bring a complaint against Martina's relatives. Doña Carmen can't bear so much fuss any longer: neither the presidents of whole countries nor the pontiffs in Rome have so much work as she. In the end, the families calm down when it becomes clear that the criminal hand of the pharmacist was in the middle of everything, and they make peace when they place a judgment against him that forbids him to sell macerated preparations, infusions, poultices, meconiums, pomades, syrups, emulsions, concoctions, potions, solutions, or enemas made by his own hands.

Doña Carmen takes a deep breath, although the root problems will never end so long as there is the Pando clan on one side and Benavides clan on the other. Each group is united by indissoluble blood ties, which are reinforced by social strata that can't be hopped over just like that, the way Marianita hopped. They are linked by political ideas: these are red while the others are blue; the Pandos identify with the left, the Benavideses with the right; the Pandos' fathers and grandfathers were liberals, the Benavides' fathers and grandfathers were reactionary *curuchupas;* the Pandos serve, the Benavideses inspect; the Pandos are dark, mestizos, of the earth, the Benavideses are blond, pale, from far away; the Pandos are poor, the Benavideses are rich; the Pandos are the people, the Benavideses the ruling class; the Pandos live in adobe houses and on the outskirts, the Benavideses live in the center of town and on haciendas; the Pandos go on foot and travel on muleback, the Benavideses go by car and travel in airplanes; the Pandos have gone as far as the capital, the Benavideses as far as Europe; the Pandos have dried, worn-out fields, the Benavideses own the generous lands.

In the beginning, however, recall the four old Pandos, more cadaverous than ever since they no longer see Magdalena and because they are consumed with worry over why the Virgin is no longer potbellied, the land belonged entirely to the Pandos and so it was recorded in the legal documents they continue to look for, but when the first Benavides showed up, he began to calmly take over all of the land: one day, a plot in the town; tomorrow, a block on the plaza; a month later, a league beside the river; the next month, four *caballerías* on the ridge; the following year, all the land on the right bank of the river as far as the bridge; the next year, all the land as far as the coast, and in this way they do to the Pandos the same thing the Spanish conquistadors did to the Indians until they are intolerably rich.

The legal suits brought by the four old Pandos when they were young accomplished nothing, the proofs are no longer in their hands, for justice is slow and lazy when the rich man fights the poor.

Doña Josefa Benavides, who was twenty times worse than Doña Carmen—according to the four old Pandos—had inherited from her grandfather lands without end in every direction of the compass rose, various dinner services of worked silver, a chest full of jewels, and a box with the documents that the Pandos should have had. The papers written not with ink, but with the blood of the brown machas that live in the damp under rocks and that were what they wrote with in those days, not on paper, but on parchment, and along with all this went the recommendation written just before his death that justice should be done when the day came. The recommendation was not very specific, since it set no date, and she could consult no one because a secret is a secret and so much the more so if written at death's door, and then she developed a whitlow and how could she suspect she would die from a simple whitlow, when no one in the world had ever died of a whitlow and yet, Doña Josefa dies. And when she has already received extreme unction and the holy oils, for her departure is imminent, though it seems like a joke, she has the Virgin—who was not then potbellied but rather of smooth belly as all virgins ought to be—brought into her presence, and with the help of the priest Santiago de los Angeles, who is the only witness, she folds the papers she inherited from her grandfather—great-great-grandfather in turn to Doña Carmen—and with gum arabic and flour and water paste they glue them to the Virgin's belly because it seems to them the most suitable place, and under solemn oath, the priest Santiago de los Angeles agrees to hand over the papers to their legitimate owners after a period of fifty years, and Doña Josefa dies peacefully and smiling thinking that she has done as she ought. But when only a few years have passed, the priest Santiago de los Angeles dies of pique caused by the Virgin de la Peña and when he is already about to die, with one foot in the stirrup like Don Quixote, the poor thing remembers his oath, but since he can't speak, he dies in despair making gestures that no one can understand.

Doña Carmen suspects that what is hidden on the body of the Virgin is so terrible for the Benavides clan that it cannot be seen without the presence of an authorized and worthy witness, and because ever since 1925 there has been no one of that description, she forbids the undressing of the Virgin. A superstitious fear keeps her from discovering the true content of the papers, although in a way she suspects, and she doesn't dare look at them, ever since a certain time when, unable to restrain her curiosity and knowing that she cannot touch the Virgin because she is married, she climbs the little staircase of the altar armed with a good pair of scissors with which to loosen the

strips of paper glued with flour and water paste that she has seen on
the body of the image and when she lifts her dress with a superstitious and sacrilegious shiver, a false move sends her sprawling and
she breaks an ankle and three ribs, and she believes that it was a
punishment from the Virgin. She isn't certain if it was the weight of
her flesh or the trembling of her legs on the narrow steps and she
who dares anything, never dares to repeat the deed.

The four old Pandos, by pure conjecture, tying together loose
ends, conclude that the old documents are hidden on the Virgin's
body, and they spend their lives watching the cathedral from afar, but
as they are men, and sinners, they dare not touch the holy icon; after
the Battle of the Mattresses they know that what they seek is no longer
where it was and they suspect that it is in Doña Carmen's possession.
They change benches. They no longer sit facing the immense cathedral because there is nothing to watch over, and above all, because
Magdalena Benavides no longer comes nor will she ever come again;
they sit on the bench that faces Doña Carmen's house to keep track
of her comings and goings.

The summer sun falls hard, it falls like the fist of a strongman
against a tabletop. Above the roofs of the ancestral homes built on
the lands that belonged to their grandfathers, according to the litany
of each and every day, the four old Pandos watch the kites with their
long rag tails swaying in the cloudless blue sky. The schoolchildren
are on vacation, for it is the dry and windy month of August. The
school is closed, and there are so many kids in the town. The four
old Pandos watch them play and become nostalgic remembering that
they, too, played the games the kids are playing, but they played less
because they had to run errands and look after the little *guaguas,* for
they didn't have vacations because back then they didn't have school,
and they laugh remembering that they killed birds with slingshots,
that they played marbles with palm nuts which they used as coins,
in the time of Don Eloy when you had two- and five-cent pieces,
and the nut was worth a half cent of a sucre, and they remember
that they had pissing contests, scratching a line in the dirt and trying to pass it, and that the late Arroba Pando, even if he couldn't

reach the line, managed to win the contest by peeing red, and he said it was pure blood, and everyone was struck by the purple color of his urine until they discovered that the kid ate dozens of beets right before the contest, which they held on the other side of town, and they remember that they, too, splashed in the fountain of the park just as their grandchildren and great-grandchildren are doing now. They have been playing all the cool afternoon under the direction of Marianita Pando who is now a Benavides and who, in order to look good to the Sisterhood, has begun to form groups of children who go to catechism so as to prepare themselves for their First Communions whenever a priest should appear and she has them play after they come out of the church learning *by memory, smooth as water,* the ten commandments of God's law and the five laws of the church, the seven cardinal sins and the seven theological virtues.

The children have come out like a herd of caged goats, and Marianita Pando, who is now a Benavides, has them form a circle and, taking each other's hands, shout themselves hoarse, singing the one about "the painted bird was sitting in the green lemon tree." Afterward a pair is set to dance in the middle of the ring, and they don't want to do it, they're embarrassed, for in school the girls are separated from the boys, and they start to dance with their heads down and their cheeks flaming, but Marianita encourages them and finally they let go and say they are "the little widow of the Count of Laurel, who wants to get married but can't find a groom." And Marianita Pando who is now a Benavides tells them to do the round of "little orange tree, little ivory comb, who's the prettiest girl in the Guayaquil school?" and when they get tired of repeating it, the Catechism Lady suggests they change songs and sing the one about the little coal seller who wants to marry the Count of Cabra, but she doesn't love the Count nor the cock-a-doodle-doo either; the ring circles to the left and they are all holding hands, and they are happy and shout that "the patio of my home is certainly the best, for every time it rains it gets as wet as all the rest"; and they stoop down to the ground saying "crouch down, and crouch down again, for the crouching girls are the ones who can dance"; and the enthusiasm becomes indescribable with the round that Marianita Pando who is now a Benavides likes best because it carries sweet memories and, in

spite of her forty years, she can't resist the temptation and grabs the
hand of a girl and that of the smallest boy and sings the old favorite
"sweet rice with milk, I want to get married, to the pretty young widow
from San Nicolás, who knows how to sew, knows how to embroider,
who passes her needle through the canvas at once"; and then they play
at *"matan tirun tirulá";* and when they are tired and their hands are red
with satisfaction and enthusiasm, the Catechism Lady breaks the circle
of "the whole party with the girl in the middle," she extends it as if it
were a ribbon of happiness to play "rum rum Felipito Felipum." When
they are worn out and can do no more, they refresh their arms and
faces in the water of the fountain and they drink from a cup made of
their hands held together, and since they are worn out from so much
movement, they sit down on the ground, seeking out the shade of the
almond tree since the benches are occupied by the four old Pandos
and by a swarm of onlookers who applaud how nicely the catechism
class is playing rather than hanging around in the streets, for no one
in the town has bothered to prepare them so well as Marianita Pando
who is now a Benavides.

And Marianita lets them take a well-earned rest, and she takes out
a bag of vanilla cookies shaped like the most varied animals, and she
places five or six in every outstretched hand, and they eat them sadly,
because they would like to save them to play with. Marianita Pando
who is now a Benavides takes out another bag that the ladies of the
Sisterhood of the Bead on the Gown of the Potbellied Virgin have
sent to sweeten up the children so they won't skip catechism class,
and she places three big, brightly-colored candies, the ones they call
gobstoppers, in each one of the hands that would like to seize the
whole bag and eat every one of them until they get sick with *güicho.*

And since there is still plenty of time and the children are still
seated in a circle, and they don't want to go back to their homes
where there is never any candy, Marianita Pando who is now a Benavides has them play sit-down games, and since they are exhausted,
with their thin legs stretched out in front of them, revealing their
poverty in their worn-out shoes, she uses the moment to have them
play "pim pim seraphim, little ivory knife, the round demands that
you hide this foot behind St. Michael's door, all but the paper."

—And speaking of papers, say the four old Pandos, rummaging in their pockets, we don't have even a scrap left to roll our tobacco.

— Compadre, what a miserable life …

And they hunt through their pockets and find nothing, and they keep watching the children who are now grouped head to head playing at the *punpuñete,* which is a little box of gold and silver guarded by a tick; and afterward they make a long line of hands that go up and down saying the one about the *chupillita* who went to carry water, and the chicken drank the water and went to lay her egg, and the priest he took her egg and went to say the Mass; and they play the game of Juan Pirulero for a long time and when they get tired they run back to where the Catechism Lady is sitting so she can lend them her knees, and Marianita Pando who is now a Benavides lays each child across her thighs and tickles its back with her elbow for the game of little *rocotín* who goes from the palace to the stove, and knows not how many fingers are up above, and each child guesses how many fingers she's holding up; and one of the children suggests that the only game they haven't played yet is "the flower I hold in my hands, that just now left my hands" and that "the Carmelite nuns wanted a turtle to see what they'd forgotten under the myrtle"; and their hands are honeyed and sticky, since to say what they were saying they had to take the big candy out of their mouths, since they couldn't talk with it in there, and the flower is a half-sucre coin that doesn't slide but rather stays glued to their palms, and you can't play like that, people just cheat; and since they've rested a long time by now they want to play at cat and mouse, and everyone wants to be a cat or a mouse, but you only need one of each, and Marianita Pando who is now a Benavides can't favor one over another, for all the children of the catechism class are equal, at least while the onlookers are watching, and she resolves the situation by means of "my granny killed a cat with a blow from a baseball bat, the bat got broken, granny got mad, one, two, three, four"; and afterward they set to playing at the little chain of *jagua* with its twenty-thousand burnt loaves, which were burnt by that Jewish dog who should be arrested as a thief; and when the chain is formed, the largest children pull on the ends and the chain breaks, like any chain, at its weakest link, which are the thinnest arms, and some fall on top of others and even hurt themselves, but no one cries, for there is no place for tears after catechism class, for there are still heaps of games to play like "let the king pass for he needs to get by for the son of the count must then stay behind."

And the four old Pandos scratch their heads, they don't know where the *guambras* in the catechism class get so much energy, now they're on to "Santa Teresa told me by way of San Roque that all the little blacks have heads like old salami," and they are infected with that lost happiness they felt so many years ago, but they don't notice that through this pure and crystalline pleasure seeps drop by drop the snobbishness of the princes, the counts, and the kings that must disavow all the ancestors, and the poison of racism is introduced as well, with its hatred of Indians, of Blacks, and of Jews. And among the four old Pandos they have only managed to find a single scrap of paper to roll up their tobacco and smoke by turns.

And when the sun goes down, it gets cold, a cold that comes down from the *páramos,* embitters their arthritis and plucks the chords of their rheumatism. All the catechism kids went home a while ago leaving at the base of the fountain a handful of yellowed papers out of which they were making little boats before Marianita Pando who is now a Benavides arrived. The old men see the papers which the wind is tearing apart, they float from one spot to another like the dry leaves of the almond tree, and the same wind carries them close to the benches where the old men collect them, stroke them, smell them and decide they'll do for tobacco. They fold the old pages in quarters, cut them with an old shaving knife that has lost its edge, they divide them equally among themselves and set some aside for the days to come:

—Damn but some paper really gives you the true taste of good tobacco.

—Amen to that, compadre.

And they smoke, throwing the curls of smoke into the air, and through the smoke they see José Gregorio Pando, standing on a chair, cleaning the windows of Doña Carmen's salon. And they keep smoking their black tobacco, for there are no more inveterate smokers than they, and they are smoking their exertions and their hopes, for the papers found lying on the ground are the famous documents that Doña Amparo bought from the lawyers and Doña Josefa hid on the Virgin's body, and which during the Battle of the Mattresses came unstuck from the icon's body and one of the kids tucked them into his pocket along with the bullet casings that he was picking up. They are the papers whose unknown whereabouts torment Doña Carmen, and while the four old Pandos smoke what they have been searching for ever since they were young, they think, where could they be, and they will have to continue searching until they die, for such is life, and *God sends nuts to those who have no molars, and crackers to those that have no teeth,* and *water that's turned the mill won't turn it again* ...

Marianita Pando who is now a Benavides is very industrious and efficient in her new appointment, and when the time comes to change the Virgin's clothes, she goes with the two bald cousins, who do their jobs very reluctantly, and Marianita has to do everything. Then she realizes that the Virgin's clothing embroidered with gold thread and precious stones doesn't look good on her, the robes are loose, as if they belonged to some other icon. She sees that she looks poorly, and in this state she doesn't inspire devotion. She tries sticking in a few pins, but it's useless, the clothes look baggy on her, careless, shabby, and then she asks Doña Carmen's permission to make her potbellied once again. The Sisterhood considers the matter and has no objection. Straight away, they set to making a precious little pillow of white satin and they fix it to her body with strips of adhesive tape and when they put on the dress indicated by the ordinances, the Virgin looks as she looked before: round, full, filled with grace and beauty.

And when the four old Pandos hear the rumor that the Virgin is potbellied once again, they don't know what to think. The only thing that occurs to them is to return to the bench they occupied before, convinced that Doña Carmen has finally found what she was looking for and returned it to its place, and they once again occupy the park bench where they always sat and they stay there until they die, and they will go one by one, single file, for they will not die of illness but rather of rage and the impotence of having been unable to do any of the many things that they said they would do.

Little by little, Doña Carmen is able to calm herself. She thinks it is
the Virgin herself who doesn't want her to find what she is looking
for and who wants what is lost to remain lost. She resigns herself
and returns to her normal life, she resumes eating and sleeping and
sending letters to Rome, all the while watching over the morality of
the town.

Around the same time, she receives a letter from her granddaughter Magdalena asking forgiveness for what she did; she says she
is happy with Figueroa, whom she has married in the church so as
not to give her grandmother more pain and she asks Doña Carmen to
send her clothes and her belongings. Doña Carmen breathes a sigh
of relief because her favorite granddaughter is not living in sin, she
sends her what she asks for and decides to forgive her, although she
forbids her to return to the town. She is also pleased because after
so many years she has received a letter from Rome acknowledging
receipt of her previous letters and very diplomatically promising to
study the matter of the deaconry. Relieved of her old worries, rejuvenated, active, without circles under her eyes, one day very early she
goes to inspect the Virgin and to confirm her suspicions as to whether
the sacristan gives a good account of the candles, which seem to grow
every day, instead of shrinking, so that she suspects they are snuffed
out at night, and she also wants to check on the cleanliness of things,
for she must look after everything. But she is left rigid with amaze-
ment when she sees that the walls of the houses are smeared with
signs and slogans. It is the first time such a thing has happened in the
town, which is an exception, every other town is a disaster, filthy with
Long live! and *Death to!* in every color and style:

—This sort of filth has never been seen here, never but never.

The first sentence she encounters reads, in huge, twisted letters
that look as if they had been written with fresh, dripping blood:

—"Down with the oligarchs!"

Doña Carmen reads it and rereads it, she is dumbfounded, for
her store of culture notwithstanding and in spite of being president
of so many prestigious institutions, she can't hit upon the interpretation of the word "oligarchs." It is the first time she has seen it written
and she doesn't recall hearing it before, and being neither a sage nor

an ignoramus, she knows that "oli" has a connection with oil, with the holy oils, moreover, which is to say, oil. And she asks herself who the oil merchants of the town are, and she doesn't remember a single one, because all the cooking oils, like Arbolito or Sabater, and the machine oils, like Mobil Oil or Singer, and medicinal oils, like castor or almond, come from elsewhere, and no one deals exclusively in oils. Oil ... oleo ... oil ... Maybe some painter, maybe her nephew, who is a painter and does still lifes in oils. But he's in Paris! He hasn't been back to the town in years, not since he married a Frenchwoman and brought her home to meet the family, and the aunts nearly died when they found her sunbathing naked on the terrace roof, it was such a scandal that they packed their bags the next day, and no one remembers the painter, but only his wife, and anyway the poor thing couldn't hurt a fly, there's no reason for anyone to bother about him and his oils. Could it have to do with Manuela Pando, who has a hog business, and makes *fritada* Wednesdays and Saturdays and sells lard in the market? Someone once claimed Manuela made *fritada* out of stray dogs; maybe she's mixing the lard with suet, or worse ... but then, why not write directly, and on her house, "Down with Manuela"? Probably these days one says oleo instead of lard. But that can't be it. How strange! She understands nothing, but at any rate it is a case of poor breeding and vulgarity that she cannot tolerate, to have people start writing on walls, *for the wall and the rampart are the slate of the upstart.*

Then she remembers that when the National Heritage people came from the capital, and stayed at her house, because they were her guests, they held a delightful soirée upon the theme of the cathedral, and during the evening they spoke of art and discussed at great length the Baroque style, and the Renaissance, and Romanesque, and Gothic, and she learned a word she has not forgotten to this day: gargoyle! And gargoyle has something of oligarchy in it ... gargoyle oil? No, that can't be it, she needs a dictionary. And she turns around quickly to look for her *Pequeño Larousse* which is on the right-hand side of her pious library, under the letter P, for Pequeño, next to the works of Pérez de Urbel, who is alongside the novels of Pérez y Pérez, beside those of Pérez de Ayala and those of Pérez Lugin, for there

are many Catholic writers named Pérez … and she sees on the façade
of her own house, on the immaculate walls that are repainted every
year, the same runny brushstrokes, dripping like fresh blood:

— "Down with the bourgeoisie."

And her indignation is again replaced by confusion. What bourgeoisie, who? Her historical knowledge points her toward the tur-
bulent days of the French Revolution and poor Marie Antoinette
beheaded and the outraged rabble committing every sort of abuse.
So, to start with, burg is town. But why on her own house, her own
walls — doesn't this have to refer to the Pandos, the townsfolk? Or
maybe it refers to the relatives of Clarisa's mother, who are Spanish,
from Burgos? But the poor thing died seven years ago! What is happening in this town? And Doña Carmen loses all desire to consult a
dictionary, thinking it would be better to visit the other ladies of the
Sisterhood and compare notes, and discover the spoiled brat who has
dirtied the walls, give him a good fine, and oblige him to clean it all
off as a warning to others. And she begins walking, worried and indignant, and two meters along she sees the odious writing yet again:

— "Up with the proletarian cause."

This really strikes her as ridiculous — prole … proli … proliferate?
progeny? She can't understand why on earth the poor want to pile on
more children, life being as expensive as it is, and this is obviously
the work of the Pandos, for no Benavides would dare to write on
the walls. Which Pando could it be? Because of the sophistication of
the words, which not even she — being who she is — understands, she
supposes it must be Manuel Pando, the ungrateful crazy who crossed
over to the other side, leaving behind the surname that belonged to
him and disdaining a good future. It has to be him, he is the only
educated one among them. But she doesn't think him so stupid as to
suggest they should have more children, nor can she imagine him, as
bold and arrogant as he is, writing on the walls under cover of darkness. And she can't believe that this lame, waddling hand belongs to
him. He's no spoiled kid, in fact he puts on the airs of a fine gentleman,
and they say he lives like one, too. What is possible is that *that* Pando
is the éminence grise behind this disagreeable event. Something will
have to be done about him. He needs to be watched. Out of all of the

Pandos in town, he is the only halfway respectable one and he even inspires fear with all the outrageous calumnies against the Sisterhood and the church and against all the Benavides family that they say he writes daily in his newspaper, and they even say that many of the priests who came and went argued with him and then packed their bags.

— Oh my Potbellied Mother, save us from the claws of that uppity cholo!

And she continues walking and she sees the four old Pandos, who are watching her, and she suspects that they know perfectly well who is behind these indecencies, but she will not humiliate herself by asking, for she has always ignored them, and she seems to sense an attitude of defiance as if the old men themselves had been the authors, but the poor old things wouldn't know any of these words, and it is impossible that they would have the energy to write such huge letters, nor the strength to go out at night with a can of paint and a brush.

Her steps ring with authority, loud and sonorous on the few meters she walks clicking her heels before she stops in front of yet another slogan written crudely as if the throat of each letter had been cut and the blood were dripping down to the foundation stones. But this bit of writing doesn't anger her, she rather likes it; in spite of its appearance, the idea moves her:

— "Triumph or die."

She thinks that it would be a beautiful motto to print up on cardboard, or even better to engrave it on metal so that it would not be ruined by rain; this motto should be found in every home, on every block, in every business, at the head of every bed. Triumph over the enemies of humanity: the world with its unhealthy pleasures, the devil with his daily temptations, and the flesh with its lust, or die like martyrs in the heroic struggle. Deeply moved, she exclaims:

—Who would have believed that morality was still maintained at such a level, in spite of the lack of good priests!

Doña Carmen continues walking, deeply stirred, and she has almost forgotten the other graffiti when she reads:

— "Down with the capitalists."

—No, no, this is too much.

She once again doubts the meaning of the inscription. Why capitalists and not inhabitants of the capital? She thinks that the Pandos are definitely a bunch of ignoramuses and on top of that, localists. They should get it through their heads that if people from the capital come to the town, they are promoting tourism, for all the outsiders who come admire the cathedral and become followers of the Potbellied Virgin. Moreover, these ignorant people are destroying the language. They need more schools, she thinks, to teach them to write *inhabitants of the capital* and not *capitalists*.

—So much work for a single soul!

She has almost arrived at the home of Doña Elena Benavides, permanent secretary of the Sisterhood of the Bead on the Gown of the Potbellied Virgin, when she reads in the same bloody characters:

—"Down with imperialism."

She wrinkles her brow in confusion: which imperialism? She tries to recall which countries aren't republics but kingdoms or empires—for it's the same thing—and she counts them on the fingers of one hand: England, with Queen Elizabeth; Monaco, with Grace and Rainier; Holland, with Juliana; Greece, with Queen Fredericka; she can't think of any others ...

—And what do we have against those poor kings? What does England matter to us, or Monaco, or Holland, still less Greece, that we should go fouling the town walls?

She is so confused that she can't decide what to do. She has to gather the ladies of the Sisterhood to exchange impressions. And when she arrives at the home of Doña Elena, she sees that they have written on her house as well:

—"Down with Yankee imperialism."

Then she realizes that imperialism refers to the gringos. She doesn't like that one bit. She knows that the best thing the gringos can do is improve the race—intermarrying with gringos has been a tradition in the Benavides family so as not to lose their blond hair. In the last few years, all of the grandsons have wanted to go to the U.S. and if they marry gringas there, it's a disaster; in the past they traveled to France and the Virgin's dressing room was heaped with blond wigs that could be changed just like her gowns, whereas now there is only one wig, which the Virgin is wearing, and one other potential wig, which is not in the dressing room but rather on the head of Marianita Benavides and:

— God forbid, if she should be left bald like the other poor handmaidens ...

Terribly vexed, Doña Carmen casts her eyes over the walls of the other houses and sees the insistent letters P C R. Uncertain what they mean, she tries to puzzle them out ...

Promote change and revolution? Praise Christian rebels? Proletarian civil residents? Private parties count reserves? Pandos' complaints redouble? Please compose republics?

And she enters Doña Elena's house bewildered, agitated and nervous. Doña Elena is dressing as fast as she can, and in her hurry she can't manage the hooks of the whalebone corset that she has to put on to leave her house and she shouts to the maid to come help her, and the maid comes, drying her hands on her apron, and when Doña Elena learns that Doña Carmen is in the house, she begins to shout to her from the bedroom, for the situation isn't one for standing on ceremony or silent waiting or cooling one's heels. Doña Elena shouts that at that very moment she was on her way to Doña Carmen's house, because she is uneasy about the writing that has mysteriously appeared from one day to the next on the white walls of the houses, and that to move their investigation along she has sent to ask the pharmacist — very by the way, as if she had no real interest — what the letters P C R mean, and the pharmacist has said in so many words that any idiot knows that it stands for Party of the Communist Revolution.

And upon hearing that, Doña Carmen charges into the secretary's bedroom like a *vaca loca,* crossing herself a thousand times. Trembling, she helps her fasten the hooks of the corset, and then helps her to dress, for one can see her improper and forbidden flesh. And when she has dressed, they mutually express their most profound sympathy and they dissolve in lamentations, and standing face to face, entirely shocked and at the same time horrified as if Satan himself with his *twenty thousand burnt horns* and his trident tail were in the town, they ask each other:

— Communists? Communists in *our* town ... ?

— Others besides Manuel Pando, who is plenty?

—And not even keeping silent, as one might have expected, but defiant, bold, advertising themselves on the walls as if they were Finalín, or Coca Cola, or El Progreso cigarettes?

—Impudently and provocatively, as if they were for sale and want even we Benavideses to buy, to tolerate them, to know that they are living safely among us?

—What shamelessness, Carmen, what nerve!

—We cannot sit on our hands in the face of such a threat.

Immediately, losing no time, for it is the gravest emergency that they have faced since the Sisterhood was founded, they send for José Gregorio Pando to inform all the ladies of a plenary session. And when they arrive at the Sisterhood meeting room, each one's face is longer than the last, for the word has already spread throughout the town that the communists have written revolution on the walls.

All of the plans long cherished by the ladies as a result of the fiestas of the Jubilee come crashing to the ground, they tumble like the walls of Jericho at the sound of trumpets and drums, they crumble like shortbread, they shatter as windowpanes do when the great bell peals. The ladies had planned to consecrate the entire republic, with all its counties and provinces, to the Potbellied Virgin, for if García Moreno could do it with the Sacred Heart of Jesus to annoy the liberals, Doña Carmen could certainly do it with the Potbellied Virgin, throwing out all the other virgins and teaching the hardened communists a lesson. But things being as they are, everything is turned upside down, because a lesson is not what they need. And they take their heads in their hands and pace from one side to the other, they bite their lips and think and suddenly they burst out in unison:

— Communists in *our* own town!

They cannot resign themselves or remain quiet. They have to organize themselves and take the bull by the horns. They have to form the same committees they formed for the '49 earthquake when Ambato, Baños, Pelileo, Patate, Guano, Huambaló, Quero, Cataló, and Pillaro were reduced to rubble. When more than twenty thousand houses crashed to the ground, crushing seven thousand Christians and the Sisterhood endured dark days, but it came out ahead with the help of Bernardino Echeverría who was named bishop in those same days. The first step in the face of such an emergency is to find the person to blame for the graffiti and send him to jail, for as the ladies meeting with their nerves on edge have all observed, the squat handwriting and the careless use of the brush in all the slogans proves there is only one guilty party.

And they send José Gregorio Pando to spread the word to the four winds that the Sisterhood is offering five hundred sucres reward to whoever finds the culprit, and one person tells another, and parents ask their children, and neighbors watch one another's steps and become suspicious and everyone looks for the evidence that will earn them a sum that is not to be sneezed at.

Not even an hour has passed. The ladies are still in their heated session when they hear a knock at the door, an insistent knock, and they look at one another, wondering if they should open the door or pretend not to notice, for with this kind of problem, they can hardly afford to be interrupted, and as the knocks continue, they decide to open the door once and for all, and the person knocking is Encarnita Pando, all jubilant and self-important, dragging her grandson Jorge Washington Pando along by the ear and carrying a lash in her other hand. And Jorge Washington Pando is red with humiliation and rage, trying to persuade his grandmother with his explanations. And his hands are stained with red paint, irrefutable proof that he was the author of the graffiti. There is no one who dares to oppose old Encarnita who has been the one in charge in the family ever since her husband left to work on the coast and got involved with a young *montuvia* and never came back. The old woman has grabbed the lash to make herself more imposing, although they have agreed beforehand that she will not use it, but five hundred sucres won't do old Encarna any harm, she plans to buy a pair of pigs to fatten up and sell for who knows how much to Manuela Tipán Pando who makes *fritada* on Wednesdays and Saturdays. And when she has entered the great meeting room of the Sisterhood, she says, as one who is fulfilling a civic duty:

—Here is the spoiled brat. Now pay up the reward you promised.

And since behind the old woman there are hundreds of onlookers, wondering how the guilty will be punished and if the promised reward is real, Doña Carmen has no choice but to open the bulging purse that rests near the minutes book and take out five crisp, gleaming new bills which she places on the extended hand without saying a word, for the prestige of the Sisterhood is riding on it. The people congratulate old Encarna, because this polluting the walls with strange words is no good, and because five hundred sucres are five hundred sucres.

And when old Encarna receives them, she counts them eagerly, she sniffs them, caresses them, and hides them away, well folded, in her bosom, and she begins to disclose by way of an apology, that *if you keep crows, they'll peck out your eyes,* that the boy began to go astray when he went to work as an apprentice at *The Voice of the People,* for they say the owner is nuts and that he has the same madness as the thin man who went on horseback followed by the fat man riding a burro, for the madness he has is that of wanting to change the world which has always been as it is and no different, but that the boy—thanks to the prayers and promises that she has made to the Potbellied Virgin—no longer goes to the press and now he doesn't have work, for the owner—crazy as he is—paid him well, but they argued a lot, for every time the boy came back from the capital, he brought a mountain of papers and the men set to reading and arguing without a break, and the scandal was such, and the fights of the owner of the press with the rest of them, that she could hear all the way from her street that the suffocating atmosphere was killing him.

And as old Encarna is in front of an important audience that listens attentively, she gets carried away talking of what she should and what she should not, and every so often she punctuates what she says by giving her grandson a pinch, and he seethes inwardly, and she says that what worries her most is not knowing for certain just where he gets the money to take so many trips, and she fears he is involved in God knows what and she will never stand for a tricky grandson, for *blood is inherited, vice is acquired,* you can't do a thing with kids these days, this matter of writing on the walls won't do at all, so that:

—I leave you the spoiled *guambra* so that your worships might get him back on track for me, *though each man kills his fleas after his own fashion* ...

And old Encarna leaves, dignified and plain, walking tall and upright like a great ladle, and behind her goes the whole village, and the ladies are left alone with the spoiled *guambra*. Doña Carmen orders the windows that give onto the street opened so as to disperse the sour stink left by "those people," she doesn't know why they are so resistant to soap and water, this is the first and last time they will enter the offices of the Sisterhood of the Bead on the Gown of the Potbellied Virgin, for this is not a public office but a private one belonging exclusively to the ladies.

And outside, on the street, old Encarna bubbles over with happiness because she has easily wrung five hundred sucres out of the old Benavides ladies, whom she detests, as is only natural, for they are a bunch of abusive old women, although today they behaved well, for this dirtying the walls of such a clean town, where the Potbellied Virgin lives, is no good at all; and upon leaving, she cast a quick and cunning look at her grandson, and Doña Carmen grabbed that look out of the air and feels it as a light bulb that turns on and off, generating ideas all the while.

When the office is cleared of people and smells, Doña Carmen begins the interrogation, for she is dying to know the nature of the arguments, because in this town when there are arguments about that which is most important—which is naturally anything related to the Potbellied Virgin—they have their discussion and there's an end to it, nobody leaves their job because of some argument.

When Jorge Washington Pando remains quiet, unwilling to talk, Doña Carmen leaves aside the interrogation and tells him kindly that she and the other ladies want to know the meaning of the words they've seen written. Then things change, the boy begins to answer with great self-confidence, he's no coward, no, he is proud and wishes the other members of the party could hear him, going whole hog, betting everything in front of such an audience, he has never felt so pleased with himself and emboldened, giving lessons in politics to the women who own the town who don't know the meaning of what he has written, and he plants himself in the middle of the room, in front of the president's chair, with his hands in his pockets and a professorial tone that is the same as saying:

—No one treats me like a nobody.

He clears his throat and answers the first question:

—"Oligarchy, similarly to plutocracy and dictatorship, indicates a form of government considered illegitimate by the opinion and the preambles of the constitutions, which explain that oligarchy designates an existing form of ideal government that affects the distribution of real authority in a political society ..."

The ladies look at him, and they look at each other, slack-jawed, they are uncomfortable, as if they had suddenly left their armchairs upholstered in purple velvet for a school bench. They are irritated, as if the insolent boy were pulling their legs without the least sign of respect. They are annoyed at this confirmation that there are things the Pandos know of which they are completely ignorant, which from any point of view is unacceptable. Flustered, they squirm uneasily, and Doña Carmen takes the floor:

—Look, son, speak more clearly.

Jorge Washington Pando looks at her disparagingly, and what luck to be able to do so from such close range, looking at them all face to face. His one regret is that he must shine without witnesses, for the others in the party will never believe it when he tells them, for it is unbelievable that the old bags don't recognize words that any beginner can manage. And he says to himself:

—The ignorant old ladies don't understand a thing.

And in fact, the ladies are completely lost. Jorge Washington Pando scratches his head, he can't find any other way to explain things that are so obvious as to need no explanation, in fact, it's almost necessary to complicate them a bit, to make them seem more important to those who are less theoretical.

—And, who are the bourgeoisie?

—"In the present it designates, collectively, all those who by their interests are linked to the owners of the means of production, as distinct from the proletarian class ..."

—And who are the proletarians?

—"Etymologically the proletariat is the group of men who have no other social utility than procreation. According to Marx the proletariat is the class to which is assigned the messianic task of liberating society ..."

—And, who is Marx?

—"Karl Marx was born in Trier, in Rhenish Prussia, in 1818 and died in London in 1883. His work is such that it is difficult to categorize simply as that of a philosopher, an economist, a social thinker, a historian, or a polemicist …"

—Look, son, Doña Carmen interrupts, what do we have to do with this Rhenish fellow if he is already dead and no one knows if he was a philosopher, a historian, or what … ?

Jorge Washington Pando jumps, this is too much, he cannot contain himself:

—What do we have to do with him? Well, everything. Everything!

—Which everything? Son, speak clearly.

Jorge Washington Pando loses his composure and his patience. The ignorant old ladies are getting him into trouble. They are so self-important and yet more ignorant than the Indians. There is a tense and defeated silence. The ladies wait expectantly on his next words: one coughs, another blows her nose into a delicate little handkerchief; another strokes the indiscreet hairs on her upper lip which, without actually being a moustache, are as impertinent as this *guambra* who doesn't give up and speaks like a trained parrot. Doña Carmen is thinking of something else. The tense silence doesn't bother her, on the contrary, it gives her a frame in which to order her thoughts. And extending and crooking her index finger as if it were a hook out of which came a very fine fishing line, she pulls him toward her as if he were a little fish, and looking at him closely as if she had already connected the lie detector that she carries in her bulging purse, she says to him:

—So, the five hundred sucres are to be split with your grandmother, eh?

—No, not an even split, she's only giving me …

And the poor sardine realizes that he has fallen into the trap and wants to escape the net and he writhes and opens and closes his mouth, and moves his gills and stammers, he is suffocating in this unexpected atmosphere, and the words finally come out, and he says no, that his grandmother brought him by force, that his grandmother is terrible, she hits him, and that how could they imagine such a thing. And Doña Carmen, paying no attention, continues unperturbed:

—And, what do you want the money for?

And her voice carries a terribly maternal tremolo and such a friendly tone that one wants to throw oneself into her arms, and she has a smile that is all promises, and she puts into play all the guile and all the powers of the female who wants to seduce the male, leaping over the barriers of age and of belief, and she looks at him with the eyes of Red Riding Hood's wolf, for she has a graduate degree in public and human relations, and she almost has him against her ample lap as if he were a frightened kitten she were petting and offering a saucer of milk.

—Tell me, son, what do you want the money for? Ask ... just ask ...

And Jorge Washington Pando is dazzled like any Adam with Eve's apple. The "ask, ask" rings in his ears, and he feels as if suddenly the genie imprisoned for centuries in a bottle that a fisherman hauled off of the bottom of the sea had appeared, and he is crazy with longing for a bicycle. And Doña Carmen is no longer seated in the Sisterhood president's seat, the armchair with a back even higher than the rest, she is seated some three meters high, the same height as the Potbellied Virgin, and it is as though her very smile says "ask, ask," and he realizes that by letting his tongue run away with him he has lost ground, and he doesn't know how it happened, for when he was explaining the graffiti to them, he was giving lessons in politics and felt himself some three meters high, a little nervous, yes, but in control of the situation, and now…. And if he dared just a little, for *nothing ventured, nothing gained* and *if you don't display, you surely won't sell,* for Doña Carmen is rich, fabulously rich, she is the owner of the whole town and even of the immense cathedral and the Virgin with all her jewels and treasures, and just look how she took out five hundred brand new sucres, as if she herself had printed them, five hundred sucres that had never passed through the sweat of other hands, five hundred sucres, as if they were five, peeled off of a fat wad. And if his grandmother refuses to give him the hundred sucres she promised if he played his part in the charade and let her haul him in by the ear … ? The hundred sucres that would be added to the three hundred and fifty that he has saved out of what they give him for bus fare so that he can pass out the party's propaganda, and he, rather than take the bus, asks truck drivers to take him, and he rides lying down on the load, or he hitches, and when it rains, he shivers with cold and hunger, but it is the only way to save for the bicycle that he wants, because otherwise, where is the money going to come from?

—All right, son, tell me …

And if he tells her, what does it matter? Most likely, it will work, for if it weren't going to work, they would have already sent him straight to jail — and that only occurs to him now, at this very minute, not earlier when he planned the whole charade with his grandmother who is also crazy to buy those pigs to fatten. What idiots! Neither one of them thought they could send him to jail for painting on the walls. And if it works … everything has its risk, and it's certainly worth risking oneself for a new bicycle, which would be the only one in the town, a green Benotto bicycle, with a bell, with colored handlebars, with a strong hand brake, with a lamp and a dynamo to go out at night and serenade the pretty girls, with a calibrated gearshift, with green fenders with a red stripe down the middle, with the Benotto label fully visible, with a leather seat, with strong pedals … and him circling and circling the park, rolling around on the sidewalks so as not to bump over the cobblestones, flirting with the girls, and he can't stand the enormous temptation any longer and he says with a tiny voice that hardly seems to belong to him:

—It's that, I'm saving up …

—Yes? For what? What are you saving for?

—To buy myself a bicycle …

—Did you ever see such shamelessness? comment the ladies of the Sisterhood, lacking the psychological insight of Doña Carmen, who silences them with the look they know well. And Jorge Washington Pando turns red, he lowers his head as though embarrassed at having ambitions, and he looks timid, shriveled, inhibited. Doña Carmen, who understands human nature and knows what it is made of, can see the boy through his pants and shirt, and she sees him transparent, just as he is, caught with his hand in the cookie jar, carrying the dream of a bicycle which he may never have, and then she hits him — sibylline, distrustful, poisonous, obstinate, and accurate psychologist that she is — with a suggestion that comes out drop by drop, slowly, as if she were walking in a bog, carefully so as not to sink, carrying in her arms the idea that she caught on the wing when old Encarna, on leaving the room, threw that look of complicity at her grandson, and since the idea has not yet fully gelled, she is afraid to just throw it out suddenly as if it were a bomb; she caresses it, pushes it, makes it roll carefully as when she shifts the case full of Limoges and Sèvres porcelain figures and Bohemian crystal so José Gregorio Pando can sweep underneath. The idea rolls along like a barrel of fuel, slithering around the boy like a snake that has found its prey:

— Look, son, and if I — she corrects herself — if we, all of the ladies here present, if we give you a new bicycle, a big one, truly, will you leave off all this foolishness?

And Jorge Washington Pando sees himself riding the green Ben- otto, weaving as if he were on horseback, looking down from above, scaring the girls of the village with the ting-a-ling of the bell, getting into the small groups of the *guambras* in bloom who meet up every Sunday in the plaza on the pretext that perhaps a priest will arrive to say Mass, and it strikes ten, and eleven, and twelve, and the whole town is in the plaza, and the girls are dressed in their best clothes and that day nobody works. And Jorge Washington Pando, in spite of seeing himself riding the bicycle, remains down below and not on top, and he asks, playing the innocent and blinking nervously:

— What foolishness … ?

And Doña Carmen looks into his soul not with a telescope but with a magnifying glass, and she also sees him riding the bicycle, weaving as her grandchildren do, for she has a bicycle for each one of them, and she responds with the tone in which the sirens sang when Ulysses had to pass the reefs of the terrible Scylla and Charybdis:

— All this foolishness of going to the capital and bringing back propaganda and dirtying the walls writing nonsense and styling yourself the communist, because the communists aren't going to give you a bicycle, old or new, are they? Go on, son, answer …

And he doesn't answer, he lowers his head and sees, without wanting to, the old canvas boots through which you can see the callus he got on his little toes from the shoes Manuel Pando gave him which he, like an idiot, said fit him just fine so that they wouldn't be taken away. And yes, it's true, because at the meetings they've never talked about bicycles, but rather of other things that should and must be done in order to halt exploitation and abuse, and at the meetings they talk about capitalism and the rights of the people and about surplus value and about Mao Tse-Tung and Lenin, and about all of those things that are difficult to understand because he can't attend all of the meetings, and all the others have the advantage over him and know how to argue, and he has to learn things from memory, and he always has to be asking, and no one has ever said one word to him about a bicycle, and that's why they have so many arguments with Manuel Pando, because he says revolution lies not in books but in attitudes and that the first revolution they have to win is that of dignity and other things that make you furious just to listen to him. He scratches his ear which still hurts from the pinches and tugs his grandmother gave it and he hesitates, he thinks, and he hears the criticism of comrade X who is the most biting of all of them and who treats him always like an ignorant bumpkin, and he thinks about the teasing of comrade Y who is always asking if he's wearing the scapulary of the Potbellied Virgin, and the sarcastic remarks of comrade Z who thinks he's so funny and thinks he knows everything and is always smoking and never shares his cigarettes. But still, not going to the capital.... But what does he have to go for if he can have his green Benotto bicycle, and he could still go once in a while, and he can even deceive the old bourgeois ladies who think that because of their money they can do whatever they want.

But Doña Carmen knows exactly what he's thinking because she can read as if on the big screen the doubts and hesitations that consume him, she is one step ahead of him:

—But no tricks, eh?

Jorge Washington Pando finds himself surprised in his own thoughts and has the feeling of standing in his underwear before them, and he wavers again, and Doña Carmen keeps dangling that tempting, brand new green Benotto bicycle, the taste of the apple of earthly paradise that can be his if he only says a simple yes:

— Come on, son, answer: Do you want the bicycle in exchange for leaving aside all this foolishness that has gotten into your head?

Well, he's not such a fool as to let the opportunity slip by, because at the rate he's going, he only has three hundred and fifty sucres that he has saved up with all his might, and if his grandmother finds them, she'll take them, and the bike has to cost more than a thousand sucres, and likely as not, once he has all the money saved up, he'll go to the store in the capital and they'll tell him calmly that the price has gone up, inflation, import duties, all those things that thieving merchants invent, and he's going to spend his whole life saving the money, always on foot. No, it's not fair. And if his comrades find out and tease him and call him a sellout, fine, he won't go see them anymore. But—and he freezes just to think of it—what will Manuel Pando think when he finds out? With his bad temper, he'll certainly smack him. And he weighs and re-weighs: which is worse, the smack or never in his life having the bicycle he wants so much? And the needle of the scale tips toward the weightier side, for a blow only smarts for a while, just a short while, and on the other hand the bicycle they're offering.... And he decides to hell with Manuel Pando and everyone else.

And in the office of the Sisterhood of the Bead on the Gown of the Potbellied Virgin, an overwhelming silence reigns. The windows have been closed again, once the sour stench of the crowd that came in with old Encarna was aired out, and not a sound can be heard from the street, and it is the silence of abdications, of dishonest pacts made behind closed doors, the silence of consciences bought and sold, the silence of Esau thinking of the steaming lentils and Jorge Washington Pando lowers his head and says yes, and Doña Carmen extends him her plump, bejeweled hand to seal the bargain, and he shudders at the touch of that powerful hand.

— Deal. In one week at the most, you will have your bicycle, and be thankful I don't send you to jail ...

And that's it, nothing more is required. When the boy has left, staggering with humiliation and pleasure, the ladies of the Sisterhood who still haven't caught on to the game rebuke—with the requisite respect—Doña Carmen:

—But Carmita, sweetheart, how can you give a bicycle to the spoiled *guambra* rather than send him to jail?

—But Carmita, honey, you didn't even make him clean the walls ...

—But, esteemed president of our Sisterhood, at this rate, all the communist *guambras* in town are going to paint graffiti wherever they want ...

—Ah, says Doña Carmen, entirely convinced that she is in the right—for *the devil knows more from long life than from being a devil*—and she explains the ideas that have been germinating, plentiful as the weeds in the fields, lush, luxuriant, soaking up the water and the nutrients of the other plants, and when the ladies hear her talk they are left open-mouthed with wonder at her shrewdness, her tact, her prudence, the hand of God visible in the gift of such a president who will liberate them from the abominable claws of communism and will return things to their proper place, where they belong, where they have always been, ever since the first wise man recognized the nature of power.

And after much more gossip, they ring the small silver bell to call for the hot chocolate and cakes and fresh cheese that they always serve after their meetings, and before adjourning the session, which has been memorable, they offer a prayer of thanksgiving to the Pot-bellied Virgin for the sequence of brilliant ideas she has put into the head of Doña Carmen, which they don't yet fully understand in all their implications, because when they are at the station, Doña Carmen has already returned; when the ladies are just beginning to see the dawn, the president is saying goodbye to the sunset and contemplating the early morning breezes of the coming days.

When Doña Carmen arrives at her house, she goes to the telephone, asks for a line to the capital, and when the connection is made—for they don't dare make her wait—she speaks to her son and asks him to buy a bicycle and send it to her right away. And her son asks what she wants a bicycle for when the warehouse at the hacienda is full of them. And he tells her that the kids don't even want to hear about bicycles any more because what they want now are sports cars. And he tells her to take whichever bike she wants, since they aren't good for anything, and do as she likes with it.

And the next day Doña Carmen, thoughtful and reliable, goes to the hacienda and chooses the oldest bicycle of them all, and she has the mud cleaned off the tires and the dust and cobwebs wiped off the spokes, and she has a wire wrapped around the bell, which is loose, and gets some screws to tighten the seat, which is wobbly. And that very afternoon, Jorge Washington Pando is pedaling around the plaza on his new red bicycle, which is the only one in town and thus appears brand new.

No sooner has José Gregorio Pando taken him the bicycle and the poor, humanly disloyal boy climbed on, than he is off like a shot, ringing the raucous bell. He forgets entirely about father Lenin and about the things Marx said and about the fights about Mao Tse-Tung. And when Manuel Pando sees him riding the bicycle and learns that it is a gift of the Sisterhood for having painted the walls, and in exchange for what he can well imagine — for in the town there are only two Machiavellian minds, his and Doña Carmen's — he summons the boy, gives him a good smack that loosens two of his rotten teeth, and calls him a bastard, a traitor, and other insults he lets fly when he is really furious. And Jorge Washington Pando receives the blow in silence because he knows he deserves it and even makes an uncertain gesture of offering the other cheek, but Manuel Pando, who thinks a single slap is little, restrains himself, and an infinite sadness envelops him from head to foot when he sees the blood the boy spits out without thinking. And he feels the loneliness of one man in a million, because revolutionaries aren't like cabbages, they are unique, rare, they are messianic. And he feels his heart break when he sees the boy jump onto the bicycle and ride off down the cobbled streets, aching and happy at the same time. And he brings his fist down on the linotype he is setting. The pieces jump and scatter all over the floor, and he feels a bitterness similar to that of the man who learns his wife has a lover he had never suspected. And he feels the pain of a father who is the leader of a guerrilla band and finds his firstborn son in political concubinage with the forces of reaction. And he knows the

Judas kiss and the pain of suffering for a necessary cause in the midst of unbearable solitude.

Meanwhile, Doña Carmen, happy with the results of her plan and with others that she has in mind, orders the walls painted with several coats of whitewash, and when she sees that the houses and everything else are just as they were before, she smiles, satisfied and sure of herself, saying:

—One less.

Immediately, word has spread through the town and everyone remarks upon the generosity of the ladies of the Sisterhood who have given a bicycle to the Pando boy rather than send him to jail. The four old men, who are the first to find out, tell the taffy maker Rosa Inés when she brings them a demijohn of pure aguardiente, just distilled; the taffy maker tells fat Maruja when she goes to buy caramels for her children; fat Maruja tells the pharmacist when he arrives with his packets of bicarbonate; the pharmacist tells Manuel Pando's neighbor when she comes to ask him to give her a bottle of Thimolina on credit; Manuel Pando's neighbor tells the magistrate; the magistrate tells Marianita Pando who is now a Benavides, and Marianita tells the truck driver who carries the tale to other towns. A few murmur with a yellow trace of envy when they see the boy pass on his bicycle:

—What a sly one, that Jorgito!

And others say, resentful or philosophical:

—In this world everything, everything can be gotten with money.

And then Doña Carmen traps Power in a single card and puts her shoulder to the wheel. Without leaving her house, she sits atop the bell tower, so as to have the whole world within her reach, and she begins to move the tokens so as to win a game of chess against an adversary who has no queen, nor rooks, nor bishops, nor knights. She knows she is going to win; before, she didn't know how, but now she is certain. She thinks that there is no force that can stop her and to begin a new and memorable match, she convenes another meeting and the ladies assemble expectantly.

When they are all together, she sends for no less than the ferocious Manuel Pando. And José Gregorio goes off on the errand, and he enters the dark printing shop a little afraid, and he greets the printer without receiving a response, and he greets him again with the same result, and he clears his throat softly to make himself heard, and when Manuel Pando raises his head and looks at him, he looks away and says, without meeting his eye:

—Doña Carmen says to be so good as to go to the Sisterhood office. They're waiting to talk to you about an important matter.

And Manuel Pando who is lost in his own thoughts laying out the old linotypes that were disordered when he slapped Jorge Washington, jumps; he rises a few inches from his bench as if to say to himself:

—Bribes, for me?

And he calms himself, considers, and says without the slightest emotion:

—Tell your boss and the other old ladies that if they want to talk to me, it's the same distance from there to here as from here to there.

José Gregorio Pando remains motionless as if he had been frozen in place. How is he going to say such a thing? Even if he went crazy, he wouldn't repeat that to her. But Manuel Pando says it again, slowly, word by word, emphasizing each one so that he won't forget. And how could he forget, when he's the best messenger the town has ever had. There is no other choice, he will take the message, happen what may, and anyway, what does it matter to him, it's all *white folks' concerns*.

And when the messenger returns, the ladies are nervous, thinking the lunatic is going to appear and knowing that it is not going to be so easy as the matter of the bicycle. The message astounds them, and they don't know how to answer. They look at each other and when the surprise of the insult has passed, for it's an insult no matter how you look at it, all they can think to say is:

—Did you ever see such an uppity cholo!

—Now you see, Carmita, why you can't treat these people as equals.

And they realize then that they are facing a powerful enemy and that war has been declared, and that it is the enemy and not they themselves who has begun and who has opened fire without having any recognized power, and that they are threatened without the aid of their ridiculous husbands who don't want to get involved in the matter, and that they are undoubtedly in danger because Manuel Pando isn't just anyone like the others; he has a certain irritating air of stateliness that is lacking in the Benavides youth educated in the United States and other parts, who don't even know the first thing about Carreño. This Manuel has a certain class, a special nobility that he came by no one knows how — well, they know perfectly well, but they are so offended that they refuse to admit it — he is a gentleman in spite of the stained overalls that he wears when he works at the press, in spite of the brown leather jacket from Cotacachi that he wears everywhere he goes, worn at the elbows, the lapels, and even the back; in spite of the unkempt beard he wears not to go along with anyone, but because he doesn't shave because he doesn't feel like it …

Meanwhile, José Gregorio Pando is enjoying his role because he thinks himself a messenger of war and his condition does not allow him to take sides with either of the eternally antagonistic bands — never so truly on the warpath as now — which puts him out of danger, and he insists in a droning and meddlesome voice:

—What do I tell him? What do I tell him?

And the ladies, who feel that the offense has touched them deeply, consult, discuss, get heated up without arriving at a conclusion. The secretary cannot transcribe the minutes and it is the longest meeting they have ever had, and the most tense, because their spirits are exalted and opinions fly across the room as if someone had stuck a twig into a wasps' nest, and it is the least productive meeting ever because they can come to no agreement, and they even forget to send the servant José Gregorio Pando out of the room, and he observes the ardent session with delight, and to end it, because it is very late and they have to retire to their homes, because they have never met until such a late hour, Doña Carmen only manages to tell the message carrier, who has become impertinent with his constant "what do I tell him?":

—Don't tell him anything for now. We'll wait and see, for *we're not going to waste powder killing buzzards,* and *you catch more flies with honey than with vinegar.*

And in the next session, the only thing they can agree on is that they can't fight Manuel Pando, and they decide to meet every day until they understand the arms at his disposal: they begin to investigate who are the enemies to be feared, how many they are, what it is they do, what they say, and what they read so as to speak that enigmatic language. And finally, they learn that there is not a single party but several and that they fight among themselves. And the skies open up for Doña Carmen with that news, because as the sacred books say, *a divided kingdom marches to its doom.* And in this case, the best and the only thing that they can do is rile them up until they finish each other off, for *all's fair in love and war,* and this is not just any war, but a holy war. And the Sisterhood goes to fight under the protection of the Potbellied Virgin, and the others have no one to protect them in heaven, but only Satan in hell, and who can do more than She, who already once and for all cracked his head ... ?

In the investigations that each one undertakes, they discover that the town is also divided into several factions who have not even greeted each other for years and that the strongest groups are: that of Manuel Pando, which seems to consist only of him, and another more numerous group that has more than a hundred members and whose leader is none other than the selfsame magistrate appointed by this very Sisterhood, and another party of the same sort that goes against the others at every turn.

—The enemy is in our own home!

The ladies shriek with horror when it dawns on them that one of those implicated is their compadre three times over. For the magistrate has three lanky daughters studying in Ambato who are named Socialjustice, Surplusvalue, and Pasionaria, and the three are goddaughters of three different members of the Sisterhood.

—And how were we to know?

The three ladies defend themselves remembering that they were chosen as godmothers in a hurry, when a priest happened through town, and there was no choice but to baptize the girls immediately, so that the poor little things, who have no fault in any of this, would not be left unbaptized. And before, they never imagined, but now that they've been studying the subject, they know what the names mean when they didn't before. They thought Socialjustice had St. Juste as a patron, or anyway, that there was a female saint by that name. And the godmother of Surplusvalue argues the same, saddened and downcast like someone who has allowed her leg to be pulled, but the godmother of Pasionaria maintains that her goddaughter's name comes from the Holy Passion of Christ, and she says that she liked the name from the beginning.

And they send for the father of the three darlings to appear before the tribunal of the Sisterhood, and José Gregorio Pando looks for him diligently in all the bars and cantinas of the town, and when he finds him, he tells him that the ladies of the Sisterhood await him urgently, and he is frightened and knocks back the last drink in a hurry. José Gregorio Pando makes him run, they arrive out of breath, the magistrate asks permission to enter, he wipes his feet again and again on the cabuya doormat while he turns his hat in his hands, and you can see on his face that he's an unbalanced drunkard. The ladies demand the reason behind the outlandish names of his daughters, and he doesn't know how to get out of the jam, and since he already has a few drinks in him he says that, although the names are not entirely Christian, they were names his friends chose and he sees nothing wrong with them, but that, if the worthy godmothers don't care for them, he has no objection to changing the names, so long as they hold another baptism ...

—Another baptism with booze?

Doña Carmen interrupts furiously, and while the man speaks with his eyes cast down so they won't catch his shady expression, she penetrates his soul and realizes that he is a dangerous individual, and she laments not having seen it before giving him his position, she sizes him up and realizes that he is sneaky and shameless, a flatterer, social-climbing and prone to double-dealing, one who smiles from ear to ear and plunges the knife into his enemy's back, more despicable, more contemptible than poor Jorge Washington Pando who after all is just a boy and suffered his own internal struggles and who no doubt still nurses some rebelliousness in spite of everything, but this one is a poor imitation of a man, and from everything she's heard and as she now observes, a drunkard like all the other men in town,

and so she orders him peremptorily to leave and return only when he
has sobered up; he insists it was only a glass among friends and that
the three *guaguas* remain at the service of their worthy godmothers
with respect to their Christian names.

— He must be dismissed immediately.

But Doña Carmen refuses to remove him from office. She knows
how to treat this class of vermin, people who have a certain prestige
in the town and don't let themselves be caught with their hands in
the cookie jar like the inexpert Jorge Washington. If they say he is a
communist, he will swear by the Potbellied Virgin that he is not, and
will ask that they make him *prioste* in the new year. Dismissing him
will create conflicts in the town and the way things are going, it is better to tread cautiously. He has to be bought cheaply, through those
lanky daughters for whom he would give his life, and the three godmothers have to cooperate, buying in their turn the three darlings
who should arrive any day to spend carnival with their family.

But Saturday arrives, and the darlings don't appear, nor on Sunday, nor Monday, nor Tuesday. And their father is desperate because
he has to fulfill his obligations to the ladies, and he plants himself at
the bus stop and spends the three days of carnival as the dripping
target of buckets of water, and the evenings he spends drinking with
his cronies, who console him by saying that his daughters are too
grown up for him to think anything has happened to them, they are
surely off somewhere having a good time and:

— Have another drink to warm yourself up, we don't want to see
you catch pneumonia!

And the father sighs and knocks back the drink, and finally on the
last bus that arrives on the last day of carnival, late in the afternoon,
the three daughters appear, shivering. They arrive happy, streaming
with water, smeared with flour from head to foot, with the odd egg
broken in their hair, looking a sight, and with all the frenzy of carnival. They apologize saying they went to the carnival in Guaranda, and
as the father knows there are no carnivals like those of Guaranda, he
looks at them enviously and forgives them, and he takes them home,
where their mother has lit a candle to the Virgin asking that they
arrive safe and sound, and the three lanky girls disturb the whole

town with their happy laughter, shouting and singing through the
streets:

> "At the beat of carnival
> everybody stands right up
> especially because they know
> who is singing, rah rah rah!
> Oh, what a lovely carnival!"

During all the days of carnival, the ladies of the Sisterhood
have been meeting daily, and in each session they have argued with
more determination and persistence than the representatives in the
National Congress. Their homes are abandoned and their husbands
are irritated with this madness of wanting to arrange the whole
world – them! – when that job has been exclusively reserved to men.
And in spite of the agreement to keep silent about what they are
doing – for it is as if Doña Carmen had imposed on them another
secrecy of the confessional – within the matrimonial yoke when barriers are broken, secrets are uncovered, and pacts fail, not because
of loose tongues as some might say but because that is when women
find themselves driven to seek out marital protection, and out of hon-
esty and in so much intimacy, how can they keep secrets ... and their
husbands listen and leave them to it, as if to say:

– Let the poor things keep busy with something, so they don't get
bored.

– Who would have thought the crazy old women would go into
politics?

And the ladies are indignant at their masculine incomprehension
and laziness, but they push on without hesitation or rest because
they have fully entered into the problem of the town's salvation and
they know if they do not check the danger in time what will suffer are
their interests and the interests of their children and grandchildren.
And in the second place, because in the absence of priests to fulfill
the mission entrusted to them, the ladies have to fill in. As things
stand, the Sisterhood of the Bead on the Gown of the Potbellied Virgin cannot exist only to care for the Virgin's dresses and safeguard

the town's morals and proper ways, but rather it must work for the defense of religion as it is threatened by godless communists who call themselves atheists without embarrassment and want to take over the property that has cost the rich so much effort.

And in the next session, which falls on Ash Wednesday, which all the ladies have celebrated as best they could so as to begin Lent — in the absence of a priest they have had to make the black cross of ashes on their foreheads with their own hands, each one seated at her own dressing table — they read what was agreed upon in the previous session and inquire about what each one has done, particularly the godmothers who were to make up for their negligence in accepting their goddaughters' names in the first place: Socialjustice, Surplusvalue, and Pasionaria. Each one more expeditiously than the last, they inform the Sisterhood that they have made their respective inquiries and have undertaken the respective interrogations of their respective goddaughters. And while they speak, Doña Carmen writes down, quickly, the ideas that come to her and traces the respective plans of attack, which in essence consist in each girl confronting her father to persuade him that it is necessary, urgent, and imperative that he dissolve the party in exchange for their happiness.

And thus, the godmother of Socialjustice informs them that the girl, as was to be expected, is not happy with her life. She is thirty years old and single. And the worst of it is that her father is forcing her, by fair means and foul, to complete her diploma as a master dressmaker in the Municipal School of Ambato. And she — it's not that she doesn't want the degree — but her father won't understand that the degree is worth nothing, because in the town, all the women make their own clothes and those of their children, and the few who can pay a seamstress go to Marianita Pando who is now a Benavides and who has cornered the market on dressmaking, although she charges an arm and a leg for each piece. And Socialjustice feels a certain bitter listlessness toward life because she is never going to earn a cent from her profession and she isn't interested in politics or her father's doings because none of that will solve any of her problems. And they talked for a long time. And the godmother, full of sympathy, sent her that night a length of chintz so she could make herself a dress for Easter Sunday.

And the godmother of Surplusvalue informs them that her goddaughter is the most pitiful of all of them because she is the victim of her name; everyone teases her with nicknames like Surplusform, and Surplousse-café and Pluperfect and Plussage and other pluses, and what the poor thing wants most in the world would be to change her name and go to live someplace where nobody knows her because she is fed up with people's teasing. And because of her name she has not even one sorry boyfriend. And she is as uninterested in politics as her sister, because those who claim to know the most about it are those who most give her a hard time about her name, and she wants to die, and the godmother says that the predicament of her goddaughter caused her such sorrow that she opened her purse and gave her a wad of bills and a silver rosary so that she could devote herself to the Potbellied Virgin and to help her bear her troubles.

And the godmother of Pasionaria informs them that her goddaughter, like in the story of Perrault's Discreet Princess, is the brightest of the three, she says the other two lanky sisters aren't good for anything because they make their father spend a fortune and then flunk every year, but that this girl, in spite of everything, has her problems, too, because she wants to study medicine. Her father says that is for the bourgeoisie and he can't afford to pay for such an education, and she should be happy with her high school diploma, which is already a lot, and the poor thing says she wants to get a scholarship to study medicine in Cuba, and she *is* interested in politics and is happy with her name and she knows in whose honor she was called Pasionaria, but she refused to tell the godmother who said Pasionaria was. And the girl is pleasant and speaks with great self-confidence and her godmother felt sorry for her, too, and that evening sent her a gift of the *Life of Santa Teresa,* inscribed and everything.

Then Doña Carmen, who has listened attentively to their reports, grants herself the floor and reads the notes she has been elaborating. And they are not mere notes, but peremptory mandates that each of the godmothers must carry out with her respective goddaughter. And the godmothers in their turn take note of what the Sisterhood demands of them.

The godmother of Socialjustice will tell her goddaughter — softly, maternally, convincingly — that if her father abandons his communist foolishness her godmother will set her up in a fully equipped, first-class workshop — first class to those people who are used to any old thing, Doña Carmen clarifies. Not in the village where in reality there is no future for a dressmaker, but in the capital, or perhaps in Riobamba, or Ambato, wherever the girl wants. A real workshop, with two Singer sewing machines, not the pedal kind, like that of Marianita Pando who is now a Benavides — not to mention our own — but Singer machines with electric motors, and scissors, and rulers, chalk, mannequins, bolts of cloth, straight pins, a full length mirror so that Justicial's clients — for that is to be her name from now on — will be able to pay more than she can even imagine, and with the money she earns she can cancel her debt for all the things she has been given. And it's little enough to put together a small workshop, to get ourselves out of this fix, because if we don't proceed in this fashion, investing a little money, the communists are going to take away everything we have when they make the revolution that for some time now they have been plotting and planning underground, without our noticing.

And she orders Surplusvalue's godmother to tell her goddaughter that they are going to help her solve her problems, and she should appear kind so as to inspire confidence, and say that she herself will undertake to have the name changed at the civil registry, for this is only a matter of an eraser, some ink, and a little good will, but in exchange for that she must convince her father to leave off his foolishness and dissolve the communist party, which is only going to cause him problems, because the ladies of the Sisterhood are aware of his activities and rather than send him to jail, they give him this opportunity because they are Christians. And that she should go with her older sister to wherever they choose, to live together in a place where nobody knows them and where they will have busloads of boyfriends — for though they're ugly, there's no accounting for taste. And the godmother will send her an allowance until the day she marries, for the matter of finding her a husband also falls to the godmother, because she's not going to send her a check every month for the rest of her life. Some five hundred sucres will be more than sufficient, *an ounce of prevention is worth a pound of cure,* and the sum won't ruin any of us, for *spending is one thing, liking another,* and besides, this is a religious crusade that we should begin right away.

And the godmother of Pasionaria, who has been getting nervous because she knows that hers is the most difficult task, is charged with convincing her goddaughter using every argument and element to hand. And she'll have to be told in a friendly but convincing fashion that it is extremely difficult, nearly impossible, to get a scholarship to study medicine in Cuba, where only hijacked planes even land, but that it is easy, child's play, to get a scholarship to study medicine in the United States, where all sorts of planes land daily.

And she has to get it through her head that medicine in Cuba is way behind the times because on the whole island there's not one thermometer, there's no aspirin, or Mercurochrome, and that by con-trast in the United States, medicine is far advanced because doctors sit in front of some machines they have invented and all they have to do is look at the patient, push a few buttons, and get paid in dollars. And since Pasionaria is sharper than the other two goddaughters, it is important to go slowly and carefully, and above all to have complete faith in her mission, for *he who doesn't hope to win is already beaten,* and *patience conquers what luck will not reach,* and *praise God and pass the ammunition,* because in fact she will find her a scholarship to study English and also to study medicine, and meanwhile, she will gradu-ally rid her of the idea that she has to study abroad because as Doña Carmen has well observed, what is needed here are doctors who can cure parasites, and in the U.S. they don't have amoebas and here they are part of daily life, over there they take vitamins and here people die of malnutrition, because they have gotten used to brown sugar and orange water which doesn't feed anybody, but they are so ignorant …

The session adjourns with a plea for the Potbellied Virgin's assis-tance. And there is an air of expectation about the next day. The three godmothers are gravely worried, and the others are eagerly awaiting news of their results. And when the three godmothers get to their homes, they immediately send for their three goddaughters, and they arrive running, hoping for further gifts, because if not to give them something, why call them again so soon? And when they arrive at their godmothers' houses, each one settles herself on a chair and answers the questions put to her, and the godmothers begin to hint little by little what they want to achieve, and they fill the girls with promises. Each of the goddaughters is delighted with her particular godmother, the ladies easily reach their goals, although the interview with Pasionaria takes two long hours, for she does not have to be convinced so much as bribed, for she knows very well her own best interest, she shows herself extremely particular until she sees just how far she can push the luck of having a godmother who is both sympathetic and rich.

And a few hours later, when afternoon falls and the people of the town all seem to have died, the three daughters are sitting on the sidewalk, seated in a row to wait for their father. Socialjustice is looking at a Lana Lobell catalogue someone loaned her in Ambato, Surplusvalue is filing her nails so as to polish them with the new enamel someone gave her in Guaranda, and Pasionaria is reading very intently the latest issue of *The Voice of the People* slipped to her by Jorge Washington Pando. When their father arrives, with his usual faint scent of liquor, they throw themselves into his arms, they hurry him into the house and make his black coffee with sweet-savory bread, and they sit on his lap and twist his sparse mustache and attack him on three flanks, and *time to call a spade a spade,* and *Daddy, Daddykins, Pops,* and can you imagine the good luck we've had, and look at the opportunity our godmothers are giving us, and you'll never believe the bargain they're offering ...

And their mother, who is in the kitchen sautéing the onions for noodle soup, lets the red onion burn when she hears what the three girls tell, and she bursts into copious tears at the lottery that has fallen to them, and she shouts that it is a miracle of the Potbellied Virgin, and it becomes not three but four angles of attack against a wall with no foundation. And the old man thinks things over and concludes that one must *seize time by the forelock,* and *a bird in the hand is worth two in the bush,* and that *he who gets close enough to a good tree, finds a welcome shade;* and why so much hard work and *sweat grubbing after potatoes,* when everything he does and has done in his life is only to provide a future for the three darlings; that the post of magistrate, which he owes to Doña Carmen, is not a life appointment, or secure, or anything of the kind, and he had noticed that something was amiss; that behind him, there are others pushing to see if they, too, can become the magistrate; that although it is a great honor, the salary doesn't go far at all; that if good luck has arrived at his house, he's not going to be such a fool as to shut the door, that he, too, can probably get his slice out of all this; for *if you've a bird, let me have at least a feather* and *when God wants to be generous, he'll knock at the door* and he's fed up with being *bald as a guava seed;* that they'll probably take away his position as magistrate, he'd already noticed that Doña Carmen and the other old ladies in the Sisterhood were against him: he noticed they were irritated by the names that, in a moment of weakness, he gave his girls, which he didn't do to go against them, but only because, after hearing them so much, he liked them; that when they fire him he's going to be left without anything, with neither bread nor crumb, *with one hand before and the other behind;* that then they will know a good thing; that at this point there's no way he can dedicate himself to tilling the soil so as to scrape out a living, and the fall from the magistrate's office to sowing seed by his own hand is going to be hard. And he wanders the desolate paths of his fall into disgrace, without power or authority, although the fall is in name only, because in fact he is just one more Benavides lackey. He has no other choice but to bet everything, for *if you want to make an omelet, you have to break a few eggs....* And he lights a black cigarette to gather his thoughts which jump like rabbits under the drizzle of the *páramos* and he lets himself be petted by Jus, Plus, and Pas—as they are called in the intimacy of the home—who think that their father has lost the ability to speak and are consumed with impatience, sitting around him, watching every movement of his lips, and they notice the eagerness with which he inhales, how he blows the smoke out in a straight line, puckering his lips as though he were about to whistle, and how he lets the ash fall to the ground, tapping the tip of the cigarette with his index finger, and how he scratches his head with the five fingers of the other hand, how he grimaces and blinks, until he finally speaks and says it will probably work out, that *nothing ventured, nothing gained,* that given that the winds look favorable, perhaps they can persuade the three godmothers so that the Benavides family will sell them — at a reasonable price, of course — a few leagues of land to increase his miserable holdings, so that some day when *Saint Peter finally lowers his arm* and he has left his post, he can work the land, hiring some Indians to do so, since he is no longer fit for field labor after having held an office job, and that in this life *the worst action is that never undertaken* and that *the clever man can live off a fool, while a fool works for his living.*

And he sees himself wearing high boots and lashing out with his riding whip at anyone in his way, for anything is possible and *you can even plow the sea, so long as you sow fishes.*

And the four women who have waited a long time, answer that *first things first,* that *once begun, nearly done,* that what should they tell the godmothers about his leaving off his communist foolishness, that from politics — up to now — he hasn't gotten anything, and he answers that there is no problem about that, so long as they're giving and giving, that everything his young ladies have laid out for him is more than reasonable, that this is nothing new, that if he got into such a quagmire it was only to see if tomorrow he might land something ... but don't even mention it, because thinking it over, this becoming a revolutionary was just because they were so disgusted with everything, that in the long run he already sees that every revolutionary ends up crucified, that he is no Manuel Mesías nor anything close, that the revolution is waged by those without godparents, that let the idiots have their revolution, damn it, he's getting old and sees no future on any side.

And when he has stopped talking, the four women cover him with kisses, Daddy this and Popsy that, *Taitico, Papito,* on and on.

And the next day, very early, Jus, Plus, and Pas, dressed in their best clothes, go to the cathedral to give thanks to the Potbellied Virgin and afterwards they head, each on her own, for the homes of their three godmothers. It is as if they carried their father's answer on a tray piled high with flower petals, and they repeat what he said word for word, for they have no embarrassment about what they think is reasonable, for no one ever taught them another way of thinking. And the godmothers jump for joy because they are serving the cause, and they give the girls little gifts, the kind they have piled up any which way in every corner of the house, things that are worth nothing, that get in the way more than anything, but which fill the poor girls with happiness, because to even out the things of this life *the garbage of a few is the luxury of many.*

And when the meeting of the estimable Sisterhood of the Bead on the Gown of the Potbellied Virgin opens, the honored godmothers make known their excellent results and everyone congratulates them:

—Didn't I tell you? One less shameless upstart.

—Four, and with his wife, five upstarts less.

—Don't forget Jorge Washington Pando.

—And counting his grandmother, seven, seven fewer!

Doña Carmen doesn't rest on her laurels. She begins to pull strings, she talks on the phone, sends letters, and when Lent arrives, the second battle is won: the old sneak dissolves the party telling his companions that a recess of two years has become necessary, that the powerful Sisterhood has the first and last names and activities of every one of the poor comrades, that they are going to send the whole bunch of them to jail together, that there will be reprisals the like of which they've never seen, that there is no choice but to cancel meetings and programs, because *once the tree falls, everyone chops wood;* and as everyone in town well knows, *the dog bites the man in a poncho, but never the man in a frock coat,* and at the very least, they need to save themselves.

And when Easter arrives, which is celebrated only by ringing the great bell a bit harder than usual because there is still no priest to say Mass, Justicial and Elena del Carmen — as they are now called — are far away, in Riobamba. The one, sewing as fast as she can in order to pay off her debts, and the other, with the plaster icon of San Antonio that she has bought and placed on an altar standing on his head until he finds her a boyfriend, and now without that name that was an embarrassment, she is busily in pursuit of a match, looking diligently for a better-than-nothing who has yet to appear, for every time she goes out to land him, in place of compliments she hears:

—*Fiera guambra carishina, nariz de pupo de lima.*

—Savage mannish *carishina,* nose like a lime navel.

And she is furious, she is consumed with anger, but she goes ahead with her search, glaring at San Antonio, still standing on his head.

Pasionaria begins to study English in a free academy that the Adventists have set up in Ambato. She studies diligently and pretends to be interested in the Bible. She learns a few verses by heart and in one of her tantrums—which are rather frequent—she tears down the yellowing, tattered poster of Che Guevara that she has had at the head of her bed for a long time and that looks straight ahead with a terribly sad expression and a jet black, very thick beard. She yanks it down and tears it into a thousand pieces, she throws it into the garbage along with all her copies of *The Voice of the People,* and she replaces it with brand new posters: one, brilliantly colored, of a couple kissing over a bottle of Coca-Cola, wearing shorts and tennis shoes and with their butts planted on the North Pole; and another poster of a stupid-looking Christ, blond and blue-eyed— all that's missing is a wad of gum in his mouth and his own bottle of Coke.

When she comes back to town, she arrives loaded down with Bibles, she says okay and *gud morning* and *see-too morrow,* and she goes out on the street swinging her hips and people comment as she passes, and even to her face:

—*Love and ambition walked out in the country, but ambition that day was stronger than love ...*

And she is furious and looks down with icy disdain on the busy-bodies meddling in her private life who throw in her face how conceited she's always been about love, for she has always said she was not one to flirt nor to set her sights on any *guambra* of the town, for the one man she's always been in love with is Che Guevara, who studied medicine just as she plans to do.

And the ladies of the Sisterhood are happy. The great religious crusade is going better than they could have hoped. Despite what their sons and husbands think, they are in no way involved in politics. Politics is dirty and best left to men, and they are clean like freshly minted silver coins, they are above all exceedingly dignified and modest and they don't want to know anything about masculinities that tear down the eternal feminine and aren't in keeping with the parable of the prudent virgins.

And the townsfolk continue to remark on the good luck of Jorge Washington Pando who spends the whole day on his bicycle because *he who has a godfather gets himself baptized* and he who doesn't, may the thunderbolt smite him; and they talk about the good fortune of the three daughters of the magistrate who have gone to Riobamba and to the capital, for *to one born to be a tamal, corn husks will fall from heaven,* for there, far from the protection of their parents, they will be doing as they please, but *a gift is not graft* and *it's not the fault of the thief if the doors are left open …*

Meanwhile, Manuel Pando has divined the intentions of the old ladies of the Sisterhood, and he has had to revise his assessments. At the beginning, they seemed to him only fit for meddling in matters that didn't concern them and sewing little robes for the Virgin, but as he sees the extent of their reach he becomes more frenzied than ever. He comes and goes through the passages of the old house where the archaic press of *The Voice of the People* runs. He scratches his unruly beard. He reads the newspapers and writes articles at fever pitch. He tries to step up the meetings with the comrades, but no one comes, and the few that do show up and call themselves like-thinkers are so pitiful that they can't measure up to him and they cannot possibly understand what is happening. And although he speaks to them quite clearly and forcefully about the power of the ferocious oligarchy, and he gives them vivid examples of the corruption of wealth and of the traffic in consciences, they listen to him because they have no alternative, but his words slide like rain over the stones, for *honey is not made for the ass's mouth,* and he is *casting his pearls before swine,* and they get bored and yawn behind their hands and they ask to meet every two weeks, for there is no reason for so much hassle, and if they at least had a shot or two of aguardiente, and those in the other party have given themselves a healthy recess, they say that this isn't a time for meetings, that *when your neighbor's house burns, look to your own.*

And when they leave the press, they are downcast, deflated, with no energy for anything. They say that Manuel Pando is a crazy visionary, that he has stuffed himself with foreign ideas, that he is out of sync with the times and with the reality of the town. They envy the others who are safe, who wisely no longer even breathe together, while they court danger with that crazy Manuel Pando with whom you can't go anywhere. They say that this is no good, they're wasting their time, that say what they might, *it's better to be the tail of a lion than the head of a mouse* in these cases, given the sort of cats that have appeared in town.

Doña Carmen cannot waste even a minute in her most Catholic crusade and she even begins to take an interest in the books they say that Manuel Pando reads. She has sent for them by special order from the capital, and they have sent her an enormous crate, and the books have been chosen by who knows what shop clerk, and as soon as they arrive, she begins to look through them, and she reads them and tries to understand them, and she more or less takes in the significance of the words Jorge Washington Pando wrote on the walls, but she doesn't entirely understand the books, they don't convince her, and she ends up stashing them in a corner. She thinks that perhaps they are right on some points, but that they weren't written for her, that *it's one song on the guitar and another on the violin,* that *it's one thing to crow and another to lay eggs,* that — as her grandchildren say — Libertad Lamarque is one thing, but it's quite another to be the marked man; that the town of the Potbellied Virgin is one thing and quite another Peking and Moscow with their Pekinese and Muscovites.

And in one of her fits, she orders José Gregorio Pando to make a fire in a corner of the patio and she burns the crate with all of the books, which cannot be kept with those that form her Christian library, and better they shouldn't fall into the hands of the unwary, and we would have to lament the appearance of further Manuel Pandos, and if they have charisma, we're all lost, for then they would identify themselves — leaving distance aside — with the Indians' Manuel Mesías, and when the flames leap as high as the second story railings, she herself stirs the ashes, for *an ounce of prevention is worth a pound of cure,* and *Johnny Careful lived a good long life,* and she would be mortified if someone saw such books in her library.

And when the crate of books has been reduced to a handful of ashes, she decides to forget about the matter and continue proceeding in her own fashion, for much as she would like to get into the head of that pigheaded Manuel Pando, who having been a member of their own house, sent them to the devil so as to go off with the others; who, while he could have used their last name, uses that of the other band; she would like to know what goes on in the head of that shameless man that everyone knows is the illegitimate child of her brother's first adventures, his son with the woman who washes the tablecloths and the white clothing in the river and who refuses to tell him she is his mother and yet lives her life watching his every step and who will never tell him it was she who brought him into the world. Doña Carmen knows the story down to the last detail, since it concerns her, and she has other details from the mouth of José Gregorio Pando who is the most skilled in town at ferreting out secrets, at sneaking into closed places, at sniffing out clandestine matters, grasping mysteries, and finding out all about any hidden thing.

There are many things that the president of the Sisterhood doesn't understand, she doesn't understand that uppity cholo, who—more bad luck for her—carries a little of her own blood, which makes him different from the other Pandos, perhaps because he was educated on the hacienda, but he is Benavides from his head to his over-large feet. She would dearly love to suss out his intentions, for of the thoughts and intentions of the others, she knows more than enough, and if he were eliminated, the matter would be at an end, *for dead dogs don't bite,* for without him everything would be easier and the ladies of the Sisterhood could concern themselves with matters more in keeping with their offices, but since this is a pivotal moment for the town, she has to follow the plan she has prepared: that they should eliminate each other by their own hands, for she will not permit that they go on living comfortably, multiplying themselves from one day to the next.

On one of those frigid nights when the limbs of the body become numb with cold and the air is icy and glacial as if all the winds of the *páramos* had fixed a date to meet in the town, and the animals curl up in their lairs and objects seem rigid and the only thing people want to do is climb into bed with hot water bottles — those that have them — and those without at least wrap their feet in a newspaper; one frightening, dark night, a night of mist and gloom when no one dares to be on the streets even to knock back a scalding, cinnamony *canelazo*, Doña Carmen remains awake. She doesn't get into bed, as is her custom, instead she bundles herself up and takes out of the depths of an enormous wardrobe — large enough to hold the entire house of any of the Pandos — a can of red paint and a brush she has ordered from the capital, so that not even José Gregorio Pando will know of the matter, because what she is going to do is so daring, so exposed and risky, that not even the other ladies of the Sisterhood know of her plans, and it is so secret that only her guardian angel knows — there was no alternative — and she commends herself to him when she has the paint can in her sure hands, while she opens it and begins to stir it with the brush she recites:

> "Guardian Angel, heavenly companion,
> please do not desert me even for a moment
> until you can place me, in peace and happiness
> with Jesus and Mary. Amen."

And for the first time in her long life, she waits until all the servants of the house are asleep. She checks, room by room, to be sure there is no light, no candle burning, that no sighs can be heard, that any murmur of conversation has stopped. She puts her ear against José Gregorio Pando's door and hears the snores that rise like the whistle of the espresso machine that one of her nephews — who arrived from abroad with a blond in tow — just gave her and which is no good to her, for she is not one to drink the tasteless coffee that has become fashionable, but rather drip coffee freshly brewed.

An incredible *fiuuuu* wheezes out of the keyhole …

His snores climb to unexpected rising flats, and afterward descend like avalanches from the highest pinnacles to the deepest chasms: *roooo* …

And she wants to laugh at José Gregorio Pando's snores, for she has never heard such an orchestra, but she doesn't laugh, for the moment is serious and carries its strictures and its own harsh austerity. And she peeks out one of the windows that looks over the plaza and sees that the town is as deserted as a cemetery, and she waits for the last night watchmen, who pass at two in the morning, to make their rounds and blow their whistle in front of her own house to make their presence felt, and she looks to be sure that not even an owl is lying in wait for her, nor a ghost, nor any creature of this world or of the next. And she puts on an old black astrakhan coat and she wraps up in a scarf that covers her nose, and she goes downstairs in slippers so as not to make noise, and she opens very slowly the small door set into the great gate, whose hinges have been oiled beforehand so they won't make rusty squeaks, for a few days earlier she ordered all of the hinges in the house greased, so as not to awaken the suspicions of that sneaky José Gregorio Pando who doesn't miss a thing and carried out the task like any routine chore.

And while she endures the cold, she plants herself determinedly in front of the white walls of her own stately house and trying to imitate as much as possible the squat letters of any of the Pandos and to disfigure the careful English penmanship that she learned from the nuns when one still used pen and ink and delicate ascending and descending strokes, she writes under the shadow of the complicit night, with all her bravery, bellicose daring, and bad spelling:

"Down with the PCR, TrAyters and SEL-Owts."

Every letter is some two handbreadths long and a quarter wide, and can be read from the plaza and from across the street, and there they stand engraved, red and dripping as if they had been beheaded in the very belly of the alphabet: the A looks as if it had been quartered; the D somehow looks pregnant with two simultaneous fruits; the S, dislocated by a hard blow; the O is an exploded ovary; the E has had its ribs torn out in chunks; the L looks like a pair of sticks to kill an injured burro; the P is the profile of a headless Raquel Welch; the C, a half-moon with a toothache ...

And she dries the brush and puts the lid on the can, and she goes back into her house and closes the little door and replaces the iron bar with its padlock, and she goes past José Gregorio Pando's room, where he is still snoring in the same tone, and convinced that no one has seen her, she hides the evidence of the crime in the back of her

wardrobe, locks it, undresses, crosses herself, and falls asleep counting the beads of the Hail Marys on the rosary of tortoiseshell and
pearl that she inherited from her mother.

And at dawn, the bread bakers who are the first to go out to
the street carrying the sweet-savory *lampreados,* the five-cent rolls,
the breads made with the tasty lard left over after frying pork,
and the water baguettes, stand staring at the graffiti and they know
this is directed at the magistrate for the bribes his lanky daughters
received and also against all of that gang of crooks who swear by the
Potbellied Virgin that never in their lives have they plotted in the
town, and the bread bakers wonder if those who have written such a
thing are those who are with Manuel Pando, or if it is the other group
opposed to the first two, and they don't know why they fight among
themselves when in fact they're all against the Benavides set.

And the next to read what has been written are the pious old
ladies of the town who go to the cathedral every morning, even
though there is no Mass, and exchange gossip, rumors, intrigues,
and chatter, while they sit on the stairs waiting for the sacristan to
open the doors so they can say their prayers to the Potbellied Virgin,
and when the pious ladies decipher what is painted on the wall of
Doña Carmen's house, they cross themselves because they sense the
makings of a fight. And next to read it is the sacristan who opens the
doors, lights the altar candles, and tucks three or four away in the
straw of the baskets of fresh eggs that he is off to sell to the stores
that are just beginning to open up with yawns of bread, sugar, and
coffee. And as the morning progresses, everyone who goes out to the
street reads and comments, criticizes and interprets the graffiti, and
everyone who reads it guesses to whom it refers.

Those in question finally arrive, led by the magistrate, to see
with their own eyes, and when they read it their wrath is confirmed,
while the members of the other two parties have somewhat sarcastic
smiles, for much as they may be comrades and despite all the shots
they've drunk together like good compadres, they can't leave aside
their constant envy—for without it the poor things would hardly be
men—that so much was given to his lanky daughters who are so ugly,
and to ours, nothing ...

And a scrap of charcoal that fell out of the bag of a pack mule appears, and the magistrate picks it up and crosses out the letters with huge, spread-eagled Xs, and when he is about to write, furiously, Down with the PCM! and a bunch of other things he's thought of, the imposing figure of Doña Carmen appears in the midst of the uproar preceded by José Gregorio Pando who has just taken word of the morning's news. Doña Carmen confirms that her stratagem is having good results and orders all those present to show her their hands, and they hold them out and the magistrate shows his to be incriminatingly blackened. Doña Carmen rebukes him for having sullied the walls of her house, and refuses to hear excuses or explanations; she fines him one hundred sucres and sends him to jail for three days, and at the same instant, in the presence of many witnesses, she relieves him of his office for being a bad example and for not behaving like the figure of authority he is supposed to be. And since the poor man tries to defend himself saying he was only crossing out the letters, he hadn't written anything, she obliges him to clean off the red letters and the black cross-outs with soapy water and a scouring pad, and afterward she sends for a bucket of whitewash and a cabuya swab so he can leave the walls just as they were before, and in this way, she establishes yet one more precedent of her authority and her justice which the people applaud because everyone knows that the disgraced ex-magistrate wasn't good for anything except to flatter the rich and sit around in bars. The man completes his task inwardly raging with humiliation and revenge.

—Hurry up, insolent man! No one is going to save you. You leave my walls just as they were, for *one nail drives out another!*

—But patrona, I didn't write anything …

—And you dare to contradict me, when I caught you *with your hands in the cookie jar*, you shameless idiot!

And she goes back into her mansion and goes upstairs and eats breakfast, and she goes through her personal files to find out who is the most recalcitrant comrade of either of the other two parties, and her notes say it is Nicasio Duque Pando whom she saw not long ago leaning against a corner post smoking, worried and out of sorts, thinking no doubt that it's bullshit that a woman runs the town. Doña

Carmen orders José Gregorio Pando to send him to see her, and after a while he presents himself in a fresh shirt and with his hat dancing in his hands, and she makes him wait a half hour, unnecessarily, so the man will be still more nervous, and when she has him sent in to her study, without returning his greeting, she blurts out as soon as he enters:

—You will be the new magistrate. I'm going to have your salary raised, so you'll be paid double what your predecessor earned.

Nicasio Duque Pando is stunned, he didn't expect anything like this, but rather the contrary. He turns red, because he is the one who has said the worst things about the old lady and about all the old ladies of the Sisterhood. He turns pale, because he remembers that he has a pile of leaflets under his bed that he has forgotten to circulate in the midst of so much commotion. And he doesn't raise his eyes from the carpet in the face of the immense honor he is offered, he does not know how to thank her, and he wants to throw his arms around her and throw himself down and kiss her feet, and say to her, *mamitica linda,* and he stutters and finally thanks her with a scarcely audible:

—*Diosolopay,* may God repay you, Ma'am.

Then Doña Carmen explains to him how he must carry out his office, how he must be a good example to the town, how he must make the insolent communists toe the line, those people who want to cause disorders and uprisings in a town that is so peaceful and Christian only because of the Potbellied Virgin and not from political games, and she emphasizes that the salary is double what the previous fellow earned, but that if he does not carry out what they have agreed upon he will be left *with neither bread nor crumb,* and without recourse, because she is in charge and will make the decisions.

And when the walls are clean, the humiliated ex-magistrate heads for the jail, walking on his own feet and by his own will, accompanied by his buddies whom he is busy convincing that they cannot just accept the offence of being called traitors and sellouts, that what was written wasn't about him, but about the party, that they are all involved here, that neither his name nor those of his daughters appeared, that *a word to the wise is sufficient.* Little by little they get worked up: they are being blamed for faults they never committed, they are real men and *let's have clear facts and thick chocolate,* let them say it to our faces, otherwise they should present proof, and they can't take that old Benavides witch any longer, she takes on powers illegally, she owns the whole town and everyone in it, and at this rate they won't even be able to breathe without her permission. His friends leave him at the jail, they say goodbye with hugs and pats on the back, they tell him they'll be back in three days to get him out and celebrate his freedom with a good binge, that three days will fly by and it would be worse to disobey the old lady, for *there is no year that goes unfinished nor debt that goes unpaid* and *it's no use crying over spilt milk.*

Doña Carmen sends the pharmacist a message to spread the word that the next time the walls are dirtied, there will be a fine of two hundred sucres and the guilty will spend six days in jail and will have to pay for the whitewash and the painting, not just of the wall but of the whole house, for *the best cure is the hair of the dog that bit you.*

And after lunch, which, since it is Monday, begins with barley and a pork chop, and *cuchi papa* with cabbage and cilantro; with a main dish of potato cakes with fried eggs and avocado; for dessert, deep-fried *pristiños* with brown sugar syrup; and although the townspeople are still without breakfast, busy discussing the event, Doña Carmen emerges from her ancestral home, and she walks very smugly yet circumspectly to the house of Doña Elena who receives her in the intimate parlor, offers her homemade hot orange peel punch and between "to your health, and to yours," tells her that she, with her own hands, wrote the graffiti.

—But Carmita, what are you saying? What are you telling me?

Doña Elena has not yet crossed the threshold of her surprise when the president of the Sisterhood orders her—since she, being a widow who sleeps alone in her bed and has her house in a central location, is the obvious candidate—to write the second graffiti. She places in her hands the packet containing the brush and the can of red paint. She tells her what she must write and how to make the letters, what is the most suitable hour, the discretion she must maintain and the precautions she must take. After she has left, Doña Elena is left trembling with fear and anxiety, she does not know how she is going to get out of this bind, for her two servants never go to sleep before she does. Doña Elena believes in ghosts, in souls in torment and in apparitions, and she has ordered the maids never to go to bed before she herself is snoring. If she happens to wake, at the head of her bed, at the foot of the great crucifix said to be the work of Pampite, there is a cord that ends in a bronze bell over the head of the servants' bed, and she always wakes them when she can't sleep in the middle of the night, for she cannot be alone even for a moment without being attacked by trembling, and this is a custom that they have observed ever since her patient husband left her widowed.

In the present circumstances, she knows that it is impossible to pretend, for if she gets into bed, she can't then go outside without catching a cold, for she is prone to them, and if she doesn't treat them as she ought she could end up with pneumonia which can only be cured by months of drinking infusions of elder, borage, salsify, aromatic eucalyptus leaves, verbena, and linseed boiled in milk by the liter, and as cold as it's been, she can't run that risk nor can she send the servants to bed without arousing suspicions:

—Those smelly know-it-all cholas.

She thinks and she thinks how she can get out of the jam Doña Carmen has gotten her into. But by late afternoon, when she still hasn't found a possible solution she sits gazing through the gratings that lead to the patio where the acacias sway in the wind, and among them, close against the garden wall is a leafy guanto tree with yellow flowers, which they say is the best soporific there is; looking at it, inspiration comes to her as if it were a lamp with twelve arms and all of the bulbs lit.

Before it begins to get dark, she goes out to the patio and plucks the great funnel shaped flowers that dangle like yellow bells ringing out dreams. She gathers them in a large bunch and, walking on tiptoe, enters the servants' bedroom while they are busy grinding coffee in the kitchen. She crushes the flowers and places them under the heavy cases of the two pillows on the bed where the two sleep together to keep each other company, for after hearing so much about ghosts and souls in torment, they too have seen them hanging about the walls, peering through the panes of the windows that are always closed and walking on the roof tiles.

At supper time, Doña Elena pretends not to feel well and takes only a sip of chicken broth with tapioca that looks like fish eyes swimming in a hot sea. She gets into bed fully clothed and when the maids come in to sit up with her they think she is truly asleep and hurry off to their own room. No sooner do they enter than they begin to yawn, they undress as fast as they can, and as soon as their heads hit the pillow they are invaded by an immense torpor and they sink into the most profound sleep, a strange sleep plagued by indecent and erotic dreams.

Doña Elena jumps out of bed and goes to their room to make sure the guanto is working. She lifts the lid of each of their eyes and the lid falls back into place like a heavy curtain, she calls them by name and they don't respond, she shakes them and they seem dead, she rings the bell and it's as though it had nothing to do with them; then she returns to her rooms to wait for the night to advance. She prays a rosary to give herself courage and she recites the prayer of the Just Judge. She hunts feverishly for the two chunks of benzoin resin that she keeps hidden for luck in the enterprise and she lights a candle before the image of the Potbellied Virgin; she crosses herself and crosses her fingers. She waits, timid and afraid, and the minutes seem like centuries.

When she knows that the appointed hour has arrived and everything is quiet and cold and no one is on the street, she goes outside, trembling with fear, opens the paint can and writes in huge, grotesque red letters with poor handwriting and worse spelling the next graffiti:

—"Down with the PCM enimys of the peopol and of the Verjin."

She finishes who knows how, crazy with fear. She almost drops the paint can in the hallway. She is sure she saw the headless priest riding along the street on a black horse, his eyes shooting flames; she thinks she saw the veiled lady coming to meet her; she is convinced that she saw the retinue of the *caja ronca* and heard the *tam tarr-AM* of the drum made with the shinbones of the dead. Her teeth chatter with terror. She padlocks the door, hurriedly hides the can of paint and the brush, desperately yanks on the bell cord and the bell rings, shaking the whole house, but the servants don't come to keep her company. She goes to their room and tries to wake them: they don't even move. Shaking with panic she pushes them to either side, she keeps seeing ghosts by the dozen and, terrified, she climbs in between the two of them wearing her shoes, overcoat, and scarf and just as she thinks a ghost is pushing at the door she faints into sleep ...

When the bread bakers get up early the next morning and go with their baskets of *lampreados* and their baguettes, they read the graffiti and remain frozen in place. The sacristan lets his basket of fresh eggs fall to the ground. The early-rising ladies cross themselves, saying:

—Holy Mother of God! This is the end of the world!

And the others when they read it murmur, frightened:

—Jeez, now there's really going to be trouble!

They form a group in front of Doña Elena's house, and those named in the graffiti are furious at the insult. The possible authors protest the J in Verjin which proclaims clearer than clear that they are a bunch of morons and ignoramuses and they look at one another suspiciously, wondering who is the worst speller. But no one dares to cross out the words, and everyone wants to go in search of the swab and the whitewash to clean the wall and get himself out of danger.

The new magistrate, Nicasio Duque Pando, who is most expeditious in his duties, goes running with the news to Doña Carmen who was ready to present herself unexpectedly before the sloppily painted walls to see how the secretary had carried out her task, and she hears the news in silence, without comment. The two set out walking quickly and behind them go the rest of the townsfolk to see what will happen. Doña Elena doesn't appear. No matter how much they knock and pound on the door, nobody opens it. Doña Carmen doesn't understand why she is hiding and decides to do without her. She orders that the responsible party be searched out and right there, in the presence of everyone, she offers a five hundred sucre reward to anyone who offers any information before midday, and when midday passes and there is no clue of any kind, Doña Carmen cunningly doubles the reward and everyone gets in on the search, for any of them could use a fortune in exchange for giving a name, and one group accuses another, but there is no proof, and you can't toy with the president of the Sisterhood, for *those who live in glass houses shouldn't throw stones* and *the man with a straw tail shouldn't go near the fire.*

Dirty linen hidden away for years comes out into the midday sun, for *in the soapmaker's house, if you don't fall, you slip.* Doña Carmen and her entourage of ladies take notes as to who is and who isn't, and nearly everyone in town *beheld the mote in his brother's eye, but considered not the beam in his own.* All of the Pandos are somehow implicated in the mess, but the graffiti was written by a single person, who must be found before the promised thousand sucres vanish.

A few cautious souls advise the others not to talk too much, for more than one will go to jail and it's embarrassing for relatives and compadres to accuse one another. They say that everyone is against everyone else because *he who says what he should not, hears what he would not* and a lot of people have already been beaten up on the street corners for disloyal gossip, that they should settle down once and for all, that *least said, soonest mended* and *a closed mouth catches no flies.*

Chaos takes over the town. Doña Carmen pretends to be furious. No one suspects that she is enjoying herself as never before. She decides to set the matter aside — let them kill each other off without her, she has done her part. And when the hour of the evening session arrives, Doña Elena still doesn't appear and they have to keep meeting without anyone to take the minutes. Doña Carmen is almost pleased that Doña Elena doesn't show up, lest she commit some indiscretion that would give away the secret. The ladies anxiously discuss how badly things are going in the town, how degraded the people are when neither jail nor fines seem to trouble them, they ask themselves what they are going to do in the future with so many sneaky, half-breed cholos and so many men, among their own, who are good for nothing and leave them alone in front of an uncontrolled rabble.

Meanwhile, the members of the PCM won't tolerate the offense and since they dare not violate the order of the Sisterhood because they would go straight to jail for six long days, and that would be putting the rope around their own necks, for behind bars they can't do anything, for *I wouldn't be a prisoner even with silver chains,* they set themselves to meeting late into the night, and since it is cold and the owner of the house where they are has a clandestine still, they drink more *canelazos* than they should and they begin to feel a violent heat and the liquor goes straight to their heads and they overflow with the courage they never have when sober. They go out to the plaza and they fill their pockets with rocks that they pull out of the streets, and in the quiet of the night *chil-LING ching ching!* they break the windows of all those who are their adversaries and who they think wrote the graffiti. The noise and the uproar reach as far as Doña Carmen's bed, and she gets up with a Mother of God! on her lips, but when she is fully awake, she guesses what is happening and she goes back to bed, plumping her pillow as if the racket were not in her town. Everyone wakes up shaken and runs out to the street in their nightshirts. They go out to see what is happening and when they see the damage they are afraid. Women run to gather and protect one by one their sons and husbands and to hide them under the bed, for more than the reprisals of the owners of the broken windows, they fear the wrath of Doña Carmen.

The whole town is standing around discussing the events, terrified that dawn will break and that daylight will clarify the facts, for there are dozens of witnesses. Everyone is trembling, except for Doña Carmen, who gets up late, and Doña Elena with her two servants who have been sleeping since the evening of the day before under the effects of the huge yellow flowers of the guanto.

While Doña Carmen sips her café con leche and dips pieces of a baguette into a large plate of cream, she hears, smiling and amused, the horrors that José Gregorio Pando tells her about the barbarities committed by the members of the PCM at the homes of So-and-So and What's-His-Name and You-Know-Who of the PCR. Well breakfasted, although she is not among those for whom *full belly, contented heart,* she dresses in her lace blouse with ruffles and pintucks, she combs her hair into its bun with twenty-one hairpins, she tells the servant to accompany her, for she is going to restore order to the ungrateful town and is going to do justice after her own fashion, for

Nicasio Duque Pando, the new magistrate, must be sleeping. And José Gregorio Pando walks, not at her side but rather behind her, unaware — like everyone else in town — that Doña Carmen doesn't give a fig about doing justice or about finding who is to blame. And when she arrives where everyone is gathered waiting, she says that she will give two thousand sucres as a reward to whoever puts her on the trail of whoever started the whole mess by writing insults on the walls of respectable homes.

Nor will the owners of the damaged houses sit with their hands folded, foregoing the sweet taste of vengeance. They are even now meeting in the back patio of one of their number, learning how to make Molotov cocktails which Jorge Washington Pando has said are perfectly easy to make, but so as not to take part in anything because he doesn't want to lose his bicycle, he pedaled off early and no one knows where he is. After many attempts and inventions the plotters manage to hit on the secret and make six or seven Molotov cocktails apiece. They spend the whole day working in silence while the women begin to sweep and to gather up the broken glass, for the barefoot *guaguas* could step on it and hurt themselves. And they tack up newspapers over the holes in the windows so that the neighbors won't see their poverty and the night cold won't come in. And they make the midday meal for their men who are working on their revenge. And they carry the food in dinner pails and casseroles to the back of the patio that smells of gasoline and kerosene, and the men avidly eat their broad bean porridge, their white rice and potatoes, in the midst of their explosive arsenal.

And when the agitated day ends amid fear and destruction and the sheltering night arrives, the comrades leave their hiding place armed with their bottles and their matches, and Boom! Boom! Boom! the town is awakened again with a Potbellied Virgin! on its lips, and everyone runs out to see what is happening, for such explosions have not been heard in the town since the eve of the Jubilee when they lit seven castles worth of fireworks, and they gaze astonished at doors yanked off their hinges, windows dancing an oblique dance and chunks of wall turned to dust, and from the depths of one of those black holes an inhuman lament emerges that shrivels the soul, brings human feeling to its knees, and sets the heart racing at an unsustainable clip and they see a half-naked woman running like a crazy person through the streets, heading for the cathedral to beg mercy, and she leaves behind huge splatters of absurdly red blood on the stones, and in her arms she carries a brutally massacred child, a child whom she had just recently sung to sleep with:

> —"Little bird singing
> beside the laaake
> asleep in his crib
> my baby don't waaake."

The chest and belly of the innocent are an open flower where you can see like spattered pistils the ribs standing on end and the head — a little head drenched in kisses and daydreams — hangs, barely supported by a bit of skin and snapped vertebrae that knock rhythmically and damply against the mother's legs, and to make everything more macabre, more cruel, the child is still smiling as if there were still life in his pale lips, lips that were just beginning to control the magic power of the word. And the woman roars, she blasphemes, curses, hollers, bellows. And the people move aside in silence, giving passage to her pain and to death before which all mortals are equals, and they look away from the dripping flesh. They are filled with panic and they cross themselves because they know that after one death comes another. Someone remembers, terrified, that this very morning they heard the bird of ill omen sing and repeats:

> "The *chushi* cries and a man dies
> it seems like chance, but it's not happenstance."

No sooner does he hear the first explosions than Manuel Pando throws himself out of bed, grabs his pants, and — half into his trousers, barefoot, with his slippers in hand — he runs to the heart of the riot, he goes from one to another, trying to convince them to listen to reason, he tells them that they are being used, he talks to them as if they were his own children, he tries to make them understand by fair means or foul that it was the Benavideses who planned all of these events. But no one pays any attention to him and they turn their backs and remain standing in front of their solitude and their blindness.

The ladies of the Sisterhood convince their men that they were right all along, that the communist revolution has broken out, they rebuke them for having left them alone and accuse them of being good for nothing.

A few well-meaning compadres take up a collection to buy a coffin and keep vigil over the dead child, and at the foot of the cathedral, in the ample atrium where everyone fits, they hold a wake amid wails and moans. Since there is no priest to say the Mass for the dead, they want to at least hold the wake in sacred space and they have no choice but to call a *rezador* to say the prayers and hire a caller of souls so that the baby will not go alone.

And the ladies of the Sisterhood do not object, indeed they give them four large candles, the Easter candles that have not been used for many years, four enormous candles for the four corners of sorrow that last until the dawn and burn down in fat drops. The man who threw the bomb laments his bad luck. He didn't want to kill anyone, still less a child, he only wanted to frighten his adversaries. He and his comrades are the only ones not present at the wake, which makes their guilt evident, and they're also absent because they are running over the hills, running the length of the twisted canyons. They flee in bands pursued by the new magistrate, Nicasio Duque Pando, who wants to perform well at the head of his troops and so keep his post, and they flee because the father of the dead child has sworn by the Potbellied Virgin, kissing his crossed thumb and index finger, that he will kill the murderer and all the rest.

The burial of the town's first victim is organized. It is a massive and sorrowful funeral, nothing like the burials of the bodies left after the Battle of the Mattresses which were attended only by the most immediate relatives, for the entire town was busy looking for the Virgin's finger in the rubble. For this burial, everyone is present. They have closed the shops and the markets, the pharmacy and the bars, the taffy maker's shop and the school.

The father and many others carry the small box on their shoulders. It seems to weigh a ton, for *the dead grow heavier when there are plenty of pallbearers.* Their eyes spark with hatred, they clench their fists and their teeth, walking in time with the funeral march played by the town band. The whole town moves toward the cemetery over the river stones that pave the narrow street. The women carry flowers and weep in maternal sympathy. The gravedigger is digging the hole in the damp earth, open like a black mouth about to swallow the communion wafer. And the sacristan, on his own initiative, has tied a gunny sack to the clapper of the great bell and is ringing out slow, rasping peals. Doña Carmen wants to wash her hands of what is happening and is unable to, she goes from one room to another unable to rest. And when they set the small white coffin on the ground, there is a profound silence, and by way of response, the mother cries out as if they were tearing out her womb and her throbbing ovaries with crude tongs:

—Aaay, my *guagua,* my baby!

And the dirt falls to cover the coffin and the father's manliness pours from his eyes in a fountain of pain and fury. And at that very moment, he feels a weight in his pocket, and when he gets back to town, he knows that he has been given an old pistol, and the weight on his tired shoulders becomes unbearable, and with hanging head he begins to search for the killer.

The ladies of the Sisterhood feel themselves spattered with warm and sticky blood, and at the afternoon session, when once again minutes are not taken, they barely speak and they feel utterly discouraged and the years begin to weigh on them, and they know that death is haunting the town.

Three days have passed since the burial and Doña Carmen finally remembers Doña Elena. She goes to her house in the company of the other ladies, and they knock on the door and nobody answers, and they knock with rocks until the wood is dented, and they send for the locksmith to force the padlocks that are on the other side, and they send for the carpenter to saw the oak planks that are so close together that the handsaw bends and can't get through, and they send for José Gregorio Pando who looks for a ladder, climbs up the wall and lowers himself through the acacias and slips down the guanto with its yellow flowers, and he removes the heavy iron bars and the padlocks from the door and opens it so that the ladies can enter as one, rushed and disconsolate, fearing the worst, and they look for Doña Elena in every corner of the house, convinced that they are going to find her murdered, and they go into the servants' room and find the bodies stretched out with the lady of the house in the middle, and they take a step back thinking they are dead, but then they see them squirm, making obscene-looking gestures. Doña Carmen attempts to wake them calling them by name, they bring a bucket of water and sprinkle their faces as if they would frighten off the bad spirits with holy water, and when they finally awake, their eyes are popping out of their heads, their lids are swollen, and they want to go back to sleep, but when they see so many people around them and remember what they had been dreaming, they jump out of bed and cannot believe that they have slept so long.

After suffering such anxieties with their aftertaste of remorse, with a bitter taste in their mouths, with little appetite, a disinterest in life, a crush of good and bad thoughts, still the ladies of the Sisterhood feel themselves pulled by the dates of the liturgical calendar that directs the life of the town and they decide to hold the hair-cutting ceremony. The Virgin needs a new wig, for after so much commotion and fuss with changes of clothing and of hairstyle and with the dust and the smoke of the candles that never go out, the Potbellied Virgin's hair is faded, yellowed and limp as if it were burlap, and the box that holds the ashes for making the cross on the foreheads of the penitent on Ash Wednesday is completely empty and it is urgent that they burn something sacred like the wig and a few dresses that are no longer used, for it is necessary to maintain the ritual, and the charged atmosphere of the town also calls for a religious release to calm the spirits, and it is absolutely essential that they ingratiate themselves with the town again, and so there is no other choice than to hold a great ceremony with a bullfight and everything, taking advantage of the fact that the priest from Pujilí has offered to come and say Mass.

Marianita Pando who is now a Benavides is ready and excited. She has made herself a new dress, long and white. And that day she gets up at four in the morning and she bathes and she washes her hair with black soap, with honey and egg yolks, and she rinses it with chamomile, elder leaves, lemon, and mint, and she covers her face with a mask of peach pits and oyster shells to hide the wrinkles that announce, plain as day, that she is no longer what she was. When the sun begins to rise, she combs her hair and dries her long locks in the first warm rays, and at precisely six in the morning she is ready, with a crown of orange blossoms and a veil that reaches to her waist, and she looks like a bride, although everyone knows that as far as that goes, nothing.

Beginning at seven, the cathedral begins to fill with curiosity-seekers and with the faithful who don't want to miss the ceremony that has not been performed for so many years. And the town band goes to the home of Marianita Pando who is now a Benavides, and she emerges looking graceful and stately and takes her place before the drum major and the cymbal player and all the neighbors come running to see her, and they form a cortege that moves solemnly toward the cathedral. And the sacristan has run up the stairs of the highest tower and begins to peal the great bell slowly while the people shout:

—Here she comes, she's almost here!

And Marianita Pando who is now a Benavides walks slowly with her eyes cast down, fully absorbed in her role of sacrificial victim, and her hair gleams like a cascade of liquid gold, and she climbs the stairs and pauses for an instant in the atrium and she touches her silky hair for the last time and shudders, and she enters the cathedral which is illuminated with large candles decorated with colored flowers made of wax, and she grows sad in spite of herself.

Nicasio Duque Pando, the new magistrate who has put on new clothes and for the first time in his life has knotted a tie around his neck—a tie printed with large yellow flowers just like Doña Elena's—greets her and she barely sees him. He is irritated, for since very early he has been diligently carrying out his duties and forbidding entry to the cathedral to all his comrades and all those who smell like them, who give him poison looks and don't speak to him, although he endures it savoring his stoicism so as not to lose his job, for before he didn't have even enough to scrape by and now he has plenty and he even thinks he can save a bit and buy land, and he must not displease Doña Carmen who is certainly keeping an eye on him, and the comrades can go to the devil, for *fair weather friends change with the wind,* and *a friend to all is a friend to none,* and he is not going to give them free access, and he tells them the ceremony is by invitation only and that they are not invited, and that *where the captain commands, sailors don't give orders,* that it isn't his fault, that *orders are orders.* And his ex-friends remain at the door, resentful and furious, and to pass the time they go and sit in the first rows of the stands that have been built in the plaza for the bullfight.

And when Marianita Pando who is now a Benavides enters the temple, the sacristan breaks into "Salve, salve gran Señora ..." and the whole town joins in on the sad, sad melody, and when the priest from Pelileo, who has come at the last minute because the one from Pujilí has let them down, gives the order for the music to cease, the sacristan stops playing and the people stop singing, and there is a thick silence interrupted only by the cry of a baby who doesn't know what is happening and who is quieted by his mother's breast when she unties the sling on her back and nurses him. The odd cough is heard from time to time.

Marianita Pando who is now a Benavides is before the altar. The ladies of the Sisterhood occupy the first row. The priest is extremely elegant in his light blue chasuble the same color as the Potbellied Virgin's gown, although *an ape's an ape, a varlet's a varlet, though they be clad in silk or scarlet.* He steps down from the altar and Doña Carmen comes forward and presents him with the silver tray that holds the cruel scissors. And the priest from Pelileo lifts the victim's veil, and the veil falls to the ground, and he takes the scissors in his right hand and with his left grasps the first lock of blond hair and cuts it off at the root as if he were cutting weeds, and the golden locks fall to the ground on top of the veil. And Marianita Pando who is now a Benavides feels an inexplicable anxiety, and when the task is completed, she feels cold at the nape of her neck and behind her ears, and she lifts her hand to her head and runs into the roughness of an unfamiliar skull and tears well up in her eyes against her will and she makes a supreme effort not to cry, for she remembers that she did not bring a handkerchief, for she never thought she would cry over what she had always wanted, for the Potbellied Virgin well knows how she cared for her hair for her. And the ladies of the Sisterhood hastily gather the locks of golden hair and place them on the silver tray which they set at the base of the altar, and the priest from Pelileo turns and begins to celebrate the Mass, and the people make the most of it for no one knows how long it will be before another is celebrated. And Marianita Pando who is now a Benavides remains standing all alone throughout the ceremony. Her head feels terribly cold and every so often she touches her skull involuntarily and gets goosebumps because she doesn't find the softness and the warmth she's used to, but rather the harshness of a brush, and she wants everything to end quickly so she can look at her face in the oval mirror in her room.

And when she hears at last the "item misa est" and the cathedral begins to empty, she remains motionless because she is embarrassed by people's looks, but Manuel Pando's neighbor, who from restraining herself with her own son, carries her maternal feelings close to the surface, has thought of everything and she approaches the victim and covers her head with a white kerchief she has brought.

And when Marianita Pando who is now a Benavides returns home, she goes alone, without hair or cortege, for everyone is at the bullfight and the town is deserted, and only Manuel Pando's neighbor walks at her side in silence, for she knows as no one else the silent sorrows of lonely women.

Everyone is at the plaza enjoying the bullfights, for the ladies of the Sisterhood have donated three bulls so that the brave men of the town can amuse themselves playing matador, although the sharp tongues of the four old Pandos insist the bulls have hoof-and-mouth disease.

And in the midst of the bullfight, when everyone is celebrating with great guffaws the tumbles of the daring *guambras* who place themselves in front of the bulls' horns, shielded only with whatever rag happened to fall into their hands, the comrades excluded from the ceremony surround Nicasio Duque Pando, the new magistrate who is at the apogee of his fame and his prestige, and using a stick that takes the place of a pistol, and without anyone noticing, they shove him toward a vacant lot and so that he won't put up any resistance they tell him under their breath:

— Come quietly, faggot.

The poor man trembles, and when they get to a place without witnesses, they give him a beating, and he can put up no defense, it's seven against one, and when they are tired of hitting and insulting him, they leave him stretched out on the grass with his teeth and his molars shattered, spitting them out in bits, just as it happens in dreams of ill omen, and his blood comes up from inside, suffocating him, and he tastes its saltiness and he doesn't want to get up, for the insults of those who used to be his friends hurt more than the blows, and he thinks that he is going to die under the hot sun that stings his wounds. And up there on the heights he can make out a pair of buzzards gliding in circles, and he feels strangely lucid, and he sees with his own bulging eyes the bad movie of his life, its grotesque presence in full color. And he wants to cry because it is a ridiculously sad movie, it's an interminable melodrama, and the protagonist is a small-town man who would have liked to have had so many things, and would have liked to live in a different fashion and to have died in his own bed with that unknown something that he never had and which is now set aside and he needs it. And he is filled with shame and nostalgia at never having had it, not because he didn't want it, but because he was never allowed, because if he had had that which is called dignity, he wouldn't be stretched out on the strangely fresh grass now, although he thinks at the same time that with dignity he and his children would have starved to death. And he hears the voice and the guitar of the shoemaker Romualdo Pando who is making jerky of his insides:

> "And we await that day
> when we will start our journey,
> that happy, happy journey
> from which we won't return …"

And he writhes under the pain of the blows and the humiliation, and he even feels sorry for those who beat him, for he is at the threshold of another existence, and he is strangely lucid, more lucid than ever, lucid enough to think that dignity is a luxury that only the Benavideses can have because they have the economic backing to send their compadres to the devil, and their obligations, and ideologies, and the bosses, and life itself.... And the wretches, he thinks—with bile rising in his throat—also die underestimating it, for they know nothing of anything, not even of that small capacity for forgiveness that is overtaking him so that he can say meekly that *when the sun doesn't shine, the wind dries the washing,* that *where three can eat, four can as well,* that *if you don't plan to drink it, let the water run* ...

And the buzzards continue circling many meters lower than they were before and he sees them descend in formation like planes with jet black feathers and hooked propellers. And he thinks of his own, of the children of the same blood that is running out of his mouth as if it were a spring, and he doesn't want to call for help, for if he shouted, pushing aside the fragments of tooth and the clots of blood, someone, some person in the town, might hear him and come to his aid. But he doesn't want to, he wants to die in his full five ruined senses, for he has finally felt that which is called dignity, that which before, when that crazy Manuel Pando—who, it turns out, is not crazy at all—said it, seemed to him only a word, like the word death, which he now tastes, he feels it and understands. And he decides to die because he has seven children, and because if he does not die now, they will never inherit anything, not even this newly learned word.... And he has to die. And he calls the Potbellied Virgin to come to his aid and kill him and, if she wishes—for her mercy is great—that she finish him off with her golden scepter and that she give him the final blow the way they do to the burros that get stuck in the ditches and can't get back out ...

And the two dirty buzzards, who have settled vigilant and greedy in the dry branches of a guabo, are gloating in anticipation, and the only thing he wants at the moment of truth is that they approach his body when he is already dead, not before—Potbellied Virgin!—he won't be able to stand it if they land on his face and empty his eye sockets with a well-aimed beak, for the eyes of their victims are the appetizer to their feasts, and he is afraid of the coarse and dirty feet on his face, and of their small jumps over his body and of the beaks puncturing his belly to tear off his skin and open deep holes to pull out his intestines in the same way that chickens pull worms from the earth. And he will be unable to push them off his body because he has no strength, his arms are heavy and he can't move them, the only thing he can move from right to left and up and down are his eyes so as to watch the eyes of the two buzzards who have come down from the branch of the guabo and are approaching with little hops, and they can look at each other and pierce his body with a glance. And suddenly, it no longer matters to him if they tear out his eyes and swallow them like dove's eggs. Nothing matters to him any longer, neither life nor death. He feels the same as at the beginning of the great drunkenness of so many tedious Sundays and he only shudders on the inside when he feels the harsh claws on his face, the miserable face of the magistrate of a small Andean town ...

And in the market square, where all the neighbors built the night before a circular enclosure, the whole town is enjoying the tumbles that the frightened bulls, not understanding why they are pestering them so, give to the valiant *guambras*. And the fiesta atmosphere infects even the murderers, who do not yet know they have committed murder and have returned pleased at having settled a debt with the new magistrate, so that he learns his lesson and never again forbids them entry anywhere, nor sets himself up as a tough guy to flatter Doña Carmen.

And no one knows that he is dead and stretched out in the sun, riddled with holes from the beaks of the hungry buzzards, with his new suit serving him as a shroud. The town band encourages the improvised bullfighters and the air carries bursts of music to the very house of Marianita Pando who is now a Benavides, who will never again be what she was, because upon looking at herself in the oval mirror in her bedroom she has seen herself old and ugly, and in a single cut they have shorn her of her illusions, which have flown out the half-open window and escaped over the rooftops, far beyond the bell tower, and they are now so high up they look like moles on the face of the sky.

And after the bullfight, the people share out the meat of the sickly and frightened bulls, and there are torrents of chicha and aguardiente that cut down their upright bodies as if the fattest and most treacherous of the Bacchae had rolled around in a wheat field flattening the ears. And at the end of the afternoon, the pitiful ballads of Romualdo Pando return to fill the streets with that aching sadness that they will never manage to shake off, ever. And only the next day, when the train of mules loaded with the milk cans comes into town, do they bring the news that they have found the body of Nicasio Duque Pando, the town's magistrate, and surprise is close on the heels of sorrow, and sorrow comes hand in hand with conjecture, and behind conjecture comes suspicion bringing with it by the hand a string of assumptions, and they begin to look for the guilty.

An hour later, the truck driver brings word that in a nearby town, in one of the narrow, zigzagging paths that lead to the river they have found another body, already decomposed, which seems to be that of the man who threw the bomb into the house of the dead child and they say that the body has seven holes from seven bullets ...

And the ladies of the Sisterhood hold another urgent meeting, but they are no longer alone. The meeting room is full, for their husbands have come to their aid, for they can no longer leave the reins of a murderous town in the hands of women whom they send off home to do their proper work of embroidering, cooking, and prayer. The men talk and discuss and organize as quickly as possible what all civilized towns have: a brigade to impose order and defend imperiled families and the traditions that cannot be allowed to disappear from one day to the next without fundamental institutions teetering, and to protect private property which is threatened, for the town is full of bandits, highwaymen, and criminals. They ask for help from the public authorities. Reinforcements arrive. The experts in violence arrive, and the Brigade of Death is formed, dedicated to the Potbellied Virgin, and the poor little image shudders and feels helpless before the force of these men.

Doña Carmen Benavides believes that she no longer has anything to do among the bossy men of the town who have distributed offices and honors and when she leaves the meeting room, she goes to her house and closes herself up in her room, and she realizes that her life has ended and that she is dead, entirely dead, and she cries as she last cried years ago, when she was young and cried so much that she was left without tears and now they crowd her eyes along with her memories, and she sees herself seated in this same chair where she swore never again to cry, and swore that she would show the world who she was, when she set her life on another course, for the Benavides women were always indomitable, even when they had to pull out their own hearts so as to stand upon them and move forward.

The four old Pandos, seated on the park bench, discuss the details of her life. They say her parents married her off very young to her uncle so that the family fortune would not be divided, that there was never another wedding like hers in the town, that people came from all over the republic, that the cathedral was fully lit, that truckloads of spikenards and orange blossoms arrived, that the eve of the wedding the groom—who was a *noble face, vile deeds*—went to the town cemetery, dug up the rotten body of his mother, and took off her wedding ring, that he put it into aguardiente with camphor to remove the smelly skin that was stuck to it, and that was the ring that he gave to the bride who could smell it during the whole ceremony, that the old man was the dirtiest old man of all the Benavides, that *a tree born crooked can never grow straight,* that once married he chased after all the girls, that he got himself entangled with the Moñuda girl and several others, that Doña Carmen pretended to look the other way, that as *you can't block the sun's glare with a single finger* his own relatives turned against him and they recognized that *even the best cloth will pick up a stain,* that Doña Carmen's life was a living hell because she was young and she loved him, that the old man would go after even a broom in a skirt, that on top of everything else he was a miser and that *the pitcher went so often to the well* that Doña Carmen herself surprised her husband in her own marriage bed, and that was when she said:

—That's it, no further.

And what happened was that she had returned unexpectedly to the hacienda, she said she had forgotten something—though she had forgotten nothing, she had a premonition—and José Gregorio Pando told them that she looked through the keyhole before entering, and she saw what she would rather not have seen, and she went in without making a sound, you could hear only the beating of her own bewildered heart, for the adulterers were asleep, that she looked for a log to break open their heads, that she searched on tiptoe for some kind of weapon, that she went to her husband's trousers and pulled out the belt that she herself had had made in Cotacachi, for *belts are made from the same leather,* that with one yank she pulled off the sheets and found them naked, that he hid under the bed, that the poor surprised lover coiled into her shame and then Doña Carmen without saying another word began to whip her, that more than eighty lashes echoed as far as the plaza, that the whole town fell silent in order to count them, and that the last—seventy-seven, seventy-eight, seventy-nine—were no longer as strong as the first, that when the woman, half dead, managed to escape from the bed, Doña Carmen followed her down the stairs with the whip, that she drove her out to the street with blows, that she was left standing on the sidewalk entirely naked not knowing what to do in front of a crowd of curious people who came from everywhere, that it made you sorry for her, that the priest Santiago de los Angeles said in the Sunday sermon that the buttocks and body of the adulteress looked like the Nazca lines, that a mule driver who was passing by gave her a jute sack to cover her privates, that she walked off barefoot down the cobblestones, barely covered by the gunny sack and her own hair, followed by hundreds of onlookers who went behind flaying her all over again.

And they tell that Doña Carmen closed herself up in her room for nine days, that she passed the time crying, without eating or drinking anything, and that when the nine days were passed, she bathed, spruced herself up, and decided her married life was at an end. She kicked the slut out of town and during nine more days she closed herself up in the living room with her lawyer to settle accounts with her husband. She filed a legal claim charging him for damages, and the claim was made public as a lesson to other men, and among other things it stated: for consensual deflowering: five hundred sucres; for two hundred sexual acts that from any angle were rapes: twenty thousand sucres; for four hundred silences so as not to disturb the peace of the home: four thousand sucres; for personal services of coffee in bed: two thousand sucres; for so many hours waiting up: so many sucres; and thus she went on making charge upon charge, and when she no longer remembered anything else she had done, given, or agreed to, she added an extra zero to each figure, clarifying that the zero was because she was who she was, and that adding up the total of all the totals, the figure was astronomical, that it rose to several million sucres in the time when the four old Pandos could have a banquet for sixty cents. They tell that the husband was ruined and that one fine day he disappeared forever, and that in the house of Doña Carmen there is a sealed room which they say gave off an unbearable stench ...

They tell how the priest Santiago de los Angeles, pained at the affront, comforted her as best he could and placed her at the head of the Sisterhood of the Bead on the Gown of the Potbellied Virgin, that Doña Carmen recovered quickly and that they have been suffering her ever since ...

But things had to get very bad for the townspeople and especially the four old Pandos to long for the days when Doña Carmen gave the orders and the Sisterhood was all powerful.

The Benavides men, absolute owners of power, do not beat around the bush. They go to their haciendas to practice and refine their marksmanship. They receive arduous training under the command of Captain Quinteros who has offered himself eagerly for any job they might have and who still has not forgotten the embarrassing defeat of the Battle of the Mattresses, which is a black page in his great dossier.

The Benavides men realize that the old, worn out rifles that they used to hunt tapir, deer, and rabbits no longer serve — for times have changed — and they need more powerful weapons which Captain Quinteros provides in generous quantities. They learn to fire while lying on the ground, standing, at an angle, from close range, and from far away. They run races and marathons to get themselves in shape, they lift weights and do push-ups, they learn to fight hand to hand and to use bayonets and, not content with all of that, they receive a short training course in the treatment of prisoners and in how to extract their secrets under torture, for *all's fair in love and war*. Two of the young Benavides men travel to Brazil to perfect their methods. And everything is done in secret and in hiding. The Benavides women have to go along with the plan, although reluctantly because they are angry at having been passed over and because after having practiced so much patience in the Sisterhood, they are not persuaded by the men's violent methods, but they now have neither voice nor vote, and obediently, they shred sheets to make lint, which is what best stanches the blood of wounds, they help prepare backpacks and place arnica and surgical tape in the first-aid kits and they never stop praying for the men who are going to war and for the town they no longer recognize. The men would dearly love to do without the women who accuse them under their breath of lacking sufficient tact to have avoided these extremes of violence and the men tell them that they aren't collaborating with sufficient enthusiasm, but the women who in times past made up the Sisterhood are not advocates of war in spite of their dislike of the Pandos and their horror of communism. They confide in no one, they are even careful to guard their tongues around José Gregorio Pando, who sniffed out what they were up to a long time since and, wounded to the depths of his dog-like devotion because after so many years of service they do not consider him one of them but rather keep secrets, carries the gossip to Manuel Pando himself who is dumbfounded, unable to breathe, for he no longer has to deal with the crazy old ladies but rather with the men, and he guesses that the entire apparatus they have built is directed against him and his ideas, for the others are easily dominated or bought.

And since it is no longer Doña Carmen who runs things in the town, or even in the family, the Benavides men, without consulting her, send for Magdalena, who was wrong about the artist Figueroa who was none of what she hoped, for in private he's a neurotic mama's boy, he gets drunk with other artists of his ilk, he thinks a Benavides should wash his clothes and cook his meals, and poor Magdalena was looking for a life companion and ended up with a conceited boss, when for a boss she already had the town on one side and the Sisterhood on the other, and she's all alone in the city and in the town there are no longer the old problems of virginities or of nonfulfillment of ordinances, and Magdalena is dying of nostalgia for the countryside and her horses and above all for an unrequited love who has written a letter offering her what the artist Figueroa could not give. And Magdalena arrives with a different smile and resumes her outings and when she passes the *Voice of the People* press, which has been closed, she no longer goes at a gallop but rather stops to chat with the owner, and when the four old Pandos see her, they become happy as rusty bells and are rejuvenated as if they had received an injection of monkey glans.

And Manuel Pando, after everything the gossipy José Gregorio Pando has told him and that his cousin Magdalena has confirmed, decides that he has to hide, that he is not going to let them kill him as if he were a rat, that Captain Quinteros' men have begun to look for him house to house, searching in wardrobes and crates, sniffing around pantries and granaries, rummaging through cellars and attics, keeping an eye on the places he goes, asking everyone if they have seen him because they have to give him a message. But no one has seen him and some claim that they don't even know him.

Manuel Pando is nowhere to be found. He is not in the town nor in the cities where they also search for him and where they say he is a dangerous cattle rustler and they offer a reward to whoever captures him dead or alive, but he does not appear, and he is not on the run in the hills nor alone on the plains, nor crossing narrow mountain paths, for to the well-intentioned, Manuel Pando is where he always has been, but he has become invisible to others. They say that one of Captain Quinteros' men affirms that he saw him smoking in the plaza, sitting beside the four old Pandos, and another swears by the Potbellied Virgin that he saw him near the Newer Bridge at the same hour, and it is not that he has become invisible, but that he has become ubiquitous, and everyone talks about him, even the children who go to catechism, and from one day to the next he becomes the idol of the town and each person has made a place for him in their heart, and the man of flesh and blood, of weaknesses and lunacy that he was until a short time ago, becomes the mystic the town needs to move ahead through so many troubles, for it seems even the image of the Virgin was wearing out ...

Then Captain Quinteros, so as not to remain passive — for he has to show the Benavides men that he is good for something and has to justify the salary they pay him — decides to present an enormous parade to terrify the enemy and he seizes upon the upcoming celebrations of May 24. The Benavides men give their approval. The captain brings his company. They build a platform on one side of the plaza, and when the day arrives, all of the houses greet the day with flags and the entire town attends the spectacle, for it is the first time there has been a military parade and they have never seen a billy club do so many tricks nor such a large drum nor such gleaming cymbals and they are left openmouthed when they see that there are so many to impose order and respect (which is why they are looking for Manuel Pando) and against whom they will have to fight if the need arises. They cannot figure out where such a large number of armed men has come from, and they count them and recount them and don't stop counting, for there are thousands and thousands and they don't understand when they came nor where they are going to find food for all of them, for although they have said they are enemies, they are also outsiders and hospitality must be observed, even if later they enter into harsh and unequal combat.

No one, not even the sharpest like Jorge Washington, nor those with most experience like the four old Pandos, imagine that it is the same men over and over, that Captain Quinteros' men who pass though the main plaza and past the reviewing platform, climb into an armored truck in whose interior they change uniforms while the truck circles around the back of the town, and the soldiers parade again as if they were another company, and they perform this operation many times while Captain Quinteros with a megaphone in his hand talks for close to two hours about honor and national pride, which the people don't understand, but "that must be what they say at military parades"; and the voice that comes out of the megaphone says that the armed forces guarantee the welfare and security of the citizens and all their worldly goods, which the people weren't worried about, since they have no goods, only ills; and he shouts that the soldiers are the heralds of the arts and sciences, and the townspeople don't give a fig about what they hear because they have never

seen a herald nor a heraldess and maybe they are something like the
horses that fly through the air and are not to be found in these parts;
and he assures them that every uniformed breast is a bastion, and
bastion seems to them to suggest volume, and they think that better describes feminine chests; and he exclaims that the bugles and
trumpets fill the town with martial voices and that true courage is
learned in war, and the townspeople know that is not how it is, for
in war you more likely learn to be a coward because no one likes to
be killed; and his voice even cracks when he shouts that they are the
example of the new generations, and the women say to themselves,
as if they had read Campoamor at some point: "I didn't raise my son
to be a soldier...." And he exclaims that the purest destiny of the
soldier is war, and they know that all wars are dirty; and he states
that a free people is an armed people, and they know that freedom is
something else; and the megaphone writhes when he says that with
their martial step they are defending the borders, and they think that
the Peruvians are probably attacking; and he yells that they are the
professionals of honor, and it seems to them that Captain Quinteros
is praising himself too highly and that it's time he stopped, heaven
forbid that the Peruvians are having their own way while his back is
turned; and he reaffirms that they are the dynamic agents of change
and development, and they don't know what a dynamo is; and he
shouts that they are the sentinels of glorious actions and of epics,
and they remember Popeye the Sailor comics.... And the soldiers
who are providing the honor guard at the improvised platform can
stand at attention no longer, for no one remembered to order them
at ease, and they have their hands up touching their caps and their
fingers white for lack of blood, and when they can bear it no longer
because the soldiers don't stop passing nor does Captain Quinteros
stop talking, they look around, and look at the Benavides onlookers who are also bored with such a long harangue — for these are no
longer the times of Doña Carmen, who would have shut him up a
long time ago — they agree among themselves using an imperceptible
sign, they count one, two, three, and they change hands, rapidly and
simultaneously, and no one notices that they are making the military
salute with their left hands.

Meanwhile, fat Maruja, who doesn't miss a detail of the parade, has begun to see familiar faces, for it seems to her that the soldier in whose eyes she threw the handful of ashes during the past skirmish of the mattresses has already passed by three times in different uniforms: the first time he was dressed in crumpled leaves, for she doesn't know what parachute troops are; and the second time he went by with his cap off balance and now he is going by in helmet and spats.... And once her suspicion is confirmed, she tells all her neighbors. Everyone begins trying to identify the soldiers shouting that one already went by and the other hasn't come yet, that he's the one who climbed up to grab the Virgin and that other one is the one who got wound up in the taffy that Rosa Inés threw, and when the one who shot one of the dead marches by, the bereaved can't contain himself and he shouts at the top of his lungs, with all the force of his old sorrow:

—I know who you are, faggot!

And the rest of the neighbors, emboldened, throw themselves into shouting insults and truths, and such a disorder erupts that no one listens to Captain Quinteros delivering the best and longest speech of his life, which is identical to every other military speech.

And the soldiers, on finding themselves discovered and recognized, for *the pitcher goes to the well so often that it is finally broken,* hesitate before they reach the place where they sense they are going to be insulted and ill-treated, they blush, they exchange their goosestep for a hawkstep, they lose the beat of the march and get tangled up.

The solemn parade, such as never was seen in the town, the epic words that came out of the megaphone that the people call the *word-sweller,* the poised rifles, the martial music, the bang bang and the ching ching of the drum and the cymbals, lose all importance: fear becomes uproar, brute force is changed to foolishness, power is dissolved into whistling and catcalls.

Captain Quinteros ends his speech abruptly, in a rush, as if his words were cookies and he were choking on them, and he has no alternative than to give the order to retreat given that he sees a certain suspicious movement, one he already recognizes as a sign that the townsfolk are really getting mad. The troops retreat almost running in the direction of the trucks that are waiting with their motors idling, just as in the last skirmish, and they clamber on like monkeys and peel out. And when the people arrive on their heels, they look around unable to believe their eyes that there were only six trucks: one of uniforms and five of troops who passed and passed again appearing to number in the thousands when they were barely a few hundred.

The town is disgusted by the trick, they haven't attended any great parade but only a crude farce, "that must be the way those people do things," and to get even for the deception they begin to cheer Manuel Pando right in front of the Benavideses, who don't know just what has happened down there below and fear begins to invade them like cold. The troops have gone, Captain Quinteros never even said goodbye, and seeing themselves defenseless and unarmed in front of a town that is looking at them ferociously, they run to take refuge in the home of Doña Carmen Benavides, as it is the closest.

The four old Pandos relate in secret, taking care that no one should hear them, that Monday morning, very early, Magdalena Benavides went to knock on the door of the blacksmith, saying she wanted a new shoe for her horse. They told her they did not know where the owner of the shop was, and she responded she would pay any sum they named to whoever would help her. They say that an apprentice appeared and shoed her horse, that she gave him — not even bothering to count them — a wad of bills in every color, that while the boy counted the money, Magdalena lashed her horse and disappeared down the road heading away from the hacienda, that that was the last day they saw her in the town. They say that her relatives have been looking for her everywhere, that they have sifted the town and believe she has been kidnapped, and they aren't going to give her away as they did when she ran off with that artist Figueroa ...

The four old Pandos say that on Tuesday at dawn, when the bakers got up to bake the daily bread, they mixed the flour, left the dough to rise, and were never heard from again, that they took the same road Magdalena Benavides had taken ...

They confirm that on Wednesday, around five in the afternoon, all of the cows on all the haciendas bawled in pain, for their udders

were swollen and the *longas* were bathing in the river as if the bellows had nothing to do with them and not one peon showed up who
wanted to get involved with the *four blasted smackers, the two looky-
lookies, and the flyswatter* ...

They mutter — placing their black tobacco on the scraps of the
papers for which they are still searching — that on Thursday when
the cocks crowed, not a soul appeared in the town to butcher the
livestock, and that no one in town has tasted meat since that day ...

They tell that on Saturday, when they went to the market, they
found it desolate, there was no one to buy or to sell, what little was
offered was spoiled and very expensive, that hunger has settled in
the town and that it is a plague because every time it is killed, it
revives ...

They tell that on Sunday, a priest arrived toward the end of the
day to say Mass, that the bells tolled the customary three peals, but
that the cathedral was deserted as never before, that you could count
the people on the fingers of one hand, that, true, all the Benavides'
kin were there, excepting only Magdalena, with Doña Carmen a mere
shadow of her former self, that they occupied the pews that were
once reserved for the Sisterhood but that anyone can sit in now
because the Sisterhood came to an end once and for all and that it
was a bad thing because in the time of the Sisterhood things weren't
as bad as they are now; that the two cousins Clarisa and Martina
were there, that they had made up and were no longer bald, that
with the treatment of beef marrow, pigeon droppings, and castor oil,
they were growing new hair, but that they looked like men in dresses,
that they were with Marianita Pando who is now a Benavides, who
did not approach the communion rail; that Jorge Washington Pando
attended, that he left his bicycle tied to a post on the corner with a fat
chain and a padlock; that the ex-magistrate went with his wife and his
three lanky daughters, Socialjustice, Surplusvalue, and Pasionaria,
who had come back to town to stay because, since there was no longer a Sisterhood, their godmothers couldn't pay their way; that the
pharmacist was there, that without Doña Carmen to control him and
keep him in line, he was once again prescribing and preparing all the
concoctions he knew; that the usual pious old women were there,

that they sat beside the real mother of Manuel Pando, who they say has lost her mind, that she crossed herself constantly and with her stiff fingers threw benedictions to the four winds, that it gave you the creeps to see her condition with her son vanished and a price on his head; that José Gregorio Pando was there, that he turned around to look every few minutes as if he were waiting for someone or perhaps counting how many were present and how many were missing; that the sacristan was there, looking haggard, that his boots were covered with mud as if he had been walking all night, and that he played and sang "Salve, salve ..." with no grace whatsoever, and finally the shoemaker Romualdo with a black ribbon on his lapel and a black armband because he had been widowed, who for a long time hasn't sung his heart-wrenching *pasillos* but rather another kind of strange music, songs they say he makes up himself, and when the men of the town get together to hear him sing and knock back a few drinks they grow quiet ... and the next day, Poof! they disappear as if by magic.

The four old Pandos say—looking knowingly at the undercover cops that the newly promoted Colonel Quinteros has placed at every corner and public site—bringing their heads close together so that not even the wind itself will hear what they say, that the men of the town are in the hills with Manuel Pando leading them, that it isn't true that they have captured him as the newspapers continually claim, that the women of those who are involved have decided to spread the rumor that the Potbellied Virgin has appeared to him and sent him to make revolution against the rich, but that they four know that the one who really appeared to him is Magdalena Benavides who—repentant like the biblical Magdalene—has left everything she had to follow him. That those who come down from the hills in search of food say that Don Eloy Alfaro himself has returned from the next world to join the struggle, but that is impossible because the dead are dead and each one must face the troubles of his own time. That those of the hamlets also maintain that it's not Manuel Pando, but the Indians' own Manuel Mesías.... That these aren't rumors or hearsay, that *when the river thunders, it's dragging boulders,* that there must be some truth in it and the proof is that after so much time, Colonel Quinteros' troops can't catch him, and they say that even the bullets respect him and that when the soldiers fire, they come zigzagging out of their rifles, that it has already been proved and proved again that Manuel Pando can split himself and be in the hills, on the plains, and on the roads at the same time, and that no one knows what will happen ...

— Compadre, it's getting dark earlier tonight. Roll us one of those that *burn without having sinned and that kiss without sinning.*

—And let's go.

—And may the Potbellied Virgin protect us ...

The End

Glossary

Alfaro, Eloy (1842–1912): Leader of Ecuadorian liberalism and president of Ecuador 1897–1901 and 1906–1911.

Father Almeida: A legendary fallen priest.

carishina: An unfeminine or manly woman; a promiscuous woman.

chaguarquero: The flower stalk of the agave plant.

Chapulos: An armed opposition movement led principally by young liberal civilians in the provinces of Guayas and Los Ríos in the late nineteenth century.

cholo: A mestizo of mixed indigenous and European origin; a country bumpkin (pejorative).

García Moreno, Gabriel (1821–1875): President 1861–1865 and 1869–1875. Closely identified with highland and Catholic interests.

guagua: An infant or small child.

guambra: A youth or adolescent.

huasipungo: A small plot of land that an Indian is given the right to cultivate in exchange for providing labor on a hacienda.

Legarda, Bernardo de (?–1773): Ecuadorian wood carver, painter, and metalsmith. Known especially for his *Virgin of the Apocalypse (Winged Virgin of Quito)*, carved in 1736, as well as the Baroque altarpieces of several Quito churches.

llacta: A small plot of land.

May 24: Battle of Pichincha, May 24, 1822. A decisive battle of independence in which General Antonio José de Sucre routed the royalist forces.

páramo: A high mountain grassland.

pasillo: A popular love song or ballad.

Pasionaria: Dolores Ibárruri (1895–1989), leader of the Spanish Communist party, known as "La Pasionaria" (passionflower), a name originally adopted as a pseudonym for a newspaper article. A passionate orator, during the Spanish Civil War she coined the Republican slogan "No pasarán!" ("They shall not pass!"). After the Nationalist victory, she spent thirty-eight years in exile in Russia before returning to Spain in 1977.

prioste: An individual responsible for financially underwriting a fiesta. Acting as *prioste* is an important rite of passage in many communities and represents a substantial economic commitment.

sucre: Ecuadorian unit of currency, named for national hero of independence Antonio José de Sucre. In 2000, Ecuador adopted the U.S. dollar.

vaca loca: Literally, "crazy cow." During certain fiestas, an individual will don a cow mask or costume; the mask's horns are lit and the dancer rushes at the gathered spectators. In some areas, torches are tied to the horns of an actual cow, rather than a costumed person.

Velasco Ibarra, José María (1893–1979): Elected to five presidential terms—in 1934, 1944 (by a constitutional convention), 1952, 1960, and 1968—he was able to complete only one (1952–1956).

Virgin of Quinche: The patron saint of El Quinche, a town near Quito.